FLATLINE

FLATLINE

by Dana Barney

Copyright © 2015 by Dana Barney
First Publication 2015 by Dana Barney
Second Publication 2017 by Dana Barney

Library of Congress Cataloging in Publication Data is available
ISBN 978-0-9965888-4-3

Barney, Dana
FLATLINE

Jacket design by
April Litz

For my mom,
In her wheelhouse

01

Prescott slid the 9mm Sig Sauer Nightmare into the back of his dress pants. It probably wasn't the most well thought out choice of the past twenty-four hours, especially since these were his lucky pants and they were deteriorating at the seams. Surely the unrestricted threads would snuggle against the barrel of the gun for a long restful sleep until someone discovered it weeks later. Probably in a lake far outside of town. He thought about that, putting the gun somewhere no one would think to look, and it would go unnoticed for years – decades even. A lake seemed like the best choice.

That's what everyone thinks. I'll outsmart you. I'm immune to the long twisted arm of the law. Until one day someone discovers the gun washed ashore. This Perfect Citizen calls the cops and the cops run the gun and the threads that have miraculously held on despite the water and new climate. The gun comes back belonging to Harvey Marcona but the threads belong to someone else, someone still alive, David Prescott, silent partner and financial backer of Harvey Marcona. The police pay Prescott a visit, want to know if he's ever been to Lake Shelton.

Never heard of it. Where is it?

About ninety miles northwest of downtown. It's beautiful this time of year.

Doesn't ring a bell.

The police take his phone and run the GPS on it. He's pretty confident the police will figure out he's lying and he's quite sure they'll prove it through the GPS. He'll turn his phone off so the internal GPS won't register the three hour drive. Maybe leave the phone at home altogether and avoid the tolls to be extra careful. Maybe he'll borrow someone else's phone or get a disposable phone at the gas station. But he won't go to the gas station near his house. Not somewhere someone might recognize him.

Forget the phone, he thought. *In fact, forget the clothes too*, too chancy that he would inadvertently leave trace evidence behind. He thought about driving there naked, shaving off all his hair too, as he shuffled over to the lab table and set the gun carefully on the resin countertop and looked down. Harvey's icy dead eyes stared him in the face. His mouth was open a slice, about to say something mid-death before Prescott shoved the gun into his abdomen and fired one solid shot below his rib cage. The air went out of his chest first, his lungs arid, then a shiny layer of crimson seeped from his chest before he hit the floor. He didn't want to shoot him, but he weighed his options and didn't see any other way. Harvey was a poison that needed an antibody and Prescott had shareholders to answer to.

"911."

"I'd like to report a fire." There was no sense in leaving the body here overnight only to have Janice discover it in the morning halfway through her latte.

"What is your name, sir?" the dispatcher said on the other end of the phone.

"Harvey Marcona. 334 Industrial Plaza East. Basement." Prescott said as he let the phone drop to the floor, hitting the pond of Harvey's stomach matter. He didn't hesitate and turned around and worked his way down a long aisle between two refurbished lab tables each with their own collection of lab equipment: centrifuges, dry baths and auto-claves – the necessities.

When he reached the end he was face to face with a panoramic glass wall that peered into Harvey's office which was raised a few feet above the main solvent and chemical resistant flooring. The east wall of the office was covered floor to ceiling with the latest in high-definition technology: televisions, computer screens; a cyclical regurgitation of information. The opposite wall, was draped with a large whiteboard which was littered with thoughts and equations that amounted to who-knows-what. In between was a three-inch thick steel pocket door with an electronic keypad next to it. Panic room parading around as an office of an academic. Prescott punched it in: 7-2-9- 2-0-1-1.

Click.

Harvey's son, Ford's, birthday. Code breaking is only as complicated as the memory of the people designing the codes.

He stepped into this lavish, newly renovated office. The floors were Pianeta Legno, some fine exotic Italian hardwood that takes weeks to settle. Hovering over the snobby Italian were the original walls; a flimsy ceramic hybrid that kept all the chemicals out and conceit in. The board of directors was kind enough to let Harvey indulge in his overseas whims but they put their foot down when it came to general safety. They didn't feel it was necessary for Harvey to have his guests inhaling whatever concoction his team was developing on the other side. Harvey managed to cover the death white color of the walls with a variety of degrees: California Institute of Technology, MIT, a masters from Northwestern. Pedigree through and through. Prescott suspected that Harvey had them enlarged to fit the space allotted and to drive home that you were dealing with someone with paramount aptitude. He felt a little better about shooting him. Guilt waved over.

Nonetheless, the place had to be demolished. Prescott unscrewed the cap to a gallon of Dimethyl Sulfide he found tucked away in the storage room. He liked the label and thought the overstated red skulls guaranteed total and complete annihilation. He poured the contents over Harvey's mahogany desk and chair. He splashed the rest on the vertical filing cabinets that lined the back wall and slowly walked out of the office back into the lab, the smell of sulfide following his trail. He stopped at Harvey's feet and let the last amounts of sulfide dribble on to his Bruno Magli's.

Prescott ignited the Bunsen burner and let the flame erupt. He knocked it over and walked out. Minutes later the flame would spread and find its way toward the Dimethyl. Prescott didn't know what sort of damage it would do or if there would even be an explosion. May be there would just be a dull roar of flame. Either way, he would be long gone by the time the flame destroyed Marcona and his lab.

Go home, kiss his wife and kids and get a goodnight's sleep knowing that he corrected some terrible evil in this world.

Who did Marcona think he was anyway?

02

"It's not working out." Were the words that came out of his mouth. The next words were: "Marie has a packet for you."

A packet of what? A packet of apologies and excuses? I gave Cleft Duvall and this network three solid years – sweat and tears – *here's your packet, and we are very – truly – sorry that we have to do this to you.*

I worked furiously to build a name for myself here, took all the punches local news had to offer and toed the line when no one else would. I even turned the other cheek and focused my attention on the factory fire when Cleft was under scrutiny for giving a graduate student herpes in the back seat of his leased Camaro. That's another story. I mean, the leased Camaro is another story, everyone knew about the herpes and that if she let him stick it to her once, maybe two or three times, that she would be on the fast track to Monday morning's on the seven's. They have medicine and support groups for that stuff now anyway. Besides, if you don't leave graduate school with at least one transferable STD clearly you weren't doing anything right. Who cares if you got the corner office at JP Morgan if you don't have a great chancroid anecdote to go along with it? Anyway.

"What do you mean it's not working out?" Were the only words that my freshly shaven face could muster. This was me asserting myself.

"K is mandating we do at least five layoffs this quarter." Cleft said as he ran his hand down the front of his burnt orange dress shirt.

K was short for Kingsman. Larry Kingsman, but no one wanted to give him credit by actually saying his last name. He made it big in adult publishing, rides around in a twenty thousand dollar wheelchair, says it's some Korean War thing, and then decided to buy a local television station and a few magazines in the early '80s when credit still meant something. All this and he still manages to give me a migraine on a Tuesday afternoon. You usually wouldn't shake a fist at five layoffs, and he was probably going to get rid of some deadweight, but I was high-up and had some merit here. I wasn't following his logic.

"I get that K is mandating, but you made the choice," I said to Cleft. He had puffy cheeks and sucked them in when he was thinking about something. It was an appalling trait and probably drove his wife insane but he is who he is.

"It's complicated, Peter." Suck suck suck, probably regretting whatever he had for breakfast.

"He gave you a directive and you chose to make the directive complicated."

"Kingsman wants you gone, so - well, you're gone."

"He said that? He said that he wants me out of here?"

"You're a liability."

Ugh.

"Those were his words." Cleft said but I could tell he didn't want to review the series of events with me. "Peter Richards is a liability to this company and the reinvigorated field of local television news as we know it."

"I got it, you didn't have to go over it word for word."

"You were asking."

I am - or was as of thirty seconds ago - the Godfather of Cleft's son, Avery. He was born five weeks premature and has a condition that prevents him from breaking down the essentials: fats, proteins, compound words. It's called fucosidosis but I think that's fancy talk for pain in the ass. He's 20 now and I'm pretty sure he's running drugs out of his parents garage. Not that I'm looking.

"It's business. Complicated business." Cleft was able to spit something out that didn't sound like horseshit. "To be honest with you, people only care about the weather and the traffic. We make most of our ad spend between 6:40 a.m. and 7:00 a.m. People don't care about who may or may not have robbed the Episcopal church Friday night. They care about the temperature and if some tractor trailer is going to jack-up their commute to work."

"I got a good lead on that Episcopal church thing." Last Friday, burglars broke into a church in the 1100 block of east 12th Street. Less than a mile away, burglars also broke into a house in the 2000 block of Chicon

Avenue, also on the east side. Police said there have also been other robberies in the area and I had a chance to speak with a witness who said he knew something was up when he saw two men he didn't recognize walking around the outside of his house. In surveillance video from the residence, the two men start to walk away when the witness runs outside to confront them.

"You've been working on that for over a week." Cleft said.

"I'm an investigative journalist. I'm investigating it."

"Nobody cares." Cleft said.

"The neighbor, Nancy Atworth, says she thought she heard two kids around 2 a.m."

"So?"

"So I think there's a network out there. A network of thieves who are orchestrating these robberies."

"A network of thieves?"

"Yes – that's what I said."

"You hear yourself? People don't orchestrate robberies on the east side. The Hope Diamond isn't buried over there, the east side is a total shit hole."

"Nancy Atworth thinks differently."

"Nobody cares."

"Eat my shit, Cleft."

I could go into detail but you get the drift. Cleft told me I was out of line so I threw a paperweight at his window. It cracked, he got upset and called security and they booted me. I never did see the packet from Marie but I'm sure I'm not missing anything. It's not like I worked for Hearst or Gray. Those guys give you a nice chunk of change if you've been toeing the line. Not the K. He's private and if you take his parking spot or he finds out you Googled his name you're pretty much out.

I was out. I'm not sure if I was ever in, *but I was definitely out.*

03

After the incident with the paperweight and Cleft's antique window my blood pressure started to rise.

When Paula got pregnant with our second daughter, name to be determined later, her doctor said that her blood pressure was above average for a woman in her mid-thirties with great hair and an above average education. Paula exercised, ate well and took overall good care of herself but the body does what it wants, especially when you're four months pregnant.

Each night she would take her blood pressure and then lean over to me so she could take mine. My blood pressure wasn't looking good. One hundred and thirty over ninety three and that was on a good day. Paula said I needed to go and see Dr. Myers and she couldn't understand why I kept putting it off. At my age, they would say, I only needed a checkup every five years. It's true. That's what Dr. Myers told me. Every five years. They don't say that to people who are on the brink of death. If he had even the slightest suspicion that something was wrong he wouldn't suggest I wait five years to come back. I was there two months ago.

"Insurance. They say those things because that's what insurance companies require," she said.

"That's bullshit." I said and told Paula that my blood pressure spikes because I'm nervous about getting my blood pressure taken. She says it's because I'm turned on by her perfume. She's my hero.

Truth was, I started spending my lunch hours with Brad, Paula's significantly older, and politically vocal brother. Around 11:30 each morning we'd meet at the newly renovated diner downtown – The All-American. Brad worked for the Drug Seizure Unit in the local police department. The DSU, as he likes to call it, was created a few years ago while the department was going through a major reorganization. The sole mission of the DSU is for officers to sit on the side of interstate 35 and pull cars over with the hope they would catch drug runners coming up from Mexico with pounds of cocaine stashed inside their car seats. It wasn't luxurious police work and he was one pay grade above a traffic cop, but he got to carry a gun, if that meant something, and haggle families heading back to Dallas. He was the front line of defense for America's war on drugs and he loved it.

Brad worked from 9 at night to 9 in the morning, five days a week and they only worked the northbound side of the freeway. The thinking was that people bringing drugs in from Mexico weren't going to head south and back home. Officers in the DSU needed probable cause to pull people over so Brad and his partner would target people going a few miles over the speed limit or cars with their brake lights out and the pickings were plentiful. Once they pulled someone over they would go through standard traffic protocol and then it was up to them to determine whether or not the suspects, that's what Brad chose to call them, were worthy of a full vehicle search. It was completely subjective and up to Brad and his partner to determine. The thing was, people running drugs from Mexico usually aren't Mexican and they usually don't look like people who would be running drugs. It was usually middle-aged white guys, probably divorced, in minivans. They were innocuous and easily overlooked which was the point. You don't make hundreds of millions of dollars running a cartel if you send your nephew to run an errand for you.

Brad was usually done filing paperwork by 11 and then had a twenty minute drive from his office which was in an old industrial park on the north side of the city, nowhere near police headquarters. Brad said that it was because it was a special department and didn't adhere to the rules of a normal police outfit. Depending on parking he would usually arrive immediately after 11:30, a few minutes before me.

I usually had a double cheeseburger: lettuce, tomato, no pickle and extra mayonnaise. Trisha brought me the pickle anyways, she always did, there was something about not bringing the pickle that was considered un-American to her. Shame on me. Brad would order a salad and eat only half of it. I always offered him some of my fries and he always declined, further supporting my theory that he was taking some sort of steroid and appetite suppressant. You can't eat kale for lunch and be OK. He had a neck as thick as his head and biceps to match. His torso and legs were thin but that's because guys don't care about that, we think women want a firm chest and arms that can lift a Cadillac. I'm pretty certain about that despite Paula wholly accepting me in my pre-middle-life corpulence.

Every time we had lunch, at least once a week, Brad would squint his small inset eyes and tell me that my political candidate of choice was part of a larger evil plan to put the United States in to default on its numerous loans from other countries. China, Russia, France, they all had it out for us. He said he had proof. In fact, we all had proof; you just had to know how to read the stock market, understand the code words on CNN and read the *New York Times* upside down after snorting enough cocaine to fill a canoe. A confluence of events, is what Brad would say. He also told me that having a double cheeseburger everyday was bad for me which is probably why I keep eating them. I'm really showing him.

"You read anything good yesterday?" I asked him. After his shift he would go to the gym for a few hours and read conspiracy blogs. That was if he wasn't hitting up the local bar scene absorbing some obscure Austin band. "Did France cut our credit line yet?" I asked.

"Nah, man," he said as he waved a hand towards me. "You don't take this stuff seriously. It's not that simple."

"Sure I do." I said and smiled. "And it is that simple."

"You don't know what you're talking about," he said. "You ever heard of October Surprise?"

"Nope." But I had heard of it, in all of its idiocy, but what was the harm in indulging him?

"It refers to news stories that conveniently happen before national elections."

"What does that mean – conveniently happen?"

"You know – the stories are planted. The news media plants them. This is right up your alley."

"They plant them for whom?"

"The government and politicians. Kissinger's speech before Nixon's re-election – that was planted."

"But why?"

He stumbled a little bit here but finally came up for air. "Money and power, Peter. It's a complicated world."

"Eh." I said and looked out the window. The term October Surprise gained some traction after President Nixon's Secretary of State, Kissinger, made his famous "Peace Is At Hand" speech during the Vietnam War. People thought this speech guaranteed Nixon's reelection in '72 but everyone had a theory. "It was a very moving speech." I added.

"Planted."

"If you mean they discussed having a speech and then someone went and wrote it and then he read the words then, yes, I would agree with you."

"But it was with intention." Brad said emphatically.

"Do you also think the republicans are behind Chappaquiddick?"

"Chappa – what?"

"Doesn't matter." I said knowing I had lost him. I liked these talks with Brad.

"I heard they were hiring over at KVAN," he said while blowing a parcel of dust off his kale.

"Who did you hear that from?" I asked as the sun took a sharp left turn through the window pane into my eye socket. I winced.

"Vanessa told me. She has it good with the head of programming over there. Guess they need some - fresh talent. I'll send her your name."

"Thanks."

"Sure thing my man," he said followed by "Someday, and that day may never come, I will call upon you to do a service for me." Brad also loved *The Godfather*, thought it was the pinnacle of American cinema. He's seen the movie no less than a thousand times and loved inserting quotes from the film into everyday conversation. I thought the movie was fine. Brad quoting the movie every chance he got became a little annoying but the movie was totally fine. I couldn't remember this particular line from the film but I understood what he was getting at. He was doing me a favor and wanted me to understand that he was doing me a favor. I picture him sitting in his house with a gaggle of homing pigeons waiting to arm one of them with a name – Peter Richards – to send to the head of programming at KVAN. With highest regards, Brad. It goes without saying that Brad is totally unaware of the rampant turnaround in the local news business – or any news business, for that matter. I might last six months and that was if I was lucky. They, as in the overarching societal they, don't like to hire married people with kids who are encroaching the breaking point of middle age and have retirement funds that require routine maintenance and grooming. Family is a liability. Family meant a higher insurance premium for them and me having a smorgasbord of conflicts when they need me to cover a robbery downtown at midnight. *Kids are sick, wife is down for the count, babysitter needs money for flute lessons.* I could go on. The only thing that didn't apply to me was the retirement account and that simply was because I didn't have a retirement account, at least not one with any funds in it. I started one when the economy was good in the '90s but then life took over and I never put a substantial amount in each month. Paula and I discussed it and we thought it was better to put money towards a house and it would pay dividends over time. Also, we could sell the house when we were ready to retire, downsize, and live off the equity from the house. Paula had a colleague who referred us to a financial planner who would help us map it all out, but I told Paula I didn't need to sit down with someone who was going to sell me investment products that probably won't be around in 30 years.

"That's fine." I said not remembering what Brad asked me.

"Vanessa is one of the good ones. She'll hook you up."

Oh, that's right. Connections. "What does she do over there?" I asked but Brad shrugged. This was his signature: A finite non-committal response. It was common for him. It applied when Brad didn't want to respond, because he either didn't know or simply didn't care. When I asked him if I could have Paula's hand in marriage eight years ago – her father has long passed – the answer was simple enough: Shrug. Old me didn't like this response. I have a deep-rooted sense of needing approval. I tell people that I don't like to be micromanaged and I don't need approval to do my job well. When in reality, if you throw a "good job, Peter" in my direction every once in a while it'll go a long way. So this quasi-funeral of a shoulder shrug was a big slap in the face to my ego. Clearly the shrug meant he hated my guts and wanted me nowhere near his sister. When I told Paula about his carefully selected response, weeks later after she said yes to marrying me, she said that it was just him. That's his way of going about life. He doesn't like to get too excited about stuff. Doesn't like to commit. Or, she added, maybe he has already moved on. Lucky me, inheriting a brother-in-law with the same mental agility as a two year-old.

This shrug in particular probably meant he didn't know. In fact, Vanessa probably doesn't even work over at KVAN. Brad, in the most realistic scenario, met Vanessa in line at the grocery store and chatted her up about where all the country's nuclear warheads are stored. 3,412 warheads in total, according to his precise records. Vanessa, making nice or putting the loony at bay, probably referenced hearing something about that on the news and then – KAZAM! – Brad has a brother-in-law in the news business.

Do I know him? What station is he on? I love The Today Show! New York is gorgeous. And so it goes…four hours later Brad is taking her to a nice steak dinner downtown.

"Well, thank you. I appreciate you sticking your neck out for me." I said as the waitress put the check in the middle of the table.

"No problem, man. I know how it goes. You got that house to pay for."

Right. That house. I reached into my pocket and pulled out a fifty and set it on the check. Grant smirking up at me. I prosecuted the Ku Klux Klan and freed thousands of slaves, what did you do? Always something.

"Don't worry about it, man." Brad said as he set his badge down on the bill and tossed the fifty back at me. That would cover lunch. I never really understood it. Maybe the All-American had a thing for cops and comped all the meals. Maybe Brad had a warrant out on the owner and used it for free kale. Maybe this is what cops did.

When Cleft hired me, he promised me a five percent pay increase each year. That was pretty good for any job, but impressive for someone working an obscure job in an extinct industry. Paula and I calculated that if we saved that five percent increase we'd have enough money for a down payment on a house in about six years. We could upgrade from our cozy one bedroom apartment to a full-fledge legitimate home. Windows, doors, yard, garage – the whole bit. State of the art homeownership. We were parents already, might as well seal the deal and continue the lie of fully functioning and capable adults. And that time came, three months before Cleft let me go.

Brad hooked us up with his realtor friend – Marvin – who had a short sale in a new development in the northwest part of the city. The prior owners, Stan and Stacy Winderson, bought too much house and went broke in their attempt to fill it with Gemelli coffee tables and

Chinchilla couches. Marvin liked to talk about stuff he didn't know about or things that simply weren't his business.

"The house is good. We like it." I said.

"I knew you would. Marvin is a genius." I think you pay an extra 50 dollars to get that printed on your online Realty School for Sucker's diploma. Genius, Realtor at Large.

I have to tell Paula to remind me to send him a thank you card.

"You should invite him to the next block party. Introduce him to people."

What's with the rundown? Did Marvin have dirty pictures of Brad at the ready?

"What block party?"

"Marvin said they do a bi-annual block party in your neighborhood. In the cul-de-sac. Right out your front door."

I wish he told us that before we bought the place. I'm not really a block party kind of guy, I'm more of a sit at home and judge type of person.

"Fantastic."

"Send me your résumé when you get home."

"Sure."

"And look, don't worry about Clover."

"Why would I be worried about that?"

"I think some people would see that as a big scar on your professional and personal résumé."

"I'm not concerned about it."

"Luca Brasi sleeps with the fishes."

"Am I Luca Brasi? Is that what you're saying?"

"It's a quote man, don't mean anything."

"People will have to make their own judgments about me."

"OK. That's fine."

But I could tell that it wasn't. When I was stationed in Boston I was approached by someone who worked for the district attorney and he wanted to create a give and take relationship with me. He would leak information to me about ongoing cases and I would site the information in stories I was doing. We met nearly a dozen times over the course of a few months. Clover became a friend until he ended up dead near the Bunker Hill monument twenty minutes after he and I met one night.

04

"135 over 82." Paula said as I yanked the fabric-covered neoprene bladder off my arm.

When I did an online search for high blood pressure, *was it really something to be concerned about?* I got a plethora of information. Collectively though, blood pressure is pressure that the blood exerts against the walls of the arteries as it moves through them. Stuff goes out of the left side of my heart, goes through a tunnel, with some arterial traffic and repeats over and over and over again – 'til death. The ideal candidate is a black male over the age of 55 who smokes and eats red meat. I was only twenty-five percent of that.

"You should go and see Dr. Myers."

"OK." I said. I just had to stop eating the cheeseburgers and develop an incessant love for kale. Where's my medical degree?

Paula and I met at UCLA under the glint of the southern California sunshine. She was a sophomore and I was a junior. I was neck deep in the highly lauded Art History department and we shared a Topics in Theory and Criticism course. She wanted help understanding Wölfflin's three theories and I was delighted to proffer whatever knowledge I had. We would spend hours in the library arguing about the meaning of da Vinci's paintings and whether or not Freud really knew what he was talking out. When the library got too stuffy for us we'd go down the street to a local bar and drink. We fell in love.

When I got accepted into the graduate program at Emerson, Paula decided to drop out half way through her senior year so she could go to Massachusetts with me. Paula didn't believe it would work with her on the West coast and me in Boston despite my assertion that we would visit each other often. She was convinced attrition would kick in and we would eventually forget about each other. So she came with me and got a job working at the Isabella Stewart Garden museum. It was our three year plan. I would finish grad school and then we would go back to California where she could go to UCLA to study bioinformatics. But that never happened. A year into grad school Paula got pregnant with Joyce, our first daughter, and deferred her admission to UCLA and we got settled.

There was a loud THUNK outside our bedroom window.

"What was that?" Paula's eyes flinted off her phone for half a second.

"I don't know." I was halfway asleep but managed to lift my head up to look out the window. Our bedroom was at the front of the house, above the garage. It had a direct line of sight of our driveway and, by invention, the cul-de-sac. I had to take out the floodlights above the garage because every time a stray cat ran in front of the house they would illuminate and send a burning white light into our bedroom and wake us up. "It's probably Roger."

Roger was the orange house cat of our neighbor, Chandler, who lived to the right of us. Chandler was a retired math teacher at the local high school. He gave education 40 solid years before he decided he wanted to spend more time at home with his wife, Alex Trebek and Roger. When we arrived with the moving truck Chandler came over and introduced himself. Behind him was his rotund orange house cat – Roger. Roger was attached to a leash which was wrapped around Chandler's hand. Chandler thought, I suspected, that giving his cat a name like Roger personified him. Roger had a job, Roger chased mice and Roger had the good life but was complete rubbish at *Jeopardy!* Chandler was enjoying retired life and dragging Roger around on a leash like a dog.

"Can you go check please?"

"Right."

I flung the duvet off my body and rolled out of bed. The room was a warm eighty degrees. I walked down the hall, past Joyce's and to-be-determined-later's room, and down our wide staircase which ended at the front door. I peered out through one of the three window panels. Darkness. Our house was built a few years ago by a company that went by the name of Ə-zero which was a clever play on eo, the Latin word for progress and advancement. Reverse the e, replace the o with a zero, spell it out. Clever. ∂-zero got its start designing robotic vacuum cleaners and then propelled itself into medical and residential technology. ∂-zero claims to be "The Builder of Tomorrow" with a tagline that claims "The Future is Ours." Besides, home ownership should be about futurism and possibility and not the practicality of today. A merger of technology and discovery. The houses in our neighborhood are all technologically state of the art. Cameras inside and out, security doors and professional kitchens designed by a sports car manufacturer. Each room is also littered with the greatest LCD and plasma televisions money can buy. It was living beyond our means, even more so that I was between jobs. We loved it.

THUNK.

I navigated my way through the sitting room and den to our back door and looked out. Roger was perched on top of our patio table licking condensation off an abandoned water glass. Roger has no boundaries. I grabbed the remote and turned on the television. ∂-zero enticed potential owners by claiming the televisions as 'Necessary Tools for your Complete Enjoyment', how could I resist a pitch like that? The television screen buzzed as I grabbed a root beer out of the refrigerator. Four in the morning with a root beer. Probably another thing Dr. Myers would hold over my head when I finally got around to making an appointment with him.

Four in the morning television is a sad state of affairs. The cable specialty channels are running programs promoting the latest in abdominal conditioning and the news channels are recycling the breaking news from the night before. But I found what I was looking for on channel two which was dedicated to local news 24 hours a day, seven days a week in perpetuity. Weather on the three's, traffic on the five's in ten minute blocks, each hour, twenty four hours a day. Comfort in the form of redundant information. I sent them my résumé a few months ago but they didn't have an Investigative Journalism department and were only in need of a part-time control room operator who had at least five years experience working in live multi-camera television and was happy with a salary akin to that of a barista. I thought about how much of my dignity I was willing to wash away for gainful employment.

Matt Hickens finished giving an update on the traffic on I-35, surprisingly busier than you would expect for this time of day. The drug runners from Mexico have tight deadlines in Dallas. Hickens transitioned it over to Virginia Hart, who was standing in the middle of an industrial business park. Behind her, a building was immersed in flames. When I was trying to decide if I knew where she was, a picture came up next to her face of a middle-aged man with dirty brown hair. I squinted. He looked important and familiar but I wasn't sure. The name, Harvey Marcona, didn't ring any bells either. I was tired and washed over with indifference. Also, this was probably nothing – filler – that would be rerun during the six o'clock hour. My eyes fluttered and I lost interest. That's the state of affairs these days.

Every station should have its own Investigative Journalist, I thought as I stared at the blackness behind my eyelids. My mind went back to Boston and Darren Clover. This is what happens in the middle of the night when I can't sleep, I think about the past and what could have been different. Most people, most Americans at least, stay up worrying about their retirement account – if they have one – the mortgage on their house and how are they going to get by, since they're already living far beyond their means. But not me. I sit and idle over the past and that which I cannot change

I was doing research on a wide receiver for Boston College, Roy Cardinal. *Allegedly*, is what we're supposed to say, Cardinal was involved in a drug ring that was selling premium grade product to Boston College's social elite. When a sorority girl overdosed at a frat party, a student by the name of Garret Waingro came forward and sold Cardinal out. Waingro claimed that Cardinal was knowingly selling shit product that was laced with a popular household cleaner. Cardinal said that he was trying to make ends meet and was working the night shift for an on campus courier service.

A month later, Waingro got shot while walking to his job in Harvard Square and Cardinal was charged with premeditated murder. He entered a plea of not guilty, claiming he was in Florida visiting his aging grandmother at the time of the murder. I was covering the story for Boston's NBC affiliate and had a lead that all but confirmed Cardinal was set up. Clover had proof. That's why he wanted to meet with me.

SLAM.

My eyeballs rolled around and I popped one eye open. It sounded like Paula slamming the trunk of her car. SLAM. I pushed myself off the couch and went towards the front window. A white van was parked across the street. The side was emblazoned with an at-home print job promoting Franks Floral Fantasies. I looked down at my watch:

5:45 a.m.

Very early for flowers and Joyce would be up soon. A figure came around from the driver's side of the van and headed up the walkway towards a Tudor style house that looked very much like ours. He was tall, maybe 6'2", pale skin and stark white hair. When he reached the front door he knocked. No answer. Knock. Knock. He wasn't carrying any flowers. A few moments passed and I thought about going over there and telling him to give it up, but as soon as that thought passed my head the door opened. Janice Walton was on the other side. Paula and I didn't know her very well. She was a widow and friendly and kept to herself, which is how it should be. When she saw her albino guest, a small gap opened in her mouth. She was unsure of her visitor but they exchanged a few words and she eventually pulled the door back and let him in. Hmm. Maybe he worked for Floral Frank and was stopping by on his way to work for a little early morning hanky panky despite being a decade or two younger than her. We've all had our temptations so I won't hold it against him. For whatever reason, I can't remember now, I kept watching. Maybe it was the hint of sunlight peering over her house or me counting the seconds until the van signage peeled off, but I couldn't look away.

The houses were designed so the front door fed directly into the living room and the kitchen was next to it. They both had large bay windows which allowed for plenty of sunlight. They also gave me a front row seat as Janice led her visitor into the kitchen. She poured him a glass of water and disappeared toward the back of the house. He managed to fill her absence by looking through her kitchen cabinets and picking his nose. A minute later, Janice came back with what appeared to be a banker's box. She set it on the kitchen counter and wiped the dust off of her hands. The albino did a cursory look through the box and nodded. Approval. It's amazing the sort of people you can find when you sell stuff on the internet. He walked out of the house and gently set the box in the passenger's seat of the floral van. He drove slowly away from the house, turned the van around in the cul-de-sac and headed on his way.

"Daddy?" I turned around. Joyce was standing behind me with her hand firmly grasping the ear of her pet rabbit. "Can you make me some pancakes?"

"Of course." I said and leaned over and picked her up. I gave her a kiss and carried her into the kitchen.

05

The rear door to the Dallas police cruiser slammed shut. Detective Fritz watched as Officer McReynolds fished around his pants pockets.

"Did you lose something?"

McReynolds pulled his hand out and dangled a set of keys. "Got 'em."

"Are you ready?"

"Yes, sir." McReynolds said as he went around and opened the passenger side door for Fritz.

"Isn't necessary."

"Of course not, sir." McReynolds scurried back to the driver's side and implanted his pre-diabetic ass into the driver's seat as Fritz got in and shifted his body towards David Prescott who was sitting in the back, flanked by bulletproof windows. His hands were shackled.

A call came in that afternoon, a fisherman spotted a suspicious car on the side of the entry road to Lake Shelton. The car was suspicious because it was nice and clean. The fisherman parked his '78 Chevy Suburban truck and approached the driver's side window of this late model import to discover one Jack Finneran with his hands gripped white to the steering wheel and a 9mm on the dashboard in front of him, the barrel staring him down. The fisherman called it in as a potential suicide but when the cops arrived, Finneran told them he was there to dump the weapon. His boss gave him a shoebox and told him to drive 180 miles and dump it. Had to be here, Shelton, remote and obscure. Untraceable. If you want to get something done in this world you have to do it yourself. It didn't occur to Finneran to look in the shoebox until he reached his final destination. When he saw the gun, and simultaneously when the fisherman arrived, Finneran was balancing his loyalty to his boss against his moral impulse to do the right thing. He was leaning towards loyalty but then the guy in the Orvis costume banged on his window.

The local cop arrived, thanked the fisherman and let him go. He then drove the kid and the gun back into town. He let the kid sit in the front of the police station while he made a few phone calls. The first was to a friend with the Dallas police, Detective Lee J. Fritz. Fritz had all the right connections and could run a history on the gun. Fritz called him back five minutes later and said that there was no 9mm registered to David Prescott and, in fact, the gun in question was registered to one Harvey Marcona – deceased. Fritz said to hold tight, he was going to drive down. It was a special situation and needed special attention. Depending on traffic he should be there within the hour. There was no second phone call.

When Fritz arrived two hours later he took the kid into one of the two holding cells and sat him down. He told the officer he was with to wait outside. He was doing a ride along and didn't have to time to ditch the deadweight so he had the deadweight play chauffeur. Fritz set a tape recorder down next to the kid and pressed record.

"State your name for the record."

"Jack Finneran."

"Where do you live?"

"Austin, Texas.

"Music Capital of the World, huh?"

"So they say."

"Breakfast tacos?"

"That's right."

"Music and tacos. Long way from home aren't you?"

Jack shrugged.

"What were you doing all the way out here?"

"Like I told the cop, I was told to drive out here and get rid of the gun."

"Who told you to get rid of it?"

"My boss."

"What's your boss's name?"

"David Prescott. Have you heard of him?" Jack Finneran didn't care for his boss all that much. Prescott seemed like a decent enough guy, had a wife and some kids, but he didn't have boundaries. A few

24

weeks after Jack started working with him Prescott took him to lunch, bought him a few drinks and told him that he was really impressed with the job he was doing. That night he called Jack on his cell phone and asked him to go into the office and get his bank key fob. It was 3 a.m. and he needed to transfer some money to Asia. Given the nature of the transaction he needed the three digit security code which he could only get from the key fob. Jack gave a hefty yes sir, went into the office and then took the key fob to Prescott at home and that was the beginning: nightly and weekend phone calls activating the inner errand boy that Jack always suspected he was. So when Prescott called him and asked him to drive to the middle of nowhere and dispose of a gun, Jack really didn't think anything of it. It was one more inconvenience in a series of inconveniences. Go to the drug store, get the dry cleaning, pick up that kid from school, and ditch the murder weapon.

"Why did he want you to get rid of the gun?"

"How should I know?"

"Do you know whose gun it is?"

"I would assume it belongs to my boss." Jack said and didn't think anything of it. Fritz asked him a few more questions, told him he could go home and to never repeat the events of the past three hours to anyone. As far as his friends were concerned he was at the movies watching something epic. The sun was starting to set and Fritz was getting hungry. He had McReynolds drive him down the street and stop at a Denny's before making their way to Austin. He figured they'd get there before 10 and he could sense McReynolds was a little peeved by this development despite whatever training, he assumed, McReynolds had about following the lead. Fritz would drive to Tokyo if it meant rubbing elbows with someone like David Prescott, innocent or not.

A few hours later, David Prescott's wife, Adrienne, opened the door to their Lost Creek estate a few minutes after 11. So what if Fritz was bad with time. Criminals don't expire so what was the point of rushing? Besides, McReynolds was a terrible driver and probably couldn't tell the difference between Houston and Austin if his life depended on it.

"How may I help you?" Prescott's wife said.

If you're so fucking concerned about who's knocking on your door at 11 p.m. don't answer it or, better yet, have your husband get off his lazy ass and do it himself, Fritz thought to himself. God knows what kind of monsters are out there.

"Ma'm, is your husband home?"

"Can I ask what this is in regards to?"

"He's under arrest for the murder of Harvey Marcona."

06

I decided to stop at a local food trailer on the east side for breakfast. The food trailer phenomenon started in the '90s with a single hot dog stand and has flourished into a multi-million dollar industry where five star chefs can serve foie gras out of the trunk of their car for a price. You couldn't go a mile without driving past a food court mecca where a double-decker gourmet hamburger bus was facing off with a vegan specialty stand. I decided on a trailer in the Hyde Park area that served biscuits covered in white pepper gravy with some kind of ale and sausage. I ordered two of them and sat on a refurbished picnic table and watched the morning traffic push its way out of Hyde Park towards Airport Boulevard and the interstate. Everyone was always in such a hurry to get to places only to head back to where they originally started.

I finished breakfast and waited until 9:45 before I got back in my car and headed down Duval. I was scheduled to meet Vanessa at the KVAN studios at 10. Without traffic it would take me five minutes at most and I liked getting places early. The KVAN studio was a few hundred yards east of the football stadium on a rundown thoroughfare near the interstate. The studio was housed in an old tire warehouse and was surrounded by what appeared to be run down campus housing. You couldn't tell the studio from a hole in the wall. Which I guess is what they were going for: complete anonymity.

"I'm here to see Vanessa Snowdin." I said as I proffered my driver's license. The receptionist glared at it as Vanessa came through a set of double doors and offered her hand.

"Follow me." She said as she swung around and headed back through the double doors into a refurbished television studio as the floor director was cuing Travis Holt behind the anchor desk. I've never seen him before. He looked like he was twelve and fresh out of journalism school. Probably aspires to write thought-provoking articles for The New Yorker and live in a palatial penthouse overlooking Central Park. It will probably take him a year to realize that he won't hit a six-figure salary until his '60s and by that point he'll be burned out and cynical. I give him another six months before he gives notice and moves to China to teach English to kids who weren't massacred by the one child policy.

"Have a seat." She pushed aside a huge pile of magazines on her plush couch and sat behind her desk. She shuffled through a pile of papers and pulled out a résumé. She ran her finger down it, squinted halfway through and looked up at me and then smiled.

"Brad has a lot of good things to say about you and you certainly have experience."

"Thanks. I appreciate that. It's certainly been an interesting journey –" but before I could elaborate on the struggles of local reporters and rant about how mainstream media attempts to dramatize the weather she tossed a manila folder down on the desk. My eyes fluttered towards it.

"Open it," she said.

"What is it?" I asked. She waved her hand towards it. I leaned forward and lifted the side of the folder with my thumb. It was an eight by ten black and white picture of Clover's body lying face up on what appeared to be a medical table. A sanitized gunshot wound was in the middle of his forehead. A ruler was above the gunshot, measuring the opening at a quarter of an inch. I'm pretty sure if you looked close enough you could see the lab table through the opening in his head, brain matter, thoughts and theories all eradicated to a small tunnel of air.

"Jesus." Was the only word that I could muster.

"Tell me about this."

"What is there to say?"

"Who is Charles Clover?"

I closed my mouth and let a small stream of air squeal through my nose. The room was silent sans the air conditioner blowing down on my head. Vanessa stared at me waiting for an explanation. "I don't know." I said. "He worked for the District Attorney with a focus on special criminal cases. I didn't really know him. This is some interview."

"What did he give you?"

"I'm not following." But I was. It was an unexpected blitz, possibly a weak tactic for information from someone who didn't know how to conduct a proper job interview, but maybe she was up to something else here.

"When you met Charles Clover that night on Bunker Hill, he gave you something, didn't he?"

"Right."

"So – what was it – what did he give you?" I looked passed her and wiped some dirt off my knee. I was thinking.

"He gave me a copy of an airline ticket proving that Roy Cardinal went to Florida the morning before Waingro was shot in Harvard Square." I said weary of where this conversation was headed. Everyone had an angle.

The DA's case was built on taking down Roy Cardinal and Clover had the one piece of information that absolved him. Allegedly, Clover gave this information to Roy Cardinal's defense team as well, or he had fully intended to. He gave it to me because he didn't trust the system. When Waingro stepped forward about the sham drugs, Roy Cardinal and the entire NCAA were put under a microscope. Some of the NCAA's biggest opponents claimed that this was a result of an incessantly corrupt system with no genuine regulations and the people making and monitoring the rules were the biggest offenders. This was all nice and par for the course until Roy Cardinal lawyered up. Cardinal acquiring a lawyer wasn't entirely unusual. These college all-stars already have under the table agreements with some of the nation's leading sports agents; it's frowned upon but generally accepted as long as you don't go parading it around. The thing about Roy Cardinal's lawyer was that he was employed by the same firm that represented Ricardo Gianetti, notorious Massachusetts mob boss, and the entire Gianetti family. About twenty years ago Gianetti was on trial for smuggling cocaine through cargo planes at Logan Airport and then he and his wife went missing. It wasn't readily apparent but I think Clover was beginning to put the dots together. Waingro had inadvertently uncovered a mob drug ring in attempt to embarrass a rising sports star.

"And you're aware that when Charles Clover supposedly approached you he was on leave from the DA's office? In fact, the DA wasn't even handling the Waingro shooting."

"So what – so what does it matter if he was on leave or not? Charles

Clover being on leave doesn't devalue the information that he had. Cardinal was framed. He may have been running drugs but it doesn't mean he's a murderer."

"It's just a rather big inconsistency in your story."

"Clover approached me with the evidence. I wrote about it in a column I did for The Boston Globe. If you have so many questions you are welcome to read the column."

"I read the column," she said and slid a stack of papers over to me proving, obviously, that having a printed copy was confirmation that she read it. "If Charles Clover was on leave it wouldn't have been possible for him to have the information you alleged he had, is that correct?"

"He got it right before he was put on leave."

"I think the bigger issue, Peter, is that you accused an innocent man of being the mastermind behind a totally fabricated drug ring."

"I thought this was a job interview not some sort of career analysis."

"It's a rather amazing story, isn't it? Too good to be true, isn't it? Ricardo Gianetti disappears and reappears twenty years later as lowly ticket counter operative." She opened the paper to a section that she highlighted. "Louis Kleiner has worked the ticket counter for American Airlines for the past three years."

"Right – so he can oversee a multi-billion dollar a year drug empire which specializes in infiltrating college sports."

"Can I finish?" She asked.

"All yours." I said and waved my hand towards the newspaper.

She looked back at the paper and continued: "Louis Kleiner has worked the ticket counter for American Airlines for the past three years. He lives in a small walk up apartment in Quincy with his wife of forty years, Theresa. Their landlord says that Louis and Theresa are wonderful tenants and pay cash each month for their apartment and currently have no lease agreement. A search of public records found that both Louis Kleiner and his wife have a five million dollar life insurance policy." Vanessa set the paper down. "Do you hear how ridiculous this sounds?"

"It's true about the life insurance policies. Also, Louis Kleiner had– has– the same attorney as Roy Cardinal and Ricardo Gianetti." I added. "The attorney works off a five thousand dollar monthly retainer whether or not he's actually doing any work for the client."

"It doesn't mean anything, Peter."

"Can you read the part again about the life insurance policies? I found that particularly interesting. Louis and Theresa Kleiner rent an apartment in which they pay cash for and have no kids – that's weird, right?"

"It's all supposition. In fact, this whole campaign to bring Louis Kleiner to trial for drug trafficking, a campaign you provoked, is based on some very broad and daring assumptions. How you got a judge to look at this is beyond me."

"I have connections." I said and smiled at her.

"Thankfully, the judge didn't think there was enough evidence to bring him in front of a jury and ridicule him. He, like most people, thought the evidence was circumstantial. Get enough people to start talking about something they'll end up believing it no matter what the actual truth is. You ruined Louis Kleiner's life. But for you, it was a magic potion for your career."

What a stupid saying.

"You're out of your mind."

"You invented a fictional mob boss, tarnished a man and his wife, all for the sake of what – a story? Recognition?"

"I was hoping for the Noble Peace Prize. Besides, I have sources."

"Of course you do," she said as she tossed another folder in my direction. I can only imagine what's in here. "This is a statement taken May of last year. Sandra Patterson called in and filed a complaint saying you offered her two hundred dollars in cash to say, on the record, that she was kidnapped at gun point by the North Central Strangler but managed to escape with a can of pepper spray." The North Central Strangler was an alleged serial killer unique to central Texas. He would prey mostly on young female students. Four murders have been linked to him. Her. Whatever.

"People are so full of shit." I said.

"Excuse me?"

"Nothing. If I made it all up why did someone shoot Charles Clover? Why is there a hole in his head? That's a pretty big coincidence isn't it?"

"Why don't you tell me? Maybe you were bribing him too."

"I don't have to prove a negative. I thought this was an interview not a crucifixion.

"Well–"

What do you want anyway, Snowdin?" I said with a strong emphasis on her last name.

"My last name has an 'I' in it, like snowed in for the winter, not with an 'e' like you're insinuating."

"But they sound the same, that's what's important. People will think you're related." I was talking nonsense but I knew it bothered her.

"I've been watching you and want you to understand that your actions have consequences."

"Good to know I have a fan."

"You're a joke to this industry. A joke and a liar, Peter."

I pushed myself off the couch and simultaneously tossed the manila folder at her. "Send your brother my regards," she said as I sure-stepped my way out of her office and slammed the door. An intern sat at a desk adjacent to the office and stared at me like I had a growth exploding from my neck. I worked my way down the hall towards the exit and pulled out my phone.

Missed call − Brad.

I bet he had a lot to say for himself.

07

It was cold outside so I hurried across the parking lot towards my car. Weather here rarely dipped below the forty's but when it did I liked it. Made me nostalgic for a nor'easter.

I slammed the door to my car and shoved the key into the ignition. Once the dashboard was up and running I hit the voicemail icon on my phone. Brad's voice echoed through the car.

"Dude, call me. Turn on the television. She set you up."

Of course she did.

08

I rolled the covers up over Joyce's shoulders. "Night, Daddy. I love you."

"I love you too, beautiful." I leaned down and kissed her. I worked myself off her bed and towards the door. "Sleep well."

"You sleep well, Daddy." She said as I shut the door and headed down the hallway towards our bedroom. Paula was half asleep and the television was running old episodes of some show she used to love when we first met. "Are you going to watch it?" Paula said as she rolled over.

"Ya."

"You can watch it up here."

"That's OK. I recorded it downstairs."

"Do you want me to watch it with you?"

"No. It's OK. I'm hungry. I'll let you know how it goes."

"Love you."

I got up and walked out of the room and headed downstairs. A little after 5 Brad stopped by the house and dropped off some dinner for us and told Paula that Vanessa had recorded our entire conversation that morning. She had invited me in for an interview with the specific intent of establishing me as a liar and fraud and recorded it for the six o'clock news. They started running promos as soon as I walked in the building. She probably even orchestrated running into Brad at the grocery store knowing that it was going to eventually lead back to me. It's common for journalists to use subversive and cunning tricks to get the story they want but her whole façade was a brand new level of crazy. I was relatively obscure in my new life but people would certainly find this interesting and it was definitely going to sour whatever job market was left for me. The national networks would probably request interviews as well and Vanessa would say that it's exactly what I wanted to happen. It's all part of my evil master plan to take over the world one mediocre news story at a time. I'm sure it's only a matter of days before Good Morning America calls asking me to join their lucrative team of hotshot journalists. Nonetheless, I grabbed the remote and turned on the television. I set the plate of royal blue tacos that Brad brought me on the coffee table. They were from a hole in the wall near our house and were a combination of chicken and pork wrapped in corn tortillas with mole sauce. It was my favorite and I was the only one in the house who liked them. I took my first bite as I flipped through an assortment of prerecorded kids shows and found the KVAN 6 PM show at the top of the list. I let my finger linger for a second before I hit play.

Travis Holt shuffled papers behind the anchor desk in attempt to look busy. He jerked his head up as the camera moved closer to him, surprised almost that he himself was on television. "I'm Travis Holt and this is the six o'clock news. There's a five car pileup on I-35 but first we have Vanessa Snowdin with a local story that may have some viewers asking, is there really any integrity left in the world?"

Fuck you, Travis.

"Thanks Travis," she said as a smile erupted from her face. "I had the unique pleasure of interviewing Peter Richards this morning. For those of you who don't know, Mr. Richards was most recently a reporter for KROQ in Austin until he was let go. Before he came to Austin he worked as a reporter for KROQ's affiliate in Boston but was fired because of his involvement in the homicide of a reputable Massachusetts district attorney." Interview wasn't an entirely inaccurate word choice. He was an aide, the DA was some other guy. Not that the viewers were fact checking

My mind trailed off as it usually does when I'm trying to consolidate my stress. Vanessa was covering all the key points in my career and created dots between events in attempt to prove I was manufacturing events and stories for my own professional gain. I don't know if it was my bias or her sophomoric reporting but everything she said sounded too precise and thought out; she wasn't letting the story cultivate itself and therefore it sounded like a load of rubbish. I am sure her viewers would agree with me, but I'm biased. She also highlighted the fact that KROQ got tired of my past following me around like a mangled dog looking for a home. Who can blame them really? Cleft was and continues to be a good friend despite what I did to his window and his professional reputation.

SLAM.

I let the recording play on the television as I went towards the front window and looked out. There it was - a police cruiser parked in front of Janice Walton's house. The side said Texas Department of Public Safety. I'd have to remind myself to look that up later. I glanced down at my watch:

11:02.

I set it a few minutes fast on purpose. It was a mental sleight on my part so I would always be a few minutes early, since I openly ridicule people for being late. But I know it's set ahead so I always end up doing the math in my head to correct it. We were looking at 10:58, since it would be too easy to set it exactly five minutes fast.

I could see Janice standing in her kitchen with her back pressed up against the kitchen sink talking to the DPS officer. He was tall, maybe 6' or 6'1", caucasian, and his skin had seen better days. Janice waved her hand towards the back of the house and as she did so the officer turned and walked out of the kitchen. While he was gone Janice turned around and faced the sink and pulled out her phone and pressed a few buttons. She pulled the phone up to her ear and cupped her hand around her mouth and spoke. She was either trying to cover her words as to remain inconspicuous or she knew I was watching and didn't want me to exercise my remarkable lip reading skills. I was going to put my money on the former but my thought process got rudely interrupted when the DPS officer came back into the kitchen. He saw Janice on the phone and, as far as I can tell, a fury sprinted across his face. He yelled something at Janice and went over and reached up to grab the phone from her. She put her hands up to defend herself which made him pause because instead of grabbing the phone he wrapped his hands around her neck and slammed her head against the kitchen window. A small crack shot down the middle of the window and Janice slumped over the sink and fell to the floor.

Oh shit.

I reached into my pocket to grab my phone. It wasn't there.

Paula has told me numerous times that my pants are notoriously too loose and that if I'm not careful things will keep falling out of the pockets. I told her the life of a reporter required my clothes to have various storage options but I was really starting to understand the merit of what she was saying; my phone was certainly abandoned between our couch cushions along with misplaced popcorn and old coins. I needed to relax, take a few deep breaths and go into the den and get my phone and call 911. But if I went back into the den I was going to miss what was happening at Janice's house and I wouldn't be helpful to the 911 operator when she asked me the inevitable series of questions about the events that transpired. There would undoubtedly be a gap in the timeline so I stayed, I would call them shortly. I took a few more breaths, started to count to five and went to the front door and emerged from my house without a plan.

One.

The DPS officer was a pawn of the state after all so maybe he had a good reason to slam her against her kitchen window.

Two.

Maybe she was running a brothel out of her house and wasn't giving him the civil service discount he felt he was entitled to.

Three.

I approached the precipice of our front yard and looked over at her house.

Four.

The officer hovered over where I presumed her body would be. There was a stillness to him that I couldn't decipher; maybe a hint of regret washed over him and he was going through the list of consequences in his head: no pension, jail, ridicule and so on; you can't bang heads against windows these days and get away with it.

Five. Relaxation, clarity, the sense that everything can be explained.

I took the first step out of my front yard and in an instant, without proper warning, two flashes erupted from her kitchen and were echoed immediately by two muffled bangs.

Gunshots.

He wasn't thinking anything over, he was getting ready to shoot her and now he was finished. Janice Walton's dead body laid no more than thirty yards from where I was standing and an unknown man was looking out Janice's double-paned temp-controlled kitchen window watching me.

09

I retreated back into my yard and took a few backwards steps over Paula's rose bushes and watched as the DPS officer leaned down and disappeared over Janice's body. I went into our house, locked the front door and pulled my phone from the couch crevice and dialed.

"911."

"Yes, my neighbor was just murdered. I'm at 1112 Candida Circle. She's at 1109, across the street. We're in a cul-de-sac. She was shot."

"What is your name, sir?"

"Peter Richards."

"She was shot?"

"Yes – shot – murdered. Can you send someone please – he's still in the house."

"Someone is on their way."

"He's a State Trooper."

"Excuse me?"

"I saw him. He shot her twice in her kitchen. Two shots. His car is out front. It says Department of Public Safety on the side. I can see part of the license plate. Z – H – 1 – those are the last three digits." This was being recorded so the information was now stowed away in a place other than my head. "And he saw me." I paced around the front room as an icy pain went down my spine. It's probably the same feeling that makes cats hair stand up on their back when they're in attack mode. I'll have to ask Roger next time I see him.

"Someone is on their way, sir."

"Did you hear me? I said he saw me."

"What is the license plate on the car?"

"What? Z – H – 1 – I just told you that."

"What are the last three digits?"

"Those are the last three digits. Are you listening to me?"

"Is he still armed, sir?"

I went to the window and pulled open the curtain. It was dark grey and heavy, something Paula picked out at a clearance sale at the mall last weekend. I craned my neck to see if I could read the first few numbers off the license plate but the cruiser was gone.

10

"Sir, did you hear me?"

"What? Sorry." The light clicked on upstairs. I turned around and saw Paula walking down the hallway. She stopped at the top of the stairs and looked down at me. She wore her grogginess well, an exhaustion that only parents could understand. I told her everything was fine. Go back to sleep. She turned around and slogged back to our room and shut the door. I guess when you hit a certain level of overtiredness you don't care who your husband is on the phone with at midnight. Maybe Paula would be concerned if I was trying to hide something. Maybe she didn't even notice the phone cradled below my chin or the panic in my eyes. I've never been good at hiding my emotions so I was sure the fear was draped over me.

"Is he still armed, sir?" the voice on the phone asked me a second time.

"He's gone. The car is gone. You sent someone?"

"Yes. They should be there in a few minutes." The average response time for police is eleven minutes and the operator undoubtedly dispatched someone a few minutes ago so I was working with about eight minutes. Cautiously, I shaved two minutes off. It's an average anyway and the police here are surprisingly efficient.

I dropped the phone, clenched the handle to our front door and opened it.

I stomped across my lawn and under the last working street light. I approached Janice's front door and checked the handle: locked. I twisted my wrist around so my watch fell below my sleeve and looked at the time: 11:09. Another minute down. A took a half step back, slighted my left foot and used it as a spring as I slammed my body into the front door knocking it open. It wasn't a clean break but it worked and I was in. The front door led to a small hallway which opened up into the rest of the house. The walls of the entryway were covered with pictures of Janice and her late husband; marriage, honeymoon, and children, a firm reminder. I steeled myself and took my first right into her kitchen and skirted myself around the island fully expecting to see Janice's body sprawled out in front of the sink. But her body wasn't there. It was just a normal kitchen waiting for its owner to come home sans the small crack in the window above the sink. When I first started working for KROQ in Boston I covered a story about a woman who shot her husband, disseminated his body and put him into the garbage disposal piece by piece. It took her two full days to fully process his remains. She only got caught when she called a plumber about a backed up shitter. The plumber found a fraction of her husband's femur lodged in the discharge. Janice's killer didn't have two full days and this sink didn't have a garbage disposal. These were homes of the future after all and compost was king. You either eat your food or compost, so where was Janice?

More importantly, what did the state trooper want and why did he kill Janice for it? I walked past the sink and through the archway which led to the dining room and subsequently the back of the house. To the left was a bedroom with a queen size bed ubiquitous enough to find in any specialty store. To the right was a small second bedroom that was converted into a home office. A computer, telephone and typewriter were perched on a long piece of unfinished pine which subsequently sat atop two filing cabinets serving as her desk. The filing cabinets were both open and empty.

Two minutes.

I pushed the top drawer closed on one of them and stopped when a piece of paper fell from the bottom of the drawer and landed on the floor. I reached down and picked it up and unfolded it. I was half expecting to find an old medical bill or an abandoned piece of her husbands will but it was a jumbled series of letters and numbers neatly typed across a heavy piece of eight and a half by eleven piece of twenty pound ivory paper. Some of them were crossed off and in its chaotic mess of nothingness it still looked like something. The top had a small imprint of a flower next to a company name: Frank's Floral Fantasies and a phone number with a local area code. I folded the piece of paper and slid it in my back pocket and went back into the kitchen. I stopped at the refrigerator where I found two plane tickets posted on the front. Cabo. The first ticket had Janice's name on it. I folded it forward to look at the name of the second ticket. The fettuccini alfredo with Italian sausage and meatballs I had for dinner dropped to the bottom of my stomach when I saw the second ticket. It didn't make any sense. Janice Walton and Peter Richards. First class to Cabo.

I turned around as a red light flashed across my eyes. The cops were already here. I was a minute off.

11

I stood above the toilet in our downstairs bathroom and stared at the picture Paula hung above the toilet a few days ago. It was of a young girl standing in the middle of a corn field with a barn behind her in the distance. It was black and white and worn around the edges and I wondered where people found stuff like this. Paula never took pictures, and she didn't know anyone who lived in a corn field or anyone who had access to a corn field, at least to my knowledge. So either she liked it enough to purchase it at a garage sale or flea market, or she just happened to find it. Find it but didn't like it enough to put it anywhere other than above the downstairs toilet where it would only be seen by me and a handful of a dispersed guests. Were we supposed to leave the wall blank?

There was a loud knocking on the door followed by a gruff voice "Time's up." I was a prisoner in my own home, allotted only seconds to pee and maybe a minute to sit on the toilet if I chose to do so with the APD stationed in the living room enjoying Paula's fresh made coffee cake. I should pray to be lucky enough to make a phone call but maintained a level head and tentative appreciation that they haven't hauled me downtown to police headquarters.

My escape plan from Janice's was poorly thought out, to say the least. I should have remembered that there's a police station just under a mile from our house and we live in a quiet community where the only crime is the thought of someone sailing through a red light. It was stupid of me to not realize that someone was sitting at the station waiting for a call from 911 about a murder in an area that was geographically convenient for the police. When I saw the cruiser lights I was staring at the plane tickets on Janice's fridge. United, first class. Departing in less than a week. Her and I spoke only a few times, mostly her passing acknowledgement of my cute offspring but nowhere in my mind did I ever think that my clever and often witty responses would lead her to book a trip for her and I to Cabo. People see what they want to see, I guess.

As the two officers arrived at her house and shut the doors to their cruiser I thought about turning and running through the backdoor and over Janice's fence and then loop back around and sneak in through the backdoor to our house. I keep a spare key or two around for situations like this. But there was no time and I was totally screwed.

I stood there as the police knocked on the front door. I even said come in, I thought it would be rude not to. They opened the door slowly and leaned in with their guns drawn. I said have a seat and introduced myself as the man who called 911 and also lives across the street. I left out the part about our secret trip to Cabo. See that nice house with the beautiful potted plants hanging over the front porch? I live there and the plants are fake. Needless to say, the officers didn't sit down. I tried as best I could to explain what I saw and why I was standing in her kitchen. They asked where the body was and I couldn't really tell them. We exchanged a few awkward pleasantries, I mentioned the DPS cruiser and they said we should go over to my house, sit down and talk.

On the way out, one of them noticed the plane tickets on Janice's refrigerator. We were supposed to leave for Cabo on the 11th he said.

Great detective skills there.

I asked them why would I leave the tickets on her refrigerator if I was just going to kill her. They said clues are everywhere you just need to know where to look. Police Academy 101 right there.

I flushed the toilet, washed my hands and opened the bathroom door to discover Detective Skelly standing against the opposing wall caressing fragments of a breakfast taco out of his beard. He looked the part: tired and cranky as if the aggregate of all worldly criminal activities were weighing heavily on him and he wasn't sure how to handle the pressure. He looked like a twice divorced alcoholic who was battling a weight problem that was a result of a working man's diet and life dedicated to hard-nosed policing. Is this what true heroism looks like or did he aspire to the role because society told him that's what we wanted? I trust someone because they are simply more stressed out than I am and he isn't focused on his diet or appearance so surely he cares about me and my needs.

"Sorry." I said as I followed him back into the living room where Paula was sitting on the couch flanked by the two responding officer's. On the way over here Officer Daniels called into police headquarters to report, correctly so, that there wasn't a body or any sign of a murder at the house in question. In fact, it looked like someone had just left for a very nice vacation despite my assurances otherwise. What good was an eyewitness account of a murder these days if you didn't have a body to go along with the crime?

"Have a seat." Skelly gestured over to a leather arm chair sitting in the corner. He pulled out a black moleskin notepad and flipped to the first page. Good to see he's starting fresh. "State your name."

"Peter Richards."

"And you-" he waved a slothful hand towards Paula.

"Paula Richards." I said. He glanced back at me, an eyebrow on the rise and a question right behind it I'm sure. "I was the one who made the call. She was upstairs asleep."

"That accurate?" he asked.

Paula nodded. It was getting early - almost five.

"What were you doing downstairs?" he asked me.

"Watching TV."

"What were you watching?"

"Something on the DVR. Doesn't matter. I heard a noise so I got up and saw the DPS cruiser vehicle out front."

"How do you know it was a DPS cruiser?" Officer Daniels blurted out after minutes of total silence where he was probably reviewing options in his head on how he can best me. That's what he came up with.

"It said – Texas Department of Public Safety on the side."

"Uh." I could tell he was thinking it over in his head, maybe coming to a realization that he was stumped. Skelly was looking down at his notepad admiring his penmanship.

"The windows were open – I could see into her house," I said "We live in a fairly private neighborhood, not a lot of people driving or walking by so I think she was comfortable leaving the curtains open from time to time."

"Did she tell you that leaving the curtains open made her feel comfortable?"

"No, it's – we're in a cul-de-sac, not a lot of people go by here. I think most people are OK leaving them open. Anyway, she was standing at the sink and he was on the other side of the kitchen. It looked tense, like he was unwelcome. After a minute or so he walked out towards the back of the house. She pulled out her phone and called someone. I think if you pulled the phone records – "

"I think we know how to do our job," Daniels said again. He must be up for a promotion.

"Of course you do. What was I thinking?" I took a pause – more for effect than anything else but I wanted to see if anyone else was going to say something. Silence. I glanced passed the other officers head to find the sun creeping over Janice's house. Maybe her body was over there and I blacked it out. We do strange things when we're in shock.

The side of Daniels belt buzzed. He pulled out a department issued cell phone and looked down at it. "I'll be right back," he said and stepped out on to the front porch.

"What happened next?" Skelly asked. I took him through the next few minutes all the way up until I let the officers in. Skelly listened and didn't write anything down until the very end and then he scribbled something, maybe a reminder to pick up milk on the way home. I looked over at Paula as she was staring off towards the kitchen probably thinking about moving here and getting settled. She was happy and just getting acclimated and now – this horrible and unbearable crime right across the street. It's not what Ə-zero promised.

"What was your relationship with her again?" Skelly asked.

"She was our neighbor, that's all. We've spoken to her maybe half a dozen times."

"She brought us a casserole when Joyce was born." Paula said.

"Is there anything else you haven't told us?" Skelly asked.

"No. I don't think so." I shifted in my seat and stared up at our dark grey and pea-yellow-maybe-green wall. The folded piece of paper I found in Janice's home office was pressed between me and the couch cushion. The second officer cleared his throat. Skelly looked over at him.

"Yes - ?" Skelly beckoned of him.

"There were two plane tickets on the refrigerator. Cabo on the 11th. The victim and –" he pointed his thumb towards me. For the first time since she came downstairs Paula looked up. "They had a trip planned," he said.

"Peter?" Paula looked at me.

"I have no idea." I said and it was true. I wasn't sure what was going on. "Maybe it's a different Peter Richards."

The second officer pulled out a Ziploc bag with the plane tickets and looked at them. "Peter Charles Richards. That is your middle name, isn't it?"

"Yes – that's it." Paula answered for me as she kept her eyes on me.

"Well, that aside." Skelly interjected. "I guess we don't have to tell you but without a body there isn't a whole bunch we can do here. We can take your statement and file a report. Maybe if Daniels has some time he'll run the plates on the cruiser but we have our priorities. Did you talk to any of your neighbors about it?"

I shook my head. "No."

"You didn't text or blog or tweet anything about it? Check-in to a murder scene on Facebook or anything?" he asked. I think he was trying to be funny, but I couldn't tell.

"No."

"Well, don't. It's the last thing our PR department needs right now, an alleged murder with no body."

"You hiring right now?" I asked.

"Excuse me?" he asked.

"For PR. You looking for a new PR guy - ?"

"Oh, Jesus, Peter." Paula said. I wasn't looking at her but I could feel the embarrassment.

"No." he said decisively to get me back on point.

"Well, it doesn't hurt to ask."

"Yes, actually, sometimes it does hurt to ask." Skelly responded and flipped his notebook closed.

There was a light knock on the back door. I turned around. Officer Daniels was standing in the backyard looking in. He waved his hand for Skelly to come outside.

"What's going on?" I asked

"Don't move." Skelly said as he got up and walked past me. He opened the sliding door and stepped outside.

"What's going - ?" I asked again as Skelly slid the door shut.

I stood up.

"Sit back down," the other officer said but I ignored him and went to the sliding door. Paula watched as I flicked the light on to illuminate the backyard. There was a rapid thumping in my chest as I watched Skelly and officer Daniels walk to the side of our yard, near Joyce's sandbox.

"What is it, Peter?" Paula asked.

"I don't know." I said as Skelly and Officer Daniels reached the side of the yard. Daniels pointed down to the sandbox. I couldn't see because Skelly was blocking my view. He leaned over and pulled up on the cover. I built the sandbox when Paula was pregnant with Joyce. I wasn't very handy but I wanted to build something for my daughter. Paula did some research online and found blueprints for a simple four by four sandbox with a cover to keep out leaves and shitty weather. When I started building it I got ambitious so I built an eight by eight sandbox instead. Seemed reasonable in my head but was quite the task and the lid was heavy as shit. Daniels had to step in and help Skelly prop the lid up against the fence. Skelly stepped aside and looked into the sandbox where Janice's body was spread out like a kid doing a snow angel.

My body was on a high and I felt like I could run two consecutive marathons. As the adrenaline reached my heart it took a sharp right turn and kept going. It was fast and I suddenly felt my heart expand and press against the interior wall of my chest. I instantaneously felt lightheaded and sensed the color drop from my face, run down my arm and find a hiding spot under my shoe. *This wasn't normal,* I thought, as my knees wobbled and I fell to the ground. My head smacked against our laminate and everything went black. My eyes rolled and I thought that maybe if I had enough light I could see the frontal lobe of my brain. This was it. One cheeseburger too many and now I was dead. A failed career, crummy cholesterol and death by anxiety all before the age of thirty-five. Paula was going to be so disappointed.

Where did I leave that life insurance paperwork?

12

A slender woman, probably mid-twenties, pushed Kingsman's wheel-chair towards a shortened podium and locked the wheels. She reached over to adjust the microphone for him but he waved her off. He tilted the microphone near his chin and looked out over the ballroom where hundreds of people dressed in their best evening wear looked up at him eagerly awaiting the words that were going to dribble from his mouth. Kingsman didn't make many appearances, not since the accident, but when he did they were sure to be of some note, not dissimilar to a technology giant announcing its latest and greatest product; there was fanfare and certainly a dose of drama. Kingsman wanted to make an impression and be remembered and tonight was no different. Kingsman called four hundred of his closest friends together at the Grand Ballroom in the Hilton downtown to honor the finest in the local news business. The award was called, appropriately enough, the Kingsman, and it went to someone who showed a total unadulterated commitment to telling the news accurately and honestly. Kingsman came up with this brilliant idea in 1997. The first recipient was Adam Chapman, who coincidentally was the owner of KROQ at the time. Kingsman said Chapman was a leader amongst leaders and a true scholar to his profession. Ten months later Kingsman offered Chapman an undisclosed sum of money and bought KROQ from him. People said that Kingsman created the award in attempt to appease Chapman but he kept giving them out years later. Some said this was to save face but here we were, nearly twenty years later and Kingsman was presenting yet another Kingsman. This time to Cleft Duvall, a leader among leaders and a champion amongst the ordinary. No one ever seemed to question the fact that Kingsman preferred giving the award to his stations and his employees. Maybe no one really cared. We were well past people frowning at shameless self-promotion.

"Cleft has been a pioneer in this business for the past three decades," Kingsman said. "He promotes the people's story and advocates for the viewer." Dribble. There are only so many ways you can shine a light on mediocrity but this is what Kingsman had to work with. "So I proudly present to him the two thousand and-" his voice faded as people stood up and applauded. The year didn't matter anyway. The year on this was only going to remind Cleft how long ago he was in his prime. He would then track back the years and make note of all his missteps. Kingsman rolled his wheelchair back a few feet as Cleft got up from his seat thirty rows back from the stage. The event was thin to begin with so padding it with an extra thirty seconds of applause here and there wasn't going to hurt anyone. Cleft moved down the aisle and nodded at people. Cleft was a little unsure when Kingsman told him he was next in line to receive this lavish honor. He thought it was ridiculous and, more importantly, he didn't want people to look at him as someone who was in the business for the accolades. He would have to make sure he said something to that degree in his acceptance speech. *Total one hundred percent humility all the way he thought.*

He reached the stage and leaned over to shake Kingsman's hand. Kingsman winked at him as chicken grease oozed from his palm. In addition to his growing media blitz Kingsman also had a small share in a local fried chicken company. You weren't anybody in this town unless you had at least a small stake in some emerging food empire. The phone buzzed in Cleft's pocket as he turned and approached the podium. He quickly brushed some of the grease off his hand as his phone buzzed again. He reached down and silenced it.

"Say something, asshole." Kingsman said as he rolled closer to him. "Anything, you pile of horseshit." Kingsman had a way with words.

"Uhhh - ?" Cleft looked up and out over the collection of guests. It had the suggestion of a bad dream but no one was actually looking at him sans one or two people who were new to this charade. People were busy sipping champagne and gossiping. He didn't have the undivided attention of anyone except for a woman who came in through the back. She pointed up at him as Phyllis came in behind her gripping her cell phone. She hesitated for a second and Cleft could see the look on her face. Desperation, exhaustion – something bad. "Uhh – excuse me for a second," he said into the microphone.

"What the fuck do you think you're doing?" Kingsman snapped. But Cleft was already off the stage and headed toward his wife.

"What is it?" He could see the panic in her eyes as the audience watched them.

"He's dead. Peter's dead."

13

It wasn't at all like it was supposed to be.

There wasn't a white light or sudden darkness followed by an inevitable spiral into hell, which in all fairness, is what I was expecting. In fact, it was more corporate than anything else. I guess God is busy granting wishes and figuring out who's going to win the World Series that the business of death needs to have a protocol and system. The last thing was remember is hitting the floor of my living room and looking up at the ceiling. We had the popcorn removed from the ceiling before we moved in and I could still see part of it behind the ceiling fan. That's what you get when you go affordable. Paula was going to be very disappointed in me, more so when she discovers that I've been knocking back burgers with her brother. This could have been avoided. Eat more greens, exercise and counterbalance any preconditions you may have. I couldn't die knowing she was disappointed in me. Maybe she knew where the life insurance paperwork was.

But here I was. Standing in a line outside a multi-story light blue office building. Among the dozen or so people in front of me was a young man who had part of a steering wheel imbedded into his chest. He said he was driving home from his girlfriend's house and an eighteen wheeler jumped the median of the interstate. It headed right for him and before he could react the momentum of the truck crippled his car into a pancake and twisted the steering wheel around so it poked right into his heart. I looked around. I knew that I wasn't in line at the DMV. We were surrounded by what seemed like an infinite loop of rolling green hills and lavish redwoods that went as far as the eye could see. It had a west coast feel to it. Maybe that's all heaven was, a small oasis somewhere outside of San Francisco and God was just another entrepreneur living the dream in Palo Alto, spending weekends sailing the Pacific and Monday through Friday he was hard at work perfecting the human race. Maybe we had it all wrong. Assuming I was in heaven, there were no clear indicators other than the fact that I was pretty sure I died and it was rather nice out here. I put away some money each year for Joyce's college fund, didn't run red lights and held the door for old ladies. What more was there? I didn't abuse any hard drugs or knock over liquor stores to fuel my addictions, which for the time being can go unmentioned. I didn't swindle any innocent people out of money either, at least not intentionally. Hell was the polar opposite of where I was. Hell was the sultry humidity of Florida to this Pacific Northwest retreat. Hell was where people were pegged to the ground while chain-smoking oral surgeons slowly extracted their wisdom teeth only to have them grow back an hour later. An hour was the perfect amount of time: it wasn't too quick and gave you enough time to convince yourself the misery was over when in fact it was perpetual. I think I could get used to Heaven.

"Step forward please," a voice said from the front of the line. I pushed my feet up to see over the people in front of me. A small elderly lady was sitting on a barstool handing out tickets to people as they went through a revolving door.

"What are you in for?" Steering Wheel Kid said to me.

"Heart attack. I think." I said.

"My grandfather had one of those. He was out – like that." He snapped his fingers as we reached the front of the line. The elderly lady handed us each a ticket. I looked down at mine. It had the letters QWA written on it in large black bold letters. Clever. I stepped forward into the first opening of the revolving door and walked in sync with it. As it sealed behind me there was a loud sucking sound and a gust of cool air blew down on me. *I lost the kid*, I thought, as the door opened on the other end and I stepped out into a large lobby which spanned infinitely from left to right. I was standing on a shiny white floor and the walls were painted with a white gloss that carried a brief refection of people passing by. A hundred yards in front of me was a vestibule of escalators each with their own sign which contained a letter of the alphabet: A through Z and then AA to ZZ and so on. The letters were printed in light blue letters

"Do you need help, sir?" a voice said to me. I turned around and the same elderly lady stood in front of me wearing a hat which said INFORMATION on it. I had to crane my neck down to make eye contact with her.

"You gave me this." I proffered the ticket.

With barely a glance she pointed to my right and said "Yes, that way. You'll see the escalator on your left just after QVZ and before QWB.

"I don't understand."

"It's OK. Have a nice day."

I shoved the ticket into my pocket and walked through lines of people waiting to get on their respective escalators. The lines were a hundred or so people long and people waited patiently for their turn to board only to ride up a few hundred feet, step off and disappear beyond my line of sight. Everyone was waiting in line or walking towards their assigned line. Maybe you got into Heaven if you were good at following rules.

"He bit his tongue off." Steering Wheel Kid was standing just behind me now, not missing a beat. "That usually happens with a seizure or stroke even but not a heart attack."

"What are you? Fifteen maybe?"

"Seventeen. What's it to you?"

"You look like you're thirteen. I was giving you the benefit of the doubt."

"That's not very nice."

"Go find someone else to bug then. I'm sure the car accident wasn't your fault either, am I right?"

"Screw you, man I don't know. That's not a nice thing to say."

"You cut in front of me in line."

"I didn't cut I appeared. I was driving and the truck hit me and the steering wheel did a Jackie Chan into my chest and now I'm here. I don't think Hell air evac's people just to drop them in line."

"Funny. I was going to say we were in Heaven."

"Are you serious? Look at this place. It's so orderly and sterile it makes me want to vomit. Maybe it's Heaven for some OCD lunatic like yourself. Heaven, I mean true Heaven, is littered with sluts and scotch, dude."

"That's it? You don't have a very expansive imagination."

"I'm only sixteen. What else do you want?"

"I thought you said you were seventeen."

"What are you - a teacher or something? I'm however old I say I am."

I looked up. AAT. I was making progress but clearly wasn't moving fast enough. Hurry up and wait was the name of the game.

"What are you in for anyway?" he said to me.

"Didn't we go over this already?" I couldn't kick this kid. Suddenly I felt like Dick Tracy driving Junior around 1930's Chicago. It was only a matter of time before Pruneface jumped out and sprayed some retrograde Nazi nerve gas and knocked us both out.

'No. We just discussed how we died not why. I cheated on my history exam last week."

"That's an awfully big assumption you have going there for yourself, kid. I don't think God sent you to the afterlife just because you scribbled the founders of the Constitution on the bottom of your sneakers."

"I also wished my girlfriend would get cancer and die. That's actually the thought I had just as the truck hit me. She was really getting on my nerves actually and I couldn't get her to understand that I needed space. You know how these girls are, right man? Wouldn't leave me alone, I'm a hot commodity, I'll admit it but - shit man, she was relentless. So, that's all I could think of: some mightier than thou condition that she had no control over. I would support her through treatment and everything, be a good boyfriend. But only because I knew that cancer was a dick and would take her life. It was the only solution. Terrible, I know, and that's why the truck hit me. I'm sure the driver is real sorry and everything but it was the only way. Careful what you wish for is the thing. God said: screw you and your evil thoughts, Dan, and SMACK - dead.

ABG. Progress. I didn't drink enough water earlier and I could feel a low-grade Charley horse manifesting itself in my calf. It was nice to walk around and stretch my legs but this counting by letters thing was getting old. I did some basic math in my head and figured I would reach my destination in the next four to five days. Appetite and bathroom breaks would add another day. I was anxious and wanted to increase my pace, ditch the kid, and see what was waiting for me at the ever elusive QWA. Another line, assuredly, but a different line and a different set of events that I could wrap my mind around. There wasn't really much else to this place other than the escalators and wide variety of people waiting to get on. It was a large clean and bright bus station sans the buses and corners filled with homeless defecation. Maybe the kid was onto something. Maybe his horrible unrelenting thought about his girlfriend getting sick was the reason God chose him. What horrible thoughts did I have that I was being punished for? Did God decide to off me because I was dietarily incapable and dishonest? Fuck you, I'm God, I'll get rid of you when I feel like getting rid of you. That must also mean that old people are inherently better than people who are young and dead. Janice was getting up there in age but by no means would I call her old, especially by today's revisionist standards. She had done well for herself but maybe one morning she was having coffee and saw Roger pissing in her driveway. Then she pictured backing out of her garage and squishing him. God probably didn't like that so he concocted this elaborate story in his head about a DPS officer coming over and murdering her in cold blood. Maybe that's why he got rid of me. I was hot on his trail.

To confirm my suspicion, I felt a sharp burn in the center of my chest followed by a light sting: indigestion on hyper drive. Yesterday's cheeseburger seeking today's revenge. I needed to find the nearest Hudson News and remedy this thing before it got out of control.

"Is there a gift shop around here somewhere?" I said to someone standing in line. Their response was an apprehensive stare in the general direction of my forehead.

"Thanks anyway." I said and kept walking.

"There's a Steak Heaven down there." Dan the kid said as he pointed behind us. It was in the other direction on the opposite side of where we came in. The sign above it said ZZZ. The presumable end, right next to the beginning.

"You might be on to something." I said as I turned around. "Come on, I'll buy you a cheeseburger."

"Nice." Dan the kid said as we retraced our steps. This place must be setup like a football stadium. You walk long enough you just end up back where you started: Right next to Steak Heaven, or as it's known in this region: Steak. It's the world's largest privately owned fast-food chain that serves steak burgers made from the meat of organically fed cows. They sell steak burgers and milkshakes. That's it. No french fries, no breakfast items, no chicken and certainly no dessert. We loved our cows when they were alive so you can enjoy them while they're dead, is probably what their slogan should say. In a competitive and every-growing fast-food market, Steak Heaven charges an average of ten dollars for your typical run of the mill steak burger, when the average cost of a fast-food burger is around three dollars. If you feel so inclined you can add cheese to your burger for an additional dollar fifty. I always add cheese, might as well. I'm sure God assembled a committee of people to come up with the perfect eating establishment that kept people satisfied and humored and not too terribly offended. All the vegans got sent to hell for not obeying the natural order of life.

Unlike our surroundings, there was no line at Steak Heaven. It was just a long open counter behind which a friendly looking teenager stared at us from under a white and black checkered visor.

"Welcome to Steak Heaven, where happy cows make happy customers. Can I take your order?" she said. I like my slogan better.

Dan stepped forward as I waited for the grumble in my stomach that usually happens when I'm within walking distance of a hamburger. "I'll have a Don Johnson."

"I'm sorry, sir, but we don't serve – that here." she said a little too apprehensively.

"Sure you do. Don. Johnson. He was on Miami Vice and Nash Bridges. He was Nash Bridges for crying out loud. He defined the '80s and he's also on your menu."

"I'll be right back." she said.

She stepped away and Dan turned towards me and winked. "Secret menu."

Of course there was a secret menu. You weren't anyone in the food industry if you didn't cater to a middle-class who wanted to reinforce their elitism by ordering from a menu that no one in the history of anyone had ever heard of. I thought about Don Johnson, the person and the burger, and felt a sharp squeezing pain in my chest again.

"Hey Peter – Peter-"a voice said. I looked up at Dan but his lips weren't moving. He just had a blank stare across his face. "Peter – asshole – wake up."

14

"Hey Peter." I heard the voice rumble around my head a few more times and then felt a light on my eyelids. I opened my right eye to see Cleft standing over me. "Hey, there you are bud-" he said as a smile came across his face. "Good to have you back."

He placed a firm grip on my shoulder and squeezed. A fierce pain shot down my arm and I winced. "Sorry – sorry – too soon."

"What happened?" I said as I opened both eyes. Cleft looked over at a rather diminutive man wearing surgical gear. Cleft always had a way of communicating important information.

"I'm Dr. Corgan, head of Cardiology and Innovation. You've had quite an eventful forty-eight hours." I looked over at Cleft. He was scrolling through his phone.

"What happened?" I asked.

"You suffered from congestive heart failure which means your heart was unable to provide sufficient pump action to sustain blood flow and your body gave out."

"Shit. Am I OK?"

"You are now. We replaced your heart."

"You did what?!" I blurted.

"They gave you a heart transplant" Cleft said. A smile plastered on his face. This was fun for him.

"I understand that, thank you."

"Just saying."

"Aren't there lists for that sort of stuff? Women and children first, kind of thing? I'm a white guy in my early thirties. You don't care about me. Besides, don't you match blood type and run me through the system?"

"We did that, Peter, and there was a match. That's why you're here. I'm happy to tell you that you are outfitted with a Ə-zero Electro-Flux heart. Series 2."

"What's that?"

"It's half-heart and half-machine. We took all the bad stuff out and put in some screws and wires and a really powerful battery. You are one lucky man." Dr. Corgan said as he stepped over and shook my hand.

"Ə-zero, that's the company that built my house." I said.

"I've heard of those. Top of the line. It will be a great place to get your rest. And to think, they used to just make vacuums. Anyway, the nurse will be in soon with some more pain medication and I'll come back tomorrow to check on you. In the meantime, take it easy and let your heart do the work." He turned around, brushed past Cleft and let the door close behind him.

"Is that it?" I said

"Can you believe that?" Cleft said as he took a seat on the bed. "I'll make a phone call and see if I can find out whose heart you got."

"Didn't you hear him? They gave me one of those Ə-zero hearts. I wanted to do a story on them a few months ago."

"Eh, just lip service. I bet if I check the obits of the last few days I can figure it out."

"It didn't come from anyone. It's a machine."

But he continued - "They can keep it on ice for only a day or two and I'm sure they wouldn't fly one out here for your sorry ass."

"Where's Paula?" I was still thinking about what the doctor said and I wasn't quite sure what was happening. I remember hitting the floor and then waking up somewhere that was for sure the afterlife. Was this just an extension of that? Maybe I was still living some weird unbalanced dream and Cleft just happened to appear. For all I know, I was probably still passed out on my living room floor waiting for someone to revive me.

"She's picking up Joyce from daycare. She said she'd come by later on after she drops Joyce off at our house."

"Why your house?" I asked. He wasn't looking at me.

"Just helping each other out. It's only for a few days so she can come here and see you and get some things sorted out."

"Can you grab my pants?" I asked and glanced over to a small pile of neatly folded clothes. I set my hand on my chest. I could feel my new heart pumping. Fierce and consistent.

He picked up the folded pile of clothes and handed it to me. I tore off the plastic wrap and pulled out my pants and dug through the pockets. Empty. "Dammit."

"What is it?" he asked. I wanted that slip of paper from Janice's house.

"Did they happen to leave a bag of valuables?" I asked.

"They did. Has your phone and wallet in it."

"Great. Where is it?"

"I can't speak to that," he said.

"What do you mean? You can't speak to it?" He wasn't making any sense.

"What are you looking for?"

"A phone number. I must have misplaced it. Cleft, where is my phone and my wallet?"

I reached my hand out to point to my pants but my arm only went about three inches before it was yanked back. I looked down. My wrist was shackled to the arm of the bed. Handcuffs.

Cleft reached out and put his hand on my shoulder again. "Look, everything will be OK. It will just take some time. I called Ramirez for you."

Ramirez was Hector Ramirez. He ran a small specialty firm out of south Austin that focused mostly on defending people who were accidentally accused of driving under the influence. For a reasonable five hundred dollar fee, Ramirez would expunge your record and work with the city to regain your reputation as an upstanding citizen. Recently, Ramirez expanded his portfolio to include defending a wide variety of criminals and alleged criminal activity, including murder.

"Why am I handcuffed to the bed?"

"They found her body."

"What?" I could feel my forehead fold over itself as I furrowed my brow. "I know they found her body. I was there when they found it. She was splayed out like a snow angel in Joyce's sandbox."

"I didn't know. All I know is you had a heart – thing and they found the body. No one was real specific on the order of events."

"Pretty simultaneous." I said.

"Well, the way they see it and with you being in her house when they got there that makes you the prime suspect. The only suspect, at least right now."

"So? I called 911 and told them what I saw. They wouldn't have been there if it wasn't for me."

"They think you have a condition."

"A condition?"

"Ya, some narcissist thing."

"What is that supposed to mean?"

"They think you want to have sex with yourself so you kill your neighbor, call it in and then play innocent just to see how they'll react. It's like setting a fire and staying there while they put it out."

"Killing my neighbor is a lot different than me wanting to have sex with myself."

"I'm just telling you what they think, Peter."

"What do you think, Cleft?"

"I don't know."

"Just cause they found her in the sandbox doesn't mean that I killed her. I was trying to help."

"You were trying to help so you put her in Joyce's sandbox?"

"No. I didn't. I called 911. I was being a good citizen. I took action. Isn't that what you and Paula always tell me – be a man, Peter, take some initiative."

"Well, that's a little harsh, the way you're – "

"I liked Janice." I added.

"Apparently. Paula mentioned the plane tickets."

"Jesus. I didn't kill her and I wasn't going to Cabo with her."

"It was your backyard, Peter, in Joyce's sandbox."

"Can you just refer to it as the sandbox? Why do you have to put my daughter's name in front of it every time?"

"OK. It was your backyard. They found her body in a sandbox," he said and looked at me for a split second and then turned towards the television. *Matlock* was on, playing in hospital perpetuity. I watched Cleft for a minute and knew that he wasn't going to look back at me. He was done. He'd watch Joyce and get me a lawyer but I could tell he was checked out. Too many strikes against me.

"That's not right." I said.

"What's not right?"

"This situation."

"Well, Ramirez is out there speaking to the officers now. Maybe he'll get it sorted for you," Cleft said. My eyes darted past him and I could see a slender gentleman standing outside the room speaking with Detective Skelly. He had on a Men's Warehouse suit and was carrying a large leather satchel. "They have a pretty good case against you, but I'll let him explain." Cleft added.

"Fuck me."

"Look, I know you didn't do it. Wrong place, wrong time kind of thing. Just like Clover, I guess. Ramirez is good. He's not the best but he gives us a lot of money to run his commercials so I have to say he's good." He laughed. "Just kidding. You'll be fine. I mean, you beat the afterlife so you're pretty much set, right?"

I guess that was one way of looking at it.

There was a soft knock on the door and Ramirez pushed his head in. "Can I have a minute, please?"

"We were just finishing up." Cleft said hurriedly. He looked down at me and winked. I could see a sense of relief come over him. He didn't know what to say to me. The deck was stacked against me and he wanted to distance himself as quickly as possible. He gave me a thumbs up and headed out, went past Skelly and down the hall. I'd be amazed if I ever saw him again.

I looked up at Ramirez. He reached out and handed me a small stack of business cards. "Hector Ramirez," he said. I didn't reach up to take them so he set them on the tray next to a pitcher of water and cup of pudding. I'm pretty sure pudding isn't good for a new heart, but who am I.

"We only have a few minutes before that sack of shit comes in here to talk to you," Ramirez said.

"Oh good, I'm glad someone has the same judge of character as me."

"I spoke to your wife. She agreed to let me represent you which, I think, is personally fantastic. You and I, I think we'll get along great. But let me make something clear: when he comes in here you're under arrest." I pulled my arm up to show him the handcuffs. "Shit. *More* under arrest then." Ramirez said. "Due to special circumstances they're going to let you stay in here with police supervision but you are now in the hands of the law. No phone, no email and no contact with the outside world whatsoever except for that nice gentleman and your wife.

Who is quite lovely, by the way. Me and my team are working around the clock to assure you get out of here and home safely but the police are pretty convinced you killed this Janet - "

"Janice." I interrupted.

"Right, Janice. Anyway, they said you did it and we're going to prove otherwise. Besides, their case is purely circumstantial. You were there, she turns up dead in your shed so it's closed as far as they're concerned."

"What you just said, that doesn't sound like circumstance, that sounds like evidence. And they found her in the sandbox."

"Right. Circumstantial evidence," he said. "Couldn't stay in your own fucking house, could ya?" He smirked. "Just giving you a hard time, buddy…" He looked at the monitors I was connected to, everything seemed to be in working order. "Oh, one more thing, before I forget. Did you happen to see a box in her house?"

"A box?"

"You know, a box − where you store files and stuff."

"Like a banker's box?"

"Right − ya, exactly."

The Albino.

"No. Why?"

"No reason. The police were doing an inventory and − ah, doesn't matter − go and help the police and they'll never let you live it down, am I right?" he said and patted my shoulder as the door pushed open. Skelly stepped in and walked over to the foot of the bed. The two officers were behind him. The three amigos, I guess. "I'm having a private meeting with my client," Ramirez said.

"Sure, sure. We won't be long," Skelly said. He stepped aside and waved his hand towards the two officers.

"Peter Richards, you're under arrest for the murder of Janice Walton." Skelly said and pointed to Daniels who read me my rights off a business card. He stumbled through most of it and slid the card back into his pants pocket when he was finished.

"Don't worry about it. It's just words. We can sue the bejeezus out of the state for harassment and wrongful incrimination later on," Ramirez said.

"Ya, go ahead and do that," Skelly said. Skelly put his hand on my shoulder and pressed down on me as he leaned in. "What about your

Commie wife, huh?" he whispered. "I'll get her kicked out of this country and back to Russia before you can say bypass." He looked down at me and a smile crept up on his face as I looked past him. "Didn't think I'd figure it out, huh?"

"I don't know what you're talking about."

"Sure you do. Paula Richards, born in Dorchester Massachusetts, February 8th, 1981. Sister to a-" he paused, pulled out a notepad and flipped a few pages. "Brad, right. Fucking Brad."

"Ya, he's my brother-in-law."

"That's not possible though, right? How can he be the brother of someone who doesn't exist?" I looked up at him. "There is no Paula Richards from Dorchester, Massachusetts, is there?"

"I'm not sure what – "

"Save it, Richards. I did my due diligence on this. This isn't my first time investigating someone so cut me some slack and play along. When I went to look up your wife all I could find was a change of name form in the Essex County court system. Natalya Olesay, born in St. Petersburg in 1976 and Oksana Olesay, born in Moscow in 2011."

Paula and Joyce.

It's true. There wasn't a Paula Richards from Dorchester, Massachusetts. That's just what we told people. In fact, I didn't remember what her real name was until Skelly said it. It's very possible I wasn't even given her real name. RussianCEMbR.com only offered a portfolio of staged images, a brief biography and catalogue number for its visitors. No names, at least no real names. If you were truly serious, sincerely invested in finding the right partner to spend the rest of your life with, you had to pay and cost was based on credits. A single credit cost approximately thirty Rubles, the equivalent to a single US dollar. Five credits allowed you to wink at a potential match and if she winked back you could then pay twenty Rubles to visit her customized page which offered additional information: family, goals, hobbies and so on. The next step was a phone conversation which usually proved difficult due to an immense language barrier. But that wasn't the case with Paula. Her English was perfect. She was on the site for a few years and spoke with dozens of suitors but never found someone she liked until she met me. All that time she was working on her English and matured to a point where the Russian heritage was almost undetectable. Our first conversation we talked about Boston and my family and where I grew up. We spoke a few more times over the course of a few months and then the site performed a comprehensive background check on me before I went out for a week long pre-marital visit. The background check cost me two hundred and fifty credits. It was pretty standard but I think they wanted to make sure I was really in the market for love and wasn't going to bring a girl back to my country and try and sell her on the black market. It happens more times than one would imagine. After I cleared the background check I flew to Moscow and we spent a week together in the final step of the process. Depending on how the visit went you offered a proposal of marriage. If she accepts, the site works with an unbiased third party to issue a marriage certificate and United States passport so we can travel back to the United States as husband and wife. The story of how we met and fell in love was completely up to us. Paula actually suggested the story about us meeting in college, since she didn't want to be frowned upon and judged for who she really was. I said people didn't care, and only think of themselves, but she didn't want to listen to reason. She said she saw the story in a movie somewhere and thought it was perfect.

"It's a pretty common name," I said. "What does this have to do with anything?"

"You have a credibility problem so I'd be careful what you tell people." Skelly said to me.

"Why don't you just pull the plug, huh? Take me out now while you have the chance? Daniels and what's his name won't stop you."

"Actually," Ramirez said. "I may have some issue with that."

"As my lawyer, I kindly ask you not to interfere."

"I wouldn't kill you if you were a bug on the bottom of my shoe. The court system will take care of your ass. By the time they're done with you, your wife will be back in Russia, her kid will be an orphan somewhere in the Midwest and you'll wish you never even heard of Janice Montgomery." He stepped back and went for the door. He jerked a finger at the officers and they followed him out. Ramirez looked over at me, concern draped his face.

"You better watch yourself, Peter."

"Sure," I said. My mind still clung to what Skelly said. "But who is Janice Montgomery?"

15

"Can you run a few names for me?" I said into the phone. It was a few hours later. Skelly left but Ramirez stuck around for a while longer to have me sign my life away on paper. After everything was said and done he chatted with the officer guarding the door and left. He probably went down to the cafeteria to have coffee with Skelly. They didn't seem too keen on each other but I know that Ramirez was posing for his client. Besides, they're both parts of the same system, each performing their own respective duty, I'm sure they'd have a lot of stories to share.

"I don't know, man. The detectives probably already did that," Brad said on the other end.

"But I thought you were connected. I thought you were the man. Was I wrong?"

"No. Just so you know, this is a very unusual request. It violates our relationship big time and the station would fry my ass if they knew I was running names for a suspect. That being said, what are the names? I won't run them, running the names would be wrong, but I am curious as to what you are up to."

I'm glad he gave me the run down. The station was known for recording calls at random and surfing the database for a friend was a fireable offense so Brad needed to make it clear that he wasn't going to do it, then he would hang up the phone and run the names. At least, I was hoping he would. It would simply be too much if he ate kale and had strict moral boundaries.

"Janice Walton, Janice Montgomery, Frank's Floral Fantasies and the tag on the police cruiser: something – something – something – Z – H – 1.

I think the first digit is an eight or a weird pregnant b. I can't tell for
sure."

"That's four things, Peter," he snapped back at me.

"Do you want them in order of importance?"

"I'm the Yellow Pages now?"

"Fine. Just the first two and last one. I'll check on the florist."

"I'm not checking this stuff for you."

"Right. Don't check the first two."

"You've heard of an internet search, right?"

"Yes, the hospital and Google teamed up so we had unfettered access right from our hospital beds," I said.

"Are Janice Walton and Janice Montgomery the same person?"

"I don't know. I was hoping you could tell me."

"Why a florist?"

"I don't know – just a hunch. The morning before she was killed a
florist came to her house – didn't have any flowers but left with a box."

"A box?"

"A banker's box."

"Interesting."

"Why is that all of a sudden interesting?"

"I can look into it for you, don't worry about it. You free for lunch
today?"

"Funny."

"Now is actually probably the best time to have a cheeseburger."

"I got another few days here until I get to go home or jail depending
on how this Ramirez guy works out," I said as the door to my room
opened. The nurse came in pushing a cart filled with various tubes and
clamps. I bet she would up my morphine if I slipped her twenty bucks.

"Let me know about lunch. I wasn't kidding. Significant life changes, a near death experience, can cause a relapse. I'm here if you need
me, Peter."

"Thanks." I said as the nurse sat on the edge of the bed. I clicked
the phone off and set it next to me. One side of the device was the
phone and the other side was a remote control for the television. Both
sides had huge buttons with large black numbers and letters. I'm in the
hospital so I must have terrible eye sight and only want to watch reruns
of *Matlock* or *The Price is Right*. When I feel up to it I'll have to take a
walk and find the control room where they're running the video loop

for the televisions and tell them to give me a few more options. My room has a thirty-two inch LCD television, I'd settle for a smaller one with HBO. Maybe I'll run for state senate and, if the news business doesn't work out, reform health care. More entertainment, hotels and gyms in hospitals for the healthy visitors and, for Heaven's sake, less medicine.

"That's a big no-no, Mr. Richards," the nurse said as she locked the wheels to her drug cart. I was about to respond but she leaned behind the bed and unplugged the telephone slash remote control.

"It's just a little *Matlock*, it's harmless." I said. I'm so clever.

"They forgot to take the phone. You aren't allowed to use the phone. It says so in your chart, right here." She took a finger and pointed to a section on the bottom of the chart.

"That's a remote too. How am I going to change the channel?" I smiled at her.

"You got a problem with Matlock?" She smiled back. It was a different smile than mine. "How are you feeling today, Mr. Richards?"

"Fine. Good, I guess. How are you, today - ?" I leaned over to try and read her name tag but it just said Carlisle on it. Not sure if that was her name or the type of medicine she was about to give me.

"On a scale of one to ten how is the pain?" She pointed to a chart on the opposite wall that had ten faces on it. They all looked miserable but each of them got considerably better at hiding their pain.

"Six." I said.

"Not too bad," the nurse said and wrote something down. This woman was all business. "I'm sure Dr. Corgan reviewed this with you but I'm going to give you six hundred cc's of liquid morphine. It sounds like a lot but it's about a third of what hospice patients get. It will help with the pain from surgery. How long have you been drug free for?"

There it was. "Six months." I said and reached for my neck to grab the six month pendant that I wore so proudly. It wasn't there.

"It's probably with your valuables. Don't worry, you'll get it back - eventually." She let the last word linger. I think she meant to say when I got discharged but then it probably occurred to her, between the visitors and the handcuffs, that my discharge would just take me somewhere far worse than this hospital. "Congratulations, by the way." She added. "My aunt just got her five year pendant. She was on crank, real messed up."

"Thanks." I said.

"Also, were you aware that you were wearing a bullet proof vest when the paramedics brought you in here?" she asked.

"Yes." I said.

"Do you mind if I ask why?"

"It's a long story but it was for my protection."

"Paranoid?"

"No. Just don't want my past catching up to me."

"Were you like a President in your past life?"

"No, just dealt with some unsavory people."

"Understood," she said and smiled.

I heard a soft beeping sound.

"Shit," the nurse said as she reached into the pocket of her nurse's uniform and pulled out a phone.

"Do you mind?" she asked.

"Not at all." I said.

She answered. "This is Carly," she said as she took a few steps away from the bed then went over and closed the door to the room. "I told you not to call me when I'm working. We can deal with this later." She turned around and held up a finger. It would be a minute. "No. That's perfectly OK. We can talk about it when I'm home tonight, *after* my shift, Todd." Todd such a strong masculine name, I bet he was tall. "It's posted on the refrigerator - use your eyeballs, Todd!" I could tell she was pissed, she used his name twice. She pressed a button on the phone and tossed it on the tray next to the pudding. "Sorry about that."

"It's fine. Everything OK?" I asked.

'My boyfriend bought me a new car - an Impala. He keeps telling me to get it registered and I'm like - OK I get it, Todd." She let his name linger like it was a disease.

"They'll pull you over if you don't have a sticker." I said.

"That's what Todd keeps telling me. Once the medicine kicks in you should start walking around. You can do laps in the hallway. The doctor said it was fine as long as one of your guards goes with you."

"Right." I said. "Hey - can I get some more ice, please? I would but, you know-" I lifted up my hand so the handcuffs would rattle.

"Oh, of course. I'll be right back." She gave me a soft smile, I wasn't Todd after all, and left the room. She said something to the officer guarding the door. He looked back at me as she walked down to the room where they kept the ice machine and water for the guests. When the officer turned around to check out the nurse I reached forward with my free hand and grabbed her phone. It was in one of those all-purpose cases that held all your necessary information. I pulled out her driver's license: Carlisle Jane Smith born June 13th, 1986. Blue eyes and brown hair. She must dye it. Cute. I slid the phone under my leg as she came back into the room and set the ice down on the tray.

"I need to attend to another patient in another room. I'll be right back."

She left again. I pulled out the phone. It was a smartphone and had a multitude of icons for applications I didn't recognize but most of them appeared to be games. I opened the internet browser and typed in Frank's Floral Fantasies. The first listing that came up was for a small flower shop on Anderson Lane, about four miles from our house. I clicked on the icon that allowed me to call directly from the website. It rang a few times before someone picked up. "Frank's Floral Fantasies, this is-" her voice was nice but I simply didn't have the time.

"Hi. I'd like to place a delivery, please."

"Sure. What would you like to send?" the voice on the other end asked.

"Just a simple arrangement, for a friend in the hospital. You can pick it out. I don't want to spend more than fifty dollars."

"Is that with or without the vase? The vase is extra."

"With the vase, please." All these hidden charges.

"What is the person's name?" she asked.

"Peter Richards."

"What's the address?" Fuck. I didn't even know where I was. I looked around the room. There was a notepad and pencil next to the bed. The notepad said Austin Heart Hospital on it. I told her.

"Got it. It will probably be there by the end of the day, is that OK?"

"Sure, that's fine. Hey - can I request the person who will deliver the flowers? The person getting them is rather particular."

"Uh, I guess so. All depends on if they're working today. Who is it?"

"The albino."

Silence. I think the guy I saw at Janice's house was an albino.

"Pedro? Sure, he's on today. I can ask him. No guarantee though."

"No, of course. I understand."

"The total is sixty seven dollars." They really screw you with the vase. "Do you want to write anything on the card?"

"Ya. Write this: Just Beat It."

16

Paula came to visit me a few hours later. We covered the basics, *hi, how are you, happy you're still alive, and no I'm not going to Cabo with the dead neighbor.* I then told her about how Skelly discovered who she really was and how we met – the true story. I added that he threatened to expose this information if I didn't cooperate with the investigation and turn myself in. It was entrapment at its best; if he couldn't get me to cooperate he would go for the wife and the kids. Skelly's thinking must have been right because the color dropped from Paula's face and she stared at a small dent in the wall next to my bed.

"Paula, did you hear me?" I asked.

"I didn't – I didn't even tell anyone – how did he find out?"

"I don't know. It doesn't matter."

"Of course it matters, Peter. I have a job – a career. I have credibility and integrity in my field. If this got out and they found out that I lied about something so significant then I would be just like – "

"Just like what?"

"It doesn't matter." But I knew where she was headed.

"He won't tell anyone. He's just using it against me."

"But how do you know? How do you know he won't tell anyone?"

"I don't know, but I don't think he's going to run around gossiping about it."

"You better hope you're right."

"I am right." I said and then told her that the only way the information was going to get out was if this went to trial and we were planning on paying Ramirez good money to make sure that didn't happen. I think Paula was mostly concerned because we really had no intention of telling our daughters when they were older. As far as they were concerned we met in Massachusetts and Brad really was their uncle. Everything is online now though so if they, or anyone for that matter, had the inclination and curiosity they could probably burn a big hole in our story. It would take a few clicks but they would get there. But kids also idolize their parents so the whole thing is probably moot. I put my hand on a large stack of paper and pushed it over to Paula. The hospital admin came to visit me shortly before Paula got there and walked me through all the paperwork I needed to sign. Shortly after she left, someone from billing called me and asked if I wanted to pay part of my enormous bill over the phone. I told them I would be more than happy to and that if someone came by the room I would gladly give them a check. They said that stopping by a patient's room was against hospital policy and hung up. I haven't heard from them since.

"It'll be fine," I said to Paula. "The worse thing is that Skelly leaks it to someone in the press, or worse, the news."

"Is there a difference?"

"Huh?" I said as I looked up at her hovering over my bed.

"Between the press and the news, is there a difference?"

"Yes, of course there's a difference." I retorted. She kept watching me. "If Skelly leaks it to the press it goes to print the next morning and no one reads it — ever. But if he calls the local news they'll send some hotshot Miami-grad student down here to stand in front of the hospital until they can get anyone to say anything about me and then they'll just replay that clip forever."

"Then what do we do?"

"Then we hold a press conference and deny it."

"A press conference?"

"Right. Get some cameras in here, do it right from this room."

"Do you think you warrant a press conference?"

"Sure. I know the right people."

"He could call Cleft."

"Nah. If he did that Cleft would ask me about it first and then I'd say Skelly was crazy and just using the media to intimidate me."

"And he isn't trying to do that?"

"No way. He knows better."

"You are kind of soft," she said. "No offense, but you are sensitive, so —" and she let it linger there. No follow-up and no explanation.

"Right. Soft. I hear ya."

"I just don't know what you've gotten yourself into, Peter. You were doing so well," she said.

"Nothing. I haven't gotten myself into anything," I said. She was really making this whole thing about her, wasn't she? I'm the one laying here after all, who cares if someone finds out she's lying about where she's from. It's not the most incriminating thing she's done. At least, I don't think it is.

Paula was about to say something else but there was a loud knock on the door. I looked up. One of the guards leaned his head in. "There's a delivery for you," he said as he held up a vase of flowers.

"Who are those from?" Paula said. "Did a dead woman send you flowers or is there someone else?"

"No on both accounts. I'll explain later." I waved my hand towards the door. "Is the delivery guy still here?" I asked.

"He just left," the guard said

"Can you go get him, please?" I want to give him a tip." He hesitated for a second, thinking about the parameters of his job and what he should really be doing. Before he said anything I asked Paula to grab some cash. She rolled her eyes and pulled a few singles from her purse. The guard retreated and headed down the hall calling after the delivery guy.

"Can you run down the hall and get me some more ice please?" I said to Paula. She looked at me in a way that suggested she knew I was up to something but didn't know what and she didn't have the energy to sit and argue with me. I was on the mend anyway and she knew I would never give it up. Have a little respect for the ill and recovering. She grabbed the ice bucket and went through the precipice passing a tall angular albino.

There he was. Pedro the flower delivering albino of greater Travis County, in the flesh. He was wearing an over-sized burnt orange t-shirt.

"Here." I said and held up my wallet in his general direction. Pedro the albino took a few steps towards me as I held out a fifty dollar bill for him. He went to take it but I didn't let go. "Step closer." I said. "Lean in."

"I'm good here."

"Just for a second." I said and retracted my arm. He didn't let go of the fifty so he followed it towards me. "Tell me what you know about the woman who lives at 1109 Candida Circle." I said softly so the guard wouldn't hear me.

"Excuse me?" he said as he ripped the fifty from my hands. Greed doesn't get people anywhere in this world.

"Janice Walton. 1109 Candida Circle. You were there last Tuesday morning. It was before six and she gave you a banker's box. Do you remember that?"

"I don't think I know what you're talking about, sir."

"Sure you do. Last Tuesday. One box."

"I'm sorry, but I don't think – "

"I saw you leave her house last week – or – the week before – doesn't matter, but the point is I saw you." *What fucking year was it?*

"I don't know what you're talking about."

"She's dead." I said. "Janice Walton is dead." I said again and watched as a gloss came over his eyes. "Is this all making sense now?" I asked.

"She's dead?"

"So you were there?" But he didn't answer. He moved his eyes back and forth, ran through events in his head.

"What is it?" I asked.

"That - asshole," he grumbled.

"Who - which asshole?" I have a running list of assholes but I figured it would be safe to check if he knew the same assholes or had a set of different assholes I needed to be aware of.

"It's who she worked for - he did this."

"Who did she work for?"

"She found something," he said.

"What did she find?"

Pedro the albino took a few steps back from the bed. He glanced at the television. CNN was rerunning the same story for the past hour. "That's the asshole," he said and pointed at the screen.

I looked up.

They were running a story about Harvey Marcona, an entrepreneur and biologist who was discovered dead in his office last week. He founded a few prominent think tanks and was an advisory board member at half a dozen established universities. A few years ago, he was named one of the "The World's 50 Most Influential Figures" by a super-important international publication. He was number 49. I only knew about him because it was someone Paula idolized and his name came up often when she was going on about work.

Last night, authorities arrested David Prescott in connection with his murder. Prescott was the financial backer for his most recent establishment – Endochrone – which performed genetic testing on chromosome 16.

I looked back at Pedro the albino. He was still pointing his finger at David Prescott's face.

The TV cut away from him and went to a tape package on chromosome 16. They interviewed a prominent professor about how it binds specific cells together and is a key contributor to learning and memory functions within the human brain. The professor was an expert. A stuffy omnipotent expert who probably eats half a grapefruit for breakfast each morning because some buddy told him it would help him live to be a hundred.

Pedro the albino and I watched intently.

In 2007, Endochrone purchased the patent rights to chromosome 16 so they could conduct research without interference or competition from other companies. The patent, which they apparently own in perpetuity, ensures they control the exclusive rights to any discoveries they make during testing and research.

In the last two years, they made a substantial breakthrough and sold their findings to Green Pharmaceuticals which incorporated the findings into the development of a drug called Memoton, an over-the-counter Alzheimer's medication that increases short-term memory function. The patent and research are strictly confidential but Green Pharmaceuticals has stated publicly that Memoton wouldn't exist without the research and dedication of Endochrone and, more specifically, Harvey Marcona.

Endochrone.

Chromosome 16.

Brain. Power. Down. I was only one man.

"Prescott?" I asked Pedro the albino. "Why him?"

"How should I know, I'm just the delivery guy." he said. "Two weeks ago I made a delivery to Endochrone. Some hot shot ordered a thousand dollars' worth of flowers to send to David Prescott. When I delivered them, Prescott asked to see me in person and then offered me five hundred dollars to pick up a box from this woman's house and bring it to his house. That's all I know."

"Where is David Prescott's house?"

"Man, I don't - "

"How heavy was the box?" *Was there a human head in the box?*

"Hey!" a voice said from the doorway. We both looked over. The guard was standing there with his arms folded across his chest.

"Do you have change for a fifty?" I asked the guard.

"No," he said and then looked at Pedro the albino. "Your time is up."

Oh, science, I thought to myself as I stared blankly at the television. I let my eyes wander up towards the ceiling. I pressed them shut and imagined floating in the middle of the Pacific, just off to the side Paula and Joyce were playing on our newly purchased seventy foot yacht. I purchased the yacht with the money the state government paid me after I proved beyond a reasonable doubt that Skelly and his department hooligans falsely incriminated me for the murder of a woman I barely knew. Yes, it's true, I spent some time in jail, but that's only because the system was doing what it does best. In my mind, Skelly planted Janice's body in my backyard and led the local authorities there with an anonymous tip from a neighbor that saw me carry her back to our house after I brutally murdered her. Motive? They didn't need a motive to convict me, a motive was purely optional, especially with her body in my backyard. Paula would be on my side but only for a while. Skelly and the system would get to her. She idolized the American legal system, there's no way it could incarcerate an innocent man even it was her husband. So, eventually, she too would turn on me. Skelly would question her over and over again and ask her repeatedly if she saw me carrying Janice over to our house and then put her in the sandbox. She'd say no, of course, but then she would question herself. *Maybe I did see him do it after all*, she would think to herself. *Maybe Skelly is right and I just blocked it out because I didn't want to admit to myself that my husband could commit such a horrendous crime to someone so nice.* That there would be the lynchpin in the trial. Paula would take the stand and I would watch her as she stated that she, for sure, and without question, saw me carry Janice's body over to our backyard. Not once, but twice, she would say. I had to cut her up as to not be suspicious. A jury of twelve would convict me and send me away for a long time and Skelly would bask in my misery. But why? Why on earth would Skelly go through this charade when he knew I was innocent? I needed to get out of here and find out what was in the box that Pedro the albino took from her house – it was the only solution. If I sat here and waited I was a dead man. If I found out what she was protecting maybe then I would have a chance at clearing my name.

There was a light nudge on my shoulder and a soft voice. "Hey – hey – Peter – wake up." I opened my eyes slightly and looked up. Carly was back. The drugs must have taken full affect. I felt good, for once. I didn't feel the post-surgical pain in my chest. I looked past her but she closed the privacy curtain so I couldn't see out into the hall.

"Where did my wife go?" I asked.

"Your wife went home," she said. "She said she'd be back – later." I noted the pause she took before she said later.

"That's too bad." I said and gave her the good old Peter Richards charm. But she just stared back at me, impervious to my magnetism.

"Can you explain this?" she said as she held up her phone. "I found it behind your pillow. I was looking for it but thought for sure I left it in my car until your head started vibrating."

"You told me to watch it for you."

"Mr. Richards."

"Call me Peter," I said. "I can explain."

"I certainly hope so,"she said and leaned towards me. "You know I have to report this, right?"

"Report what exactly? That you left your phone in a room with a patient who's under arrest for murder? Do you even know how aiding and abetting a criminal works?" I could throw out some more non-sense but I could see her take a beat, she wasn't sure, which was good because I was in no mood to start explaining legal terms I didn't fully understand. "That's at least five years in prison," I said. OK, I couldn't help myself. "And the way the legal system is these days, you being a nurse, they'll put you away for as long as possible. So – go ahead – tell the officer that I stole your phone. See what he says."

Silence. She thought about it for about five seconds and then said "I'm sorry, Peter." and pushed herself up. I reached out and grasped her wrist as she was turning around. I squeezed as hard as I could. "Ow!" she said. "You're hurting me."

"Sit down – now." I snapped at her and pulled her back towards the bed. "I don't know what they told you, but I didn't kill that woman.

I just needed to make a phone call, that's all. I had to call my lawyer. They promised me unfettered access to him but they took my phone away. I didn't have a choice. I'm sorry."

She yanked her wrist free from my grip. It was clear that she wasn't happy but I think she understood and I was willing to accept her compassion over her approval.

"Is everything OK in here?" the guard leaned his head in.

"Everything is fine," she said. "We're just going over some discharge information." She pointed down to her chart. The guard left and Carly shoved the phone back into her pocket and sat on the edge of the bed and looked over at me not missing a beat. "You're healing pretty well and should be done with the intravenous medication some time tomorrow pending the doctor's approval."

"That's it, huh? He comes in and waves the magic wand?"

"Pretty much as long as the heart biopsy shows no sign of rejection. In fact, I can go ahead and order that for you today to speed things up. If that comes back and the doctor gives the go ahead you'll be out of here in the next day or so." They have to say that: with the doctor's approval. They don't want patients getting too excited and walking right out the front door because the nurse promised something. Didn't apply to me though, I already had my exit planned. All I needed to do was talk to the doctor and make sure my heart wasn't going to implode on itself when I took a step out of this room.

"Here is a list of the medications you'll be taking over the next few days." Carly added as she handed me a sheet of paper. "It has the names, dosages, schedules, side effects, and reasons for taking each drug." She ran her finger over the list. "Please make sure to ask me any questions you have about each one."

"Fuck. There must be about fifteen drugs on here." I said.

"That's the reaction most patients have. Most of these you have been taking already intravenously and will continue to take over the next few days and weeks. As your heart gets strong you'll stop needing certain ones. Column D has an estimated dosage amount but when the doctor comes in he'll go over specific amounts as it fits your lifestyle."

"What if I just forget to take them – or – don't take them?" I asked.

"This system has been specifically designed to help you recover at a normal pace. It's the right balance of antibodies and pain medicine to ensure your heart's optimal performance so I'm sure you won't forget," she said. Rote. She didn't know and probably didn't care. Maybe she knew but was withholding important health information because I took her phone.

"OK thanks," I said and gave her that smile again. She smiled back, patted my shoulder and waved her phone at me to make sure I knew she had it this time. She walked out of the room and let the door shut behind her. As the door clicked the guard turned and looked at me through the window. He took an exasperated breath and turned back around and continued to check out the staff at the nurse's station. I looked down and flipped Carly's hospital badge around between my thumb and index finger. She was so distracted by the fact a patient took her phone then grabbed her that it probably didn't occur to her that I was also going to take her badge which proved an easier feat than taking the phone. She was so confused by my aggression she didn't feel my other hand reach out and rip the badge from the bottom part of her shirt.

I looked up at the clock. 11:46. The changing of the guards was scheduled for midnight but Peterson liked to skip out a few minutes early so he could go home and see his kids or run across the street and pound a few beers before it got too late. I wasn't sure which it was but I was leaning towards the kids, he seemed decent enough. He was scheduled from noon to midnight and usually showed up about five to ten minutes late each day. Arnold was on from midnight to noon and always waited around, toed the line, and made sure I was well supervised even though he was pretty sure I wasn't a flight risk. I think he even takes notes on my various activities: watches television, changes channel, pees, eats pudding, sleeps. Peterson was the opposite. He arrived late and left early, sometimes fifteen minutes early, even if Arnold wasn't here. But he knew Arnold and knew that Arnold wouldn't be late and wouldn't inconvenience him under any circumstances. Peterson must have felt like I wasn't a flight risk either, since he kept leaving a minute or two earlier each day leaving me to my own devices. It started out a minute or two before midnight and then five minutes and so on. He even gives me a generous nod when he leaves. We both know he's breaking protocol but he doesn't care and doesn't care that I know.

Peterson turns around, shoves his phone into his pocket and winks at me, but before he can turn and leave I wave him over.

There was a tinge of irritation on his face as he opened the door. "What do you want, Richards?" he asked.

I pulled on the handcuffs. "I want to do a few laps," I said. "It's been two hours."

"Not now, I'm leaving." he said.

"Fine, just uncuff me and I'll do it by myself. I promise I'll be back in bed before the other guy gets here. He'll never know."

He took a breath and walked over to me and pulled out his keys. "No funny stuff, OK?" he said as he unlatched the cuff from my wrist and left the other end attached to the bed rail.

"Deal," I said. "Besides, I didn't do it."

"That's what everyone says. We're all innocent," he said as he walked out and shut the door. He passed the nurses' station and gave them all a big wave. I'm leaving and there's nothing you can do about it.

I swung my legs around and stood up. Per the nurses instructions I unplugged the IV monitor from the wall and wrapped the excess cord around my arm. I needed to stay connected to it while I did my laps around the floor. I grabbed my pants, shirt and bulletproof vest from the chair and put them on. I took the stack of prescriptions and shoved them into my front pocket and walked towards the door. It felt good to stretch my legs and the bulletproof vest felt nice against my chest. It's true: I was paranoid and thought someone from Boston was going to catch up to me and shoot me in the chest. I knew it was illogical but I thought it was perfectly fine to take unnecessary measures and the vest was extra protection against my new heart.

The charge nurse looked up at me as I came out of my room. She didn't say anything so I started my journey. I was supposed to get up and walk every hour, which I did, but Peterson and Arnold would usually follow me from a distance. Not dissimilar to a toddler learning to walk with a worried parent trailing behind. I went past the nurses' station and turned left. Thirty feet down the hall on the right was the nourishment room where patients could replenish their water and ice supply or indulge themselves with a juice box. The room was open to all. Directly across the hall was the staff quarters where the hospital staff ate, slept and changed. That's where I needed to go.

The walking felt nice and each time I got up to do a lap I felt less lag than the time before. I had a brand new hi-tech heart and it didn't need a lot of time to get warmed up. The medicine was helping with the healing and pain from surgery so the only thing really holding me back was the haze from the drugs. But I knew how to handle that. I spent a large portion of my adult life living behind the smog of prescription meds that I acclimated myself and manipulated my lifestyle so I could function and succeed even when I was doped up. My current situation was really no different sans the fact that I haven't had any sort of drug in my system for the past six months. And the hospital drugs were the best. They want one hundred percent patient satisfaction, it meant less trips to the patient rooms and less patient complaints. Keep us at bay and dopey and we'll leave the friendly nursing staff alone.

I reached the door to the staff quarters and looked around. It was just a few minutes before midnight so there weren't any visitors and the nursing staff was sequestered to the charge station. I pulled out Carly's badge and waved it in front of the image sensor. There was a soft beep and click to indicate that the door was unlocked.

I went in.

On the left was a seating area with a television and couch littered with empty fast food containers and junk food wrappers. On the right was a restroom and a small station with about ten lockers. I went over and scanned the lockers. They were all nondescript so I started opening them and rummaging through the contents. I hit pay dirt with the fourth locker. When I opened it up there was a picture of Carly and a person I presumed to be Todd. He was tall, wide shoulders and grey hair. Not my type but I could see where Carly might find him attractive. They were at the Grand Canyon and looked happy, it was probably before Todd bought her the Impala. I fished through her belongings. There wasn't much there, a few dollars in cash and some old receipts. I took the cash and then found the keys to the Impala. I stuffed them into my gown and turned around.

Arnold was standing there. A grin the size of Montana plastered across his face. "What do you think you're doing, Richards?" he asked.

"Arnold, you're early." I said.

"You know there are security cameras up here, right?" he said. "You know every time someone opens a door here a bell goes off, right?" I get it, we're in a hospital.

"I was just stretching my legs," I said. "Look, I know you might not get this but I needed a hit. It's been six months. I thought the nurses had something. You know how the medical industry is these days. The doctors and nurses are the worst offenders."

"Whatever, you piece of shit," he said. Just because you're punctual doesn't mean you're nice, I guess. "Get over here." He pulled out the handcuffs and waved his hand at me.

"If you want me to get back in that bed you're going to have to come over here and force me." I said, standing my ground.

"As you wish." He took a few steps towards me and started to reach out. When he was about two feet away I grabbed his arm and pulled him towards me. I took a half step to the left so his body would go past me. Just as he passed, I grabbed the back of his head and shoved his face into Carly's locker. His nose cracked on the metal and his legs gave out. I leaned over and grabbed his hand, put it in the locker and slammed the door on it. I could hear the bones in his finger split. He didn't make a sound. It's remarkable what shock can do to a man. Hospital drugs also give you false confidence. It's as if they found a concoction where they can fit a martini into something the size of your fingernail.

I checked to make sure I still had the keys and the small amount of cash that Carly kept in her locker. Check. Check.

I stepped out into the hallway. It was still empty. I went to the left and through a doorway that led to the stairs. I was on the fourth floor. I went down a few flights until I hit the first level of the parking garage and found Carly's blue Impala parked right next to the stairs.

I pressed my thumb down on the unlock button on the key. The lights on the car flashed. Half a second later an alarm went off. It sounded like an air raid siren from the Second World War and it pulsed through my head. I looked up and saw flashing lights on the ceiling of the garage. Was there a fire in the hospital or did they have this noise specifically on hold for my escape? They were really making a big deal about me.

I opened the car door and got in, turned the car on and put it in reverse. I anticipated a guard wielding a weapon at the exit but there was nobody so I sailed straight through. My first stop would be the pharmacy to pick up some meds. It's possible they called every pharmacy in town in the last five minutes to alert them of my conceivable arrival but I was willing to take a chance that they didn't.

Once I got the meds I was going to pay a visit to David Prescott's house and find that box, then call Skelly up and tell him to suck it.

17

Adrienne Prescott was still awake. Since her husband's arrest she would stay up late and watch old movies and pass out around four or five in the morning. She looked over at the half empty bottle of wine. Her husband had been in lock up for forty-eight hours and Harvey was dead and she had her marching orders: Stay home and don't talk to anyone. She had grown close to Janice over the years and considered her a friend and the fact that she was killed, by a neighbor nonetheless, was heartbreaking. *How could everything fall apart so quickly?* she thought. In the few minutes she had to speak with David he said Harvey was fixing the research and messing with the test results. She never would suspect that Harvey would do something like that but she knew that a man would do just about anything for money and to provide for his family and Harvey would do anything for his son. She despised her husband for what he did to Harvey but knew that David was methodical. Maybe killing Harvey was the only solution even if it ruined their life. As backwards as it sounds, maybe killing Harvey was the only way to tell investors that the problem had truly been eliminated. If David only exposed the virus, people would say Harvey still had some play at Endochrone no matter the reassurances. Death was the ultimate absolution. Janice was another story. Adrienne first met her when she visited David in the office years ago. They became friends, started going to lunch together and then she and David would go boating with Janice and her husband until he passed away. After his death, Adrienne and Janice stayed in touch but Adrienne knew that Janice was broken and couldn't keep up appearances.

The news said that her neighbor came over and murdered her in cold blood. He chopped her up and then buried her in his backyard. He was married with a young daughter and another on the way. According to reports, he and Janice entered a romantic relationship months ago and she became jealous of his marriage so he decided to extinguish her. *How grown up of him*, Adrienne thought, *to make decisions based on fear*. It was easier for him to go through the process of killing Janice and disseminating her than it was to take responsibility and own up to the affair and make the necessary changes in his life. Murder was rarely a justifiable act, unless it was to remove a toxin like Harvey Marcona. Just before this has-been-investigative journalist was to be arrested he suffered from cardiac arrest and was rushed to the hospital where he received a heart transplant. Adrienne would love to pay him a visit and show him what true suffering was. Maybe teach him to be a man like her husband. Maybe tomorrow.

There was a knock on the door. It was probably Fritz again. He had horrible timing, always had strange questions at odd times and probably, she suspected, wanted to sleep with her. That's why he kept coming to the house at odd hours. She took a quick sip of the wine and stood up. She worked her way across the living room and opened the front door. She was lonely so maybe tonight Fritz was going to get lucky.

But it wasn't Fritz.

It was a guy in tattered clothes that needed a good cleaning. He was average height, with a weak stubble and unkempt brown hair. He smelled like vinegar and pudding.

"Don't close the door," he said. "Do you know who I am?" His breath smelled like stale coffee. "I need to ask you about Harvey Marcona." Just as he said Marcona a picture of Janice appeared in her mind and then flashes of footage from the suspect's backyard and the sandbox where they found her body. Adrienne couldn't scratch it from her mind. Then a picture she saw of the suspect on TV – average height, shit beard and diminutive posture – it was him.

"I'm calling the police," she said.

18

"Don't – don't call the police." I said as I reached out and pushed one hand against the door and reached out to her with the other hand, as if I was offering some sort of peace treaty. She took a step back and looked up at me. There was a gloss over her eyes from too many pain killers or alcohol. I knew the look.

"Why shouldn't I?"she asked. But there wasn't any fear in her voice it was just a very straightforward question, plain and simple. She looked me up and down, stared at my feet and then worked her eyes slowly up towards my face and then pursed her lips. The Candyman could show up at her door and she would just dismiss him like he was working the block for the Jehovah's Witnesses. This woman didn't care to address fear and I was impressed. Maybe the late nights she spent glaring at the television while her husband was in jail got to her. She needed a little adventure.

"Trust me." I said. I didn't have much time to think this over and I was running purely on instinct. I wasn't afforded the luxury of sitting down and mapping this out. It was late and the drug stores were closed and I needed my meds. I was on the lamb and I needed information and I needed it now. She probably hit a secret button in the floor and alerted the police of my arrival and they were probably headed over. A hot pursuit sort of situation, I guess, reserved for the Boston Strangler and the Zodiac Killer. Maybe her house was wired with microphones that connected to loudspeakers in the police commissioner's office and he was sitting around his office at 4 a.m. playing cards with Skelly waiting for a moment just like this. You pay a premium for that sort of information.

"Come on in," she said. "Do you want anything to drink?" she added.

This was fantastic. I thought for sure I was going to have to tie her up, restrain her in some way but here I was coming over for an unannounced nightcap.

"What do you have?" I asked as she left the entry way and took a few steps down into a large living room which was the size of a basketball court. There was a hefty sectional in the middle and a massive television on the wall above the fireplace. She walked around the sectional and up a few stairs into the kitchen. I looked around. "Don't worry. It's just you and me. There isn't anyone else here," she shouted as she turned and stood behind the counter and picked up a phone. She waved it around like it was a loaded gun. "Just in case you get funny with me," she said as she reached for a bottle of wine. "Is shiraz fine with you?"

"Perfect." I said. "So you know who I am?"

"You're all over the news," she said. "The police said you killed Janice Walton and I believe them."

"I didn't do it." I said. This repetition was waning on me.

"Is that why I should trust you, because you claim innocence? I can claim a lot of things but it doesn't make them true. How did you get out of the hospital?"

"A little bit of luck and some good timing. Mostly luck."

"Ah, good for you." I could tell I had a fan. "I still think you killed Janice."

"I saw the person who did it."

"Ohhh," she said, letting the h linger. "Now I believe you."

"It was a State Trooper. I was sitting in my living room and saw the car pull up. He went inside, they talked about something and then he went into the back of Janice's house. When he was back there Janice called someone but he came back out before she could finish saying whatever it was she needed to say. He then slammed her face up against the window and she went down. I got the license plate and I have someone running it for me."

"You have someone?" she asked as if I was wasting her time.

"Ya, a friend with the police."

"Must be a real good friend."

"He's my sponsor." I said.

"You're what?"

"My sponsor. I'm a recovering drug addict." Step 37, I believe, repetitive admission. "One of the very first things they do when you choose to go into recovery is assign you a sober buddy. Someone who's already been through recovery and can guide you through the highs and lows. Well, lows, we aren't allowed highs." I said and smiled. She stared at me. I knew she wouldn't get it. She looked like she was a decade past a good recovery meeting. Maybe her pious husband would get released from jail, give me the banker's box, and send her off to rehab. I never understood alcohol. Alcohol had too much sugar and made your confidence too readily available. I suppose it didn't matter to her that Brad was my sponsor but I needed some credibility here and going with the brother-in-law bit didn't seem appropriate. I wanted to put all the cards on the table, with the hope she would understand and give me something in return.

"What about Cabo?" she asked.

"What about it?"

"I heard there were two first class plane tickets to Cabo in her house. You and her. You were going to flutter away together," she said. "You expect me to believe you weren't having an affair with her – you didn't have plans?"

"I don't know – I haven't figured that out. I don't know why there were two tickets there."

"Maybe because -"

"No, we hardly knew each other. We saw her a few times and she was friendly, her husband passed away, but that's all I know."

"We were supposed to go to Cabo – celebrate. Wouldn't it be funny if we ran into each other there? Maybe we would stay at the same resort. What do you think we would have thought of each other? Do you think I would have figured out you were having an affair?"

"What are you celebrating?" I asked.

"Oh, haven't you heard? Endochrone is about to go public. Big deal and big money, I'm told. David and I we going to go to Mexico – live it up. Doubt that will happen now."

"I'm looking for a banker's box that someone delivered here a few days before Janice was killed."

"Why do you think someone delivered a box here?"

"Before Janice was killed someone went to her house and picked it up and brought it here."

"How do you know that? If you hardly know her, I mean."

"I was watching. I was awake – saw it. There was an albino. He worked for a flower company and he said that David Prescott paid him a handsome sum of money to bring the bankers box back to his house – here."

"You and the albino pals?" she asked.

"No, but like I said, I saw him at her house so when I was in the hospital I ordered myself flowers and requested him."

"You really are something aren't you?"

"Where is it?"

"We have lots of banker's boxes here."

"An albino delivered it."

"You mentioned that."

"Please?"

"What's it worth to you?" she asked but I didn't say anything. I didn't know what it was worth and I didn't know, with any confidence, that I knew what I was doing except chasing after something that might turn into something bigger. Maybe the banker's box would absolve me. I was hoping it would be that simple. She would proffer it to me and then I would call Skelly up and we'd grab coffee and laugh the whole thing off.

"That's what I thought," she said as she handed me a glass of the shiraz. "Come with me." She grabbed the phone and I followed her out of the kitchen and down a long hallway that was draped with pictures of her, her husband and what I presumed were their children. She stopped at a doorway near the end of the hallway. "I think we put it down here," she said as she pulled out a key and unlocked the door. "You first," she said as she opened the door. "The light's broken so be careful."

I looked down the stairs which led to uncertain darkness. It didn't have the same sense of warmth and hospitality that the rest of the house had.

"You have a basement?" I said. "Not a lot of houses here have basements. They says it's because of the limestone."

"We had it added on. Paid extra. David's paranoid about a nuclear holocaust. Part bomb shelter, part panic room, part something else."

"An anomaly."

"You're an anomaly," she said as a cool draft worked its way up the stairs and brushed past me. She leaned into me. I could smell the wine in her breath mixing itself with the draft. "You scared?" she asked. Her voice taunted me. I could feel my heart beat intensify and my hands clam up. I think at this point I was pretty sure I had made a mistake. I probably should have stuck it out at the hospital and trusted Ramirez to clear my name. It was all a big misunderstanding. People had to recognize the confusion at hand. Ramirez was respected, aside from his list of criminal clients, and maybe he really was the one who could prove my innocence. I'll go into the basement, check out the situation with the box and then make my way back to the hospital and slip back into bed and work it out with Arnold. No harm done. At least then I didn't have to worry about getting my prescription filled.

"Walk," she said as she pressed her hand into my back. I gripped the railing and followed it slowly down to the bottom. The light from upstairs quickly faded. She reached past me and flipped on a light switch at the bottom of the stairs. The overhead lights flickered. The basement was small. It was completely disproportionate to the rest of their lavish house as if it was hiding a bunch of secret basements behind its walls. It was newly painted and smelled like air freshener and floor cleaner. I looked to one side where there was a neat and tidy stack of banker's boxes but it didn't hold my attention for long. My eyes shot to the opposing wall which appeared to be covered in black leather wallpaper. In the center of the wall were four chains with cuffs at the end of them. Two of them were towards the top and the other two were near the bottom of the wall.

"How's your heart, Peter?" she asked.

"What is that?" I asked. But I was pretty sure I knew. This woman was certifiable and this wasn't an art installation. It was a full blown pleasure den with banker's boxes.

"You and your husband play down here?" I asked.

"Sometimes," she said. I felt her getting closer to me. "You wanna play?"

"Can I have the box and go?"

"You wanna try it?" she asked.

"I'd rather not, actually." I said. "Does that offend you?" *You lunatic.* A hospital bed seemed rather nice right now. Grass is always greener, I guess.

"Just go over there. Two minutes. Tops. Then you can take the box and be on your way."

"Ehh, I don't think that is a really good idea."

"I'll never tell," she said as she pushed lightly on my shoulder. I looked over at the boxes.

"Two minutes?"

"Tops."

"OK. But no funny business this is just-"

"Go please," she said as I took a few steps back until my back hit the soft leather padding on the wall. It smelled like lavender. She ran her hand down my arm until she reached my wrist. Didn't she know I was married? We were both married. I was about to speak up again but she squeezed my wrist and pulled my hand up towards one of the chains. She clamped my wrist in one of the cuffs and went for the other hand. "Tight enough?" she asked. My wrists dangled as she lowered herself towards my feet. I could feel her breathe on my crotch as she went lower. I didn't move.

"You OK?" she asked. I nodded as I stared longingly at the wall of box's counting down the seconds. "You dead?"

"What?" I asked and looked down at her.

"Your limp. You dead or something?"

"I'm focused."

"Whatever," she said as she cuffed my ankles and stood up and looked at me. Not sure if it was possible but she seemed slightly more drunk. The alcohol had time to catch up with her and work its magic but she didn't seem to mind. She had light brown hair that went just past her shoulders and a dark blue eyes. She looked like she just woke up or spent thirty minutes on the treadmill. The look worked for her.

"You have a minute left." I asked.

"How does your heart feel?" she asked.

"Good." I said not caring to explain to her that half of it was nuts and bolts sustained by a nine volt battery with a hundred year life span. My new heart, this appliance inside me, was in unsurpassable condition. My old heart got a jump start, a dedicated intravenous line of Red Bull for eternity. Don't get me wrong, my heart needs medication to sustain itself, but I was indestructible. I'll have to see if Ɔ-zero has any other upgrades available.

"I think this position suits you," she said.

"How's that?" I asked.

"Dangling out there for all the world to see," she said. She and Vanessa must be friends too. This woman knew everyone.

"Do I have your trust now?" I asked.

"Almost" she said as she ran her finger down my chest. She reached the top of my pants and pulled on the button until it popped off. She clenched my zipper between her thumb and index finger and pulled down. "I like that. You are fucking rock hard."

"No I'm not. I'm actually pretty uncomfortable. Your two minutes is up." I said as she looked down. She pulled out her smart phone and snapped a picture of me and all of my manly glory. "What the fuck," *you stupid maniac*, I said.

"It's just in case," she said. "How long were you sleeping with Janice?"

"What?" I must have heard her wrong.

"How long were you sleeping with her?" she said as if the answer would magically vomit itself from my mouth.

"I wasn't sleeping with her." I hardly knew her. "Get me out of this thing!"

"Sure you were. She told me about you. Tall, dark hair, neighbor. Somewhat – eh, baseline - attractive. She was keeping it a secret until you started coming over and beating the shit out of her. Then she had to tell me."

"What? I hardly knew her. We were just neighbors and I love my wife. I thought we reviewed this."

"Which is it? You weren't sleeping with her because you were just neighbors or you weren't sleeping with her because you love your wife?" she asked. I imagine reasoning with a drunk person isn't much different than taking a shower in the middle of a burning building.

"Both." I retorted.

"If you admit it, this will go much better for you. I couldn't believe my luck when you showed up at my front door. I was going to visit you in the hospital and tell you how I feel but, nope, you came right to me. A fugitive on the run. I can do whatever I want to you and no one will ever know, will they?"

"Look. I told you what happened. It's the truth. You can believe it or not but you need to let me go. I wasn't sleeping with her. I didn't beat her."

"What about that fucking cat, huh?"

"Excuse me?"

"Janice said you would come over to her house and bring your creepy orange cat. Janice said you kept him on a leash so he wouldn't get away. You smacked her around while the cat sat there and watched. What kind of sicko are you?"

Roger. "Dammit."

"Gotcha."

"No, you don't got me."

"Oh ya I do."

"That's my neighbor, Chandler."

"Excuse me?" she said.

"That's not me. I don't have an orange cat. I wasn't sleeping with her and I for sure didn't kill her, so can I use your telephone now please?" I needed to call Brad and see if he found out anything about the license plate. I didn't care about the florist or Janice really now that the banker's box was within reach, but I'd still like to know who that police cruiser belonged too and how it tied back to this Marcona fellow. Send that info to Ramirez and clear my name for good. "Come on now." I said as I pulled my wrists down in the cuffs.

"You have a lot of demands for someone who shows up unannounced at four in the morning," she said.

"I appreciate what you're trying to do for your friend but I didn't kill her. I just want to find out who did so I can get on with my life."

"Is that what this whole thing is about − getting on?"

"I just need to find out − I need something."

"When we're finished," she said and looked me over. I had no idea what she was thinking. Maybe she was going to kill me or cut my nuts off. If I really did kill her friend and beat the shit out of out her I probably deserved to have a nut or two removed. Come to think of it, this explains the long walks Chandler would take with Roger. People always thought parading your cat around on a leash was strange but I had come to accept it. We live in a progressive world and people do strange things, I wasn't about to pass judgment on a guy who put a leash on a cat. It was his only companion. But sleeping with Janice was a whole different story. Sleeping with her and beating her up, that was just plain bizarre. I looked up at Adrienne and she was still watching me, deciding something. She still probably thought I killed Janice but she couldn't do anything to me because she couldn't prove it. She was drunk and crazy but she wasn't insane or a killer or a nut cutter.

"Fine." she said as she moved towards me. "Unzip me." she said.

She was wearing a grey blouse that had a zipper that ran down the front of it.

"I can't." I said as a waved my hands around to illustrate the futility of my position.

"With your teeth. You won't need your hands."

"No." I said and squinted my eyes to let her know that I meant business and wasn't going to get pushed around like this. The squinting thing usually worked with people, somewhat similar to Brad's endless shrugging, but she moved in on me so her chest was close to my face. She smelled nice, a little raw from the alcohol but nice nonetheless. I leaned my head forward and clenched the zipper between my teeth and moved my head down as she arched her chest back. She let out a sigh as I lowered her shirt and revealed her cleavage. There was a gloss of sweat on her chest from the humidity outside. I let go.

"You're good with your teeth. Do you want me?"

"Why did Harvey Marcona want Janice dead?" I asked.

"Marcona didn't kill her. He loved her. Do you want my body or not?" she said taking a breath. I wasn't playing her game and she was getting irritated by my line of questioning.

"But if she found out that he was manipulating the research he would have to kill her, right? There must have been millions on the line."

"If Marcona was manipulating anything Janice would have known about it."

"Why did your husband take the box from Janice's house?"

"Why do you care? Can't you just fuck me?"

"Because someone is insistent on putting me away for a long time for her murder-"

"Ah, forget it." she said and pulled away. "We were about to be audited and he was going through a bunch of stuff. Janice kept things at her house, against policy of course, but some things were safer out of the office. Competition and stuff. Happy?"

"What sort of stuff?"

"Bills and shit, I guess. Office stuff." She took another step back. "I don't really know."

"So your husband had the box removed just before Marcona killed Janice and your husband killed Marcona?"

"Coincidence." she said as she reached over my head and unlatched my hands.

"Done so soon?" I asked.

"You're pretty boring," she said. "You know what Janice's last words were? What she said on the phone before she was murdered?"

"No." I said.

"She said 'he's back and he's going to kill me this time.' "

"How do you know that?"

"Because I was the person she was talking to when she was murdered," she said. "You can use the phone in the office. It's right next to the kitchen. Come on, I'll show you." She freed my legs and then grabbed banker's box and headed up the stairs. I followed her. When I reached the top she was already in the office adjacent to the stairs. The desk lamp was on and the banker's box was sitting on the desk.

"I am going to get more wine. Can I get you anything?"

"Thanks. I'm good."

"OK. Make it quick. My kids get up for school in thirty minutes," she said.

I looked at my watch. It was almost six. Shit. I was down there for a while. The events with Janice didn't sit right. You don't pay a florist to go to a house at four in the morning to transport a box of bills and shit unless you don't want anyone to know about it. Also, as bothersome as their relationship was, Chandler didn't kill her. I understand why Adrienne would think so, especially after the phone call from Janice, but that just told me that the State Trooper had been there before. Adrienne didn't know enough to put two and two together. But I did. I picked up the phone on the desk and dialed. It rang a few times before Brad picked up.

"Brad here," he said in a voice that made him sound like he was awoken from a very deep sleep.

"You working today?" I said.

"It's the weekend, man." For him that was Tuesday and part of Wednesday. I guess today was Tuesday.

"Sorry, I thought you'd be halfway through breakfast now."

"Peter?"

"Ya…"

"The cops are looking for you, dude. Where the fuck are you?"

"I'm - around."

"You're in some serious shit, my friend."

"Thanks. I'm aware of my situation but I appreciate the refresh. Did you find out anything on the license plate?" He was pretty buttoned-up about this stuff at work but I was calling him on his personal phone and he wasn't at work so he was free to say whatever he wanted. The chances of someone listening in were slim to none and if someone was listening in there's very little they could do about what Brad was going to tell me. The NSA does what it wants, and that's cool, but the local police have very strict guidelines about snooping on their own.

'Is that Peter?" a voice said in the background. It sounded familiar.

"It's just - no one," Brad said "Go back to sleep."

"Glad to know things are going well with Vanessa," I said.

"It's nothing, man. Hold on." I waited and tapped on the desk as I listened to him get out of bed. I slid the top off the banker's box. It was filled with a few dozen green folders. Each of them had a tab with a number on it and they were arranged from least to greatest.

"OK. The plate I think you're looking for is 2F5 ZH1. It belongs to a Crown Vic that is housed in the Texas State Police compound in Dallas."

"Who was driving it?"

"It was signed out to an officer Darren Bales, badge number 3629. He had it out for a special assignment."

"What was the assignment?"

"That's all I got, man. You want to know about that lady?"

"I think I got that. She worked for Harvey Marcona at a company called Endochrone."

"And you know he's dead, right?"

"The story is all over the news."

"You're all over the news, Peter. Do you want to hear this or not?"

"Sure."

"Darren Bales used to work for a private security company in Austin called Mach 10 Relations."

"Like the razor?"

"Right, like the razor," he said. "Mach 10 was shut down after clients discovered some of their employees were stealing money and valuables from clients. And you know who one of the biggest clients was?"

"Harvey Marcona?"

"Right."

It was something but it hardly cleared my name. All it did was suggest that maybe Harvey Marcona didn't kill Janice. Maybe Darren Bales did.

"What about her last name?"

"What about it?"

"Well, her last name is Walton but Skelly said Montgomery."

"Oh, right. Maiden name mix-up, I think. Her husband was Montgomery so that's what it probably still says in the public records and Skelly probably took a look at those, got his wires crossed."

"Strange."

"Nope, not strange. Shit happens. People get confused. Maybe you heard him wrong. Ever think of that?" he said. "Why don't you tell me where you are and I'll get Ramirez and we'll get this all sorted out. You have a family, Peter. Responsibilities greater than yourself."

"No. I need to see this through."

"You need to see this through – who are you? John Wayne?"

"No. That Skelly guy is out for me."

"That's his job, Peter. He's an officer of the law and you're a suspect. He's doing exactly what he should be doing whether you like it or not."

"But – "

"Right, I know, you didn't do it – I hear ya." Brad said. "Maybe in the end this will all work out in your favor. In the meantime, you need to get buttoned up and do this the right way, by the order of the law."

"I want to see this through. That's what I meant to say before."

"All the better to come back in. You're going to start coming across with an O.J. complex."

"I really think that was an entirely different situation." I said.

"You do what you think best but I really think we should pick you up and follow protocol here."

"Do people fall for that line?"

"Sometimes."

"I'm good, trust me on this one."

"You staying clean?"

"Ya, ya, I'm good."

"What number are you calling me from?" Brad asked.

"Doesn't matter," I said and hung up the phone. I looked across the room. There was a Prescott family portrait above the fireplace. David stood behind his wife and two kids, a good foot taller than all of them.

There was a wide grin on his face, a grin that suggested that he knew he was lucky. He seemed like a decent guy. I picked up the phone again and dialed Ramirez's office. It was early but he kept a twenty four hour answering service. It was customary when the weight of your clients were drunk drivers and no-class criminals. Night hawks.

"Law office," a woman's voice said.

"I'm a client," I said. "Is he available?"

"Name and contact number?"

"Tallahassee." I said.

"One moment, sir." There was a soft click and faint buzzing noise as she tried to connect me. Tallahassee was the code word. It gave the answering service the go ahead to contact him no matter the time of day or year. 7 a.m. on Christmas Day and Tallahassee would bring Ramirez to life.

Tallahassee meant the shit was real.

"I'm putting you through, sir." she said.

"Thanks."

"Hello?" a faint voice said.

"I need you to do a background check on Darren Bales," I said. Between Brad and the answering service someone was sure to be tracing this call so I didn't have time for formalities.

"Peter? Where are you?"

"I think he's the guy I saw kill Janice. He's in Dallas. My brother-in-law, or whatever you want to call him, has the information."

"You Tallahassee'd me for this?"

"Get to it, boss."

I hung up.

19

I pressed my finger against the ignition button in Prescott's Tesla Model X, an eco-family friendly car that had the body of a minivan but the spirit of a Porsche. In my heyday, shortly before Cleft dropped the bomb on me, I was flirting with a purchase. I took a few test drives and even spoke to a very friendly lady in California about my financing options. There was some appeal in a family car that could go from zero to sixty in five seconds, in case I wanted to rob a bank before dropping Joyce off at school. I had the ability to do that.

After I got off the phone with Ramirez, Adrienne was nice enough to give me some coffee, two hundred dollars in cash and the keys to her husband's car under the condition that I return it after going to Dallas to visit Darren Bales. Her husband was supposed to come home soon and she didn't want to go through a whole thing with him about how she loaned his car to a fugitive. I think she finally came around and understood my position on things. I wasn't the malevolent fraud people made me out to be. I was a good guy with a nice family and people needed to understand that. I was just a line item on a police report to Skelly, a door that needed to be closed so they could move on to the next suspect-looking person.

Adrienne stood on the front porch, sipped shiraz from a coffee mug as her daughter sat next to her trying to put her shoes on for school. She waved at me as I backed the car out of their garage. It was a nice experience and I imagined Prescott doing this each morning before going off and saving the world through genetic science and research. The daughter didn't take note of me, and if she did, I couldn't tell. Maybe the repetition of these mornings wore on her. The interstate was a few miles east of here. There was a gas station and convenience store just short of the onramp and I figured I would stop and pick up some provisions to sustain myself on my way to Dallas. Absorb the alcohol and shake the weirdness of the past few hours.

I gently rolled the car into one of the open spots directly in front of the entrance to the convenience store and pressed the ignition button. I went inside and headed towards the back to stock up on bottled water and donut holes. Shake the weird and absorb the crazy. Next to the plethora of portable donuts was a collection of disposable cell phones ranging in price based on the amount of minutes you wanted to use. I grabbed one that gave me thirty minutes of talk time. I figured that would be plenty of time to touch base with Paula and let her know that I was alright. Given the nature of recent events I was working under the assumption that since the authorities couldn't find me that they would put a bug in Paula's phone. When I called they would trace the line and be able to locate me. I would call her once I got on the interstate and then pull off and drop the phone in a parking lot a few miles north of the city. Skelly's determination multiplied by morning rush hour would equate to how quickly the police would find the phone. I was estimating that would give me a good hour head start until Skelly figured out where I was going. At that point it was just a matter of luck.

"Hello?" I heard Paula's voice say.

"It's me. —"

"Peter-" She sounded exhausted "It's you." She never made a habit of saying my name. It's not something married people do unless they're upset with each other and need to express it in a passive aggressive manner. Close friends Bill and Bob don't go around addressing each other by their first names. 'Hey, Bill.' and 'Good to see you, Bob.' Over and over again into perpetuity. You only use someone's first name if you just met them and are getting acclimated or you have a second class police detective breathing down your neck wanting information on the whereabouts of your husband. I was pretty sure this was a setup but I had to make sure.

"Is detective Skelly there?" I asked. No code words, no hints or allusions to our trust being broken just a simple, straight to the point no fuss question. Maybe Skelly was there having coffee and playing with my daughter. Maybe he took up camp in our guest room waiting for a moment like this. He may have thought I would even come home and pay a visit to my family.

"He got here about an hour after you left the hospital," she said and that's all I needed to know.

"I'll make it quick then. How is Joyce?"

"She's OK. Woke up a few minutes ago. Curious as to this crew of people in our house."

"I bet. Look, I know this is a crummy situation and it's entirely my fault but I promise you that I am going to get us out of it. No matter what."

"Peter, I don't think Joyce and I can go through this with you," she said in a very point of fact manner. The sky is blue and one plus two equals two and this is simply the current state of everything."

"I'm not asking you to go through this with me, I'm just telling you that I am in the process of fixing this."

"How do you feel?" she asked

"Good. Better than ever actually."

"Are you taking your meds at least?"

Shit. "Yup, as ordered." I could feel the lump of prescription notices in my front pocket. Begging me to take them out and exchange them for drugs. "What else is going on?" I asked not sure what else to say. It was a natural dip in the conversation and the events of the past few days have been rather unusual. There was plenty to discuss but I couldn't find the words or the feeling behind those words. I guess I wasn't my usual self. It didn't matter though, Paula had the words.

"I'm out Peter," she said "I'm done with your charades and your stories. They said this and told me this and they're wrong sort of bullshit, Peter. I'm out."

"If this is a way to buy time so the police can – "

"It's not." she said.

"I didn't kill her. You know that I didn't kill her."

"All I know is that you were downstairs watching television and the next thing I know is the police are banging on the door. They found her body in our backyard, Peter, and you were in her house."

"I shouldn't have done that. It was a misstep."

"I was awake, Peter! I couldn't sleep so I was awake and I heard you leave the house. I heard you go over there."

"If that's true then you would have heard me call 911."

"Such shit, Peter." she said and it's true, since I didn't call 911 until

I was out of the house. She wouldn't have heard. "They said that you were sleeping with her!"

"I didn't sleep with her. They have me confused with someone else. You know Chandler."

"Who doesn't have you confused with someone else?"

"That's not fair. You can believe me. You have to believe me. For the sake of our children." I was pleading now not sure what direction this was headed.

"I don't really know what to believe, Peter. Between her and that other guy in Boston and you escaping the hospital and getting fired. It adds up."

"I'll prove to you – I'm on to something here."

"What's that?"

"That Harvey Marcona had her killed."

"Great. I want a divorce."

"I'll show you – just tell Skelly to back the fuck off."

"I'm not backing the fuck off, Richards. You are going to fry for this." Skelly's voice said from a distance.

"You're a good man, Skelly. Think about this."

"Eat my shit, Richards." he barked at me with an intensity built up from years as an underpaid and under insured local law enforcement official.

"We're getting a divorce." Paula said with the same matter of fact tone.

"What? That's nonsense. You don't know what you're talking about. We're going to work on this. Also, what about Joyce and all the paperwork we're doing so I can legally adopt her? So we can become a whole family."

"Nope. We're finished, Peter." she said. The sky is blue and one plus one equals you're fucked. If your wife won't back you on something like this you are in some serious shit. Your wife leaves you, you can't see your children, you're good as dirt. Those are important steps to building credibility for yourself but without those you're shit. Having them and losing them is a far worse crime than never having them in the first place. A wife leaving you, for good reason or not, reveals to the world your weakness as a man and a person.

"I left the papers with Cleft." she added.

"You already have papers?

"I decided. You can choose to not sign them and make this harder on all of us but I'm sure that isn't something you want to put your family through. You're a decent guy, Peter." Years of marriage a beautiful daughter, one on the way and all I can get is a weak acknowledgment of decency.

"What about your citizenship?" I said, the words marching out of me before they could be processed.

"You don't have to worry about that, it's all taken care of."

"What does that mean?"

"It means Joyce and I aren't your responsibility anymore, Peter. I have to go. There's a neighborhood association meeting in a few minutes"

"They're still having those? It's not even nine a.m. yet."

"Yes, there's a lot going on here. Good-bye." Click went the phone and she was gone. I shut the phone off and stepped out of the car. There was a homeless guy lurking by the entrance to the convenience store.

"You need to call someone?" I asked.

"Sure, man." he said to me "Got a girl in Houston." Houston was a good three hours east of Austin and there really were only two ways to get there and they were both terrible, in the fact they were equally protracted and boring, which was a fair indication of the kind of time you were going to have when you reached Houston.

"I got about twenty-minutes left on this. It's all yours." I said as I tossed him the phone.

"Thanks, buddy. Hey, you look familiar. I know you from somewhere?" he asked as he squinted his eyes.

"Afraid not. I'm not from around here." I said. "You got the time?"

"It's about eight thirty," he said.

"Tuesday, right?" I asked.

"Last time I checked." he said.

"Thanks."

"I've seen you on TV – that's it. That's cool, man. I like you." Well, at least there was someone.

"Have a good one." I said as I made my way back to Prescott's car. On the other side of the freeway was a rundown motel. A ubiquitous chain that hasn't seen a makeover in about twenty years. Free HBO, telephone and Wi-Fi, everything the worldly traveler needed short of a Cracker Barrel. I got into the car and pulled on to the feeder road. I took my first left and went under the freeway. I was on the other side of the freeway in a matter of seconds and went south a hundred feet and turned into the parking lot of the motel. It was a small parking lot and all the spaces faced out to the feeder road. I didn't have much choice. I needed to get up to Dallas and see Darren Bales and get him to confess that Harvey Marcona hired him to kill Janice and I needed a recording of it. No tricky wiring needed just some simple diversion and the simple click of the recording feature on a smart phone. The ubiquity of portable recorders and smart phones made them a staple in court rooms around the world. You didn't need a court order and you didn't need a crack team hiding behind a studio sound system in a van around the corner. You just needed determination and time and I was very short on time. I needed to go through the contents of the banker's box and determine why Marcona was after it, figure out how to get my meds and then patch things up with Paula. I'm sure she can come to some sort of understanding, especially if I can prove that Marcona was the monster people say he was.

"I just need a room for a few hours." I said as I pushed a twenty across the counter. The front desk lady looked up at me.

"We don't do that."

"Just an hour, that's all." I said as I set another twenty on top of it. Between this bribe and my provisions at the store I was already halfway through the generous purse Adrienne gave me and the few dollars in Carly's locker.

She took the forty dollars and grabbed a key from the box behind her. "Room 17. Go outside and up the stairs. It will be on your left. You have one hour."

"Thanks" I said.

"No funny shit with the bed, it's broken." she added "Some guy brought his wife in here and they shorted the motor on it. God knows what she was doing to him." she said as she smiled at me.

"It's just me. All by myself."

"For now." she said.

"Can I have room 13?" I said "It's my lucky number."

"Let me check." she said. I was burning through that forty dollars rather quickly. I looked down at my watch. It was just past nine.

"Actually, I may need it for just over an hour." I said

"Of course, you will." she said as she set the key on the counter. "When you go outside head up the stairs and take your first left."

"Will do." I said as I took the key from her.

"And no messing with the bed."

"Right. No messing with the bed." I said as I left the lobby. I went back to the car which stuck out like a sore thumb in this empty parking lot. I pulled the banker's box from the trunk and headed up the stairs. I took a left, passed room twelve and stopped at thirteen. Once I was inside I set the banker's box on the bed and relieved myself in the bathroom. The walls were a dingy salmon color with a grey dusty overtone due to years of neglect and cigarette smoke. I counted. Between the queen sized once motorized bed, the small sitting area and bathroom there were no less then four ashtrays. Despite how diminutive the table in the sitting area was it held two ashtrays. It must be hard for people to share a room for their sexual escapades when they wouldn't dare consider sharing the community of an ashtray. Being in a room like this, where the very soul is ill, makes me want to be healthy and eat kale and go running at five each morning. Doctor did say to take it easy on the exercise for a few months though, until the heart got acclimated.

I flipped the top off the banker's box and set it on the end table. It was about half full with dark grey end-tab fastener folders with reinforced tabs. Standard weight and common in hospitals. I grazed through them and counted fifty folders organized numerically front to back with the lowest number being up front. The first folder labeled 001 and opened it up. On the left side was an eight and half by eleven black and white picture of a woman straight from Central Casting. She had short brown hair and a nose that sloped upwards. She was also wearing a pair of reading glasses that made her look older than she probably was. I liked the look. It was conservative but at any minute she could remove the glasses and become an entirely different person. With her it was glasses, with me it was a new heart. Whatever works. Her name was written across the bottom of the picture in red ink: Carol French. And then it occurred to me: 001-FRENCH. That's what was scribbled on the piece of paper I found at Janice's. 001-FRENCH, 002-DAVIS and so on. Janice wrote them all down. Just in case, I guess. On the right side of the folder was what appeared to be an application for medical services form, common for people who are requesting to be part of a medical study. It went through a list of all the vital medical history questions: high blood pressure, high cholesterol, trouble sleeping, dizziness and so on. There were pages of questions but Carol French was in perfect physical condition and didn't smoke, didn't have more than five to seven alcoholic beverages a week and didn't engage in the use of heavy narcotics, at least not admittedly. The only anomaly was that she suffered from occasional but temporary memory loss. On the very last page was her signature followed by a printed date: October 5th, 2011, only a few years ago. Above the signature and date was the word *APPROVED* stamped across the page.

Congratulations, Carol, you passed.

I put Carol's folder back and pulled out the next one: Peter Davis. *APPROVED*. Then Roger Reddinger, Padima Limaye, Becky Wilkens and so on. Fifty people, half male and half female, none over the age of 50 and all of them suffered occasional and short-term memory loss. They were also all approved for the trial of Memoton, a hot new drug that was supposed to curb the symptoms of early onset Alzheimer's. It was scheduled to hit the market at the end of the year – only a few weeks away – and be responsible for twenty percent of revenue for Green Pharmaceuticals. They don't disclose actual projections, but it's a significant chunk of change and Endochrone will receive a percentage every time a doctor signs the prescription pad. Some analysts have suggested that Endochrone will get upwards of a hundred million dollars annually just from the residuals for the research it did on Chromosome 16 and its contributions to Memoton.

A door slammed outside.

I jumped and looked up.

Silence.

I went over and peaked through the curtain out on to the narrow walkway. It was empty. "I only have about fifteen minutes so you better get to it, boss." a woman's voice said in room 12 next door.

"Sure, sure." a man's voice trailed behind her and then I heard the bathroom door shut. I looked at my watch. It was just after 9:30. They were late. I stuffed the folders back into the banker's box and put the lid back on and went outside. The cold morning air blew past me and the frost was just burning off. I preferred this to the heat of the long summers. I raised my hand and knocked lightly on the door to room twelve. "Who is it?" the woman asked. "Room service." I said, being clever. I heard the two talking on the other side of the door, the woman pressing the man to answer it. After a few seconds the door opened about half an inch. A man peaked out. It was Cleft. "Peter, Jesus." he said.

"Let me in, Cleft." I said.

"What the fuck do you think you're doing out there?"

"Let me in, man."

"Who is it?" the woman's voice asked

"Peter. It's fucking, Peter."

"Jesus – is he OK?" the woman asked. It was Marie from work. Cleft's secretary.

"How did you find me?" Cleft asked stunned that I tracked him down.

"9:30 a.m., first and third Tuesday of every month. It's in your calendar."

"I pick up dry cleaning the first and third Tuesday of every month. That's what it says in my calendar." he retorted. A man of wisdom this Cleft Duvall.

"Yes, but her calendar says Cheap Motel off the Interstate at 9:30 a.m. the first and third Tuesday of every month. She drew little hearts around it." I said as I pushed the door open and looked at Marie. "Hey there, Marie." She was on the bed with her hands tied to the headboard and feet anchored to the foot board. Her blouse was opened revealing part of her chest.

"Jesus, Marie." Cleft said. "I told you not to write this shit down." He took a gulp from a large water bottle.

"I'm sorry, Cleft. Sometimes it's hard to remember stuff, I need to write these things down. You know that about me." she said, not missing a beat.

"Do you know what could happen to me if a divorce attorney found that? I would be years of unwarranted alimony payments."

"You're not getting divorced, you've told me that numerous times."

"Do you two need a minute?" I asked

"Fine, it's fine – don't worry about it." he said as he opened the door some more and waved his hand at me to come in.

I looked over at Marie. "What are you two up to in here? I feel like I am interrupting."

"You are interrupting." Cleft said.

"How is your heart, Peter?" Marie asked, resigned to the fact that an active fugitive was in a motel room feet away from her exposed chest.

"Good, considering. You know how things are. Things are going along as planned and then you're on the run from the law because you killed your neighbor."

"Oh my God, it's so true, Peter. Just yesterday my sister was telling me about her boyfriend and how he was going to-" Marie was letting the thoughts loose in her mind.

"Peter –" It was Cleft's turn now "You're insane if you think they won't catch you."

"Where's the confidence, Cleft?"

"Don't push your luck, Peter. You're good as dead. You know Skelly found your letters in Janice's house?"

"What are you talking about? My letters?"

"They found love notes from you. This whole time you were denying it but they found the letters – pictures, Peter."

'I don't understand," I said. I felt that pinch in my chest again and my breath changed pace but I had to keep it together. Keep my cool or I was going to end up in a hospital bed again and there was assuredly no way I was going to get away this time. "Let's take a step back." I said calmly. "I think you mean the letters from our mutual neighbor – Chandler. Because he was sleeping with her and then he was beating the crap out of her. I think Roger made him do it."

"Who's Roger?"

"His Cat."

"I don't think so," Cleft said. "They say, love Peter, all of them."

"That's not right."

"Jesus, Peter." Cleft snapped at me. "You were screwing around with her and sent her love notes and pictures of your – junk. The police showed me the letters. They were on our stationary. It was your handwriting."

"That's not possible."

"Sure, of course not. If you're gonna fool around on Paula don't insult her and get caught. Be a man, Peter."

"I am a man. For once, I am." Trying, at least.

The tension left Cleft's shoulders. He looked over at Marie and then back at me. "Peter, what can I do to help? Anything. I owe you at least that." I could see a sense of helplessness in his face. Maybe because I caught him in the act of his not-so-secret secret or maybe because he laid me off and felt partially responsible for the continuous downfall. Either way, I hit pay dirt. I pulled the crumpled prescription notes from my pocket and handed them over to Cleft.

"I need you to get my medication." I said "By the end of the day, if possible."

"Peter, you know how this goes – I can't go in there. Your name is on those. I'm sure they have an officer at every pharmacy from here to San Marcos with the hope you'll turn up."

"Well, I as fuck can't do it, Cleft. You owe me."

"Peter – be reasonable"

"Fine, forget it. My dealer can probably get me something – black market. Better than the original."

"Alright, alright – fine. You got me." Cleft said. It appeared he didn't want to be responsible for me falling off the perpetual wagon. "Marie can do it."

"What?! I ain't doing shit, Cleft."

"Sure you are, Marie." He took the prescriptions from my hand and bunched them together so they were on top of each other like a neatly packed deck of cards. He then proceeded to rip one side of them.

"What the hell, man – I need those."

"They're already crumpled, they'll never suspect a thing." he said as if pilfering was his thing. "Marie goes in, hands them over and they never suspect a thing."

"The fuck I will."

"Yes, you will, because Peter needs this. Innocent or not he needs our help."

"Thank you." I said.

"Go now," Cleft said. "There's a pharmacy on the other side of the freeway. It's off Twelfth Street. Peter and I will wait here for you."

"Fine." She pulled on the bed. "You going to untie me?" Cleft went over and pulled on the rope to free her hands. She buttoned up her shirt and slipped her shoes on. She walked over and gave Cleft a kiss on the cheek and grabbed the prescriptions and went on her way.

Cleft looked at me. "Want some coffee?"

20

"It's called the Kabuki cleanse." Cleft said to me as I sipped the last of my coffee. I had made the terrible mistake of asking him how the sex was with Marie. He said it was good, an outlet for him. I know it wasn't my place, and I wouldn't normally ask something as brash, but I didn't really care. I was curious why he would put his marriage and family on the line for something he would regret when he was confronted with a post-ejaculate reality. Apparently, the appeal was this thing that Marie learned about on a trip to Japan with her sister. Evidently, and this is according to a tour guide who Marie's sister, Lisa, was sleeping with, but the traditional Kabuki performers would urinate on each other after the performances to wash away the makeup and sweat built up after each show. Lisa was so dubious about this tale, and rightfully so, that the tour guide insisted on showing her. He did a little sweet talk and finally got her to agree. She put on some heavy eye-liner, jogged four miles, and he pulled out his thing and did his business and then she goes and tells Marie how amazing it is. Which brings us to present day, where Cleft and Marie meet every other Tuesday. Marie puts on a variety of makeup and Cleft spends the morning chugging bottles of water in preparation for their 9:30 rendezvous. Apparently, this Kabuki cleanse is the new black, the new brown loafer without any socks. I would put my money on Marie being a nutcase who fabricated the whole trip to Japan just so she could say Lisa tried it and vouches for it. I was going to proffer my theory to Cleft but I couldn't stop looking at the urn that was sitting on the bedside table. I know bibles are customary in hotel rooms across the country but an urn seemed a little out of place.

"Is that common for motels these days?" I asked Cleft. He was sitting on the bed devouring the free HBO.

"What?" he asked. I flicked my finger towards the urn. "Oh no. I brought that with me. I have to make a stop after this. Sorry. It's weird, I know."

"Who is it?" I asked. How could one not ask that question. I misplaced my business plan for the urns with name tags not dissimilar to wine charms.

"You mean, whom is it?" he said.

"Excuse me?"

"Whom is it. Not who. Who and whoever are subjective pronouns but whom and whomever are in the objective case."

"OK." *What the fuck.* "What's the point here?"

"I'm just saying that who and whoever are always subject to a verb, and that whom and whomever are always working as an object in a sentence. It's just easy to get them confused is all."

"So, whom is in the urn?" I asked with the eager hope that I passed Cleft's Grammar 101 crash course.

"You actually." he said with a big Cleft Duvall smile like it was nothing. Maybe it was nothing.

"Funny." *What an asshole.*

"No, it's true. There was a mix up at the hospital." he said as his smile wavered. "See, the people who manage the patients aren't the same people who manage the corpses, if you can believe it. The hospital has orderly's and administration staff to do the back and forth. When you went under they thought you were dead. They even put a time on it – seven a.m., right on the spot. The nurse wrote the time down and went back to the nurse's station to take a phone call. An orderly came by and picked up the form and sent it to the morgue. A day or two later, someone from the morgue calls me and tells me you're ready to be picked up. They tried your house first but whomever answered said they had a wrong number. I told them that they have made a mistake, clearly they made a mistake because I was in the room talking to your former boring self. Two days later, Paula calls me to tell me that they sent someone to the house with this urn. She was all about this divorce thing so she didn't want anything to do with your former self so now I have it. I was going to go back to the hospital and tell them they are insane. You're welcome to come with me. In fact, I encourage it. What a great headline: Wanted fugitive apprehended at hospital returning own ashes. It would get great coverage. Maybe even national."

"What's the point? Giving you an empty urn?" I asked. "Didn't they check?"

"They did and there are ashes in there."

"What do you mean?"

"Take a look." he said as he picked it up and handed it to me. It was a shiny bronze and heavy. I guess if you take the core of a person and burn it down, it still has some weight and purpose to it. I took the top off and looked in. "Spooky, huh?" he said.

"Who do you think it is?" I'm telling someone about this urn charm idea. You can reuse the same urn for different people, just switch out the charm. Millions.

"I don't know who it is. For all I know they just have a bucket of ashes on hand that they fill these with and then cut up the bodies and sell them on the black market. How would I know, I'm just throwing a theory out there."

"I should tell Avery about it. He would appreciate it. He's a good God son."

"Stop calling him that. You aren't his God parent. You're in your mid-thirties and he's a teenager. It's creepy."

"We're close, that's all I mean. It's a compliment, Cleft." I said.

"It's weird."

"I can call him whatever I want."

"But you aren't his God parent so it's misleading and, frankly, doesn't make any sense."

"Do you have a pen?" I asked. His perspective on my relationship with his son was tedious.

"Sure, what's going on?" Cleft asked.

"I think I'm going to sign those divorce papers. You don't happen to have them, do you?" He just stared at me. He was happy hanging out watching HBO and poking fun at the hospital mishap throwing a few jabs here and there but I needed to take him out of his comfort zone. I didn't feel too bad about it either because Paula gave him the papers so she was really to blame for me bringing the whole thing up.

"Don't you want to try, at least?" he said to me like I was about to jump off a cliff without a contingency plan. It's as if this whole time I wasn't trying and then when it mattered I just gave up, exhausted from being inert. In fact, I was trying. Despite the circumstances, Paula and I were a good fit and we made things work. I wanted to be a husband

and a father and she wanted be a citizen. We still managed to find love and admiration for each other. At least, I thought we did. Every relationship has issues but you work through them, resolve them, you don't just throw it all away. I was confused. Maybe she wasn't happy after all and this was her out. "What about Joyce?" he added. He knew I was working on adopting her, making it official. But I didn't say anything, I just stared down and thought it through. "Shit, I don't care." he said as he handed me a pen. "Just leave me out of it." Those were the words of support I was in search of. I looked down at the pile of paper and the signature line that was beckoning me. It couldn't be this easy. You can't decide a life-changing event like this quickly and sign your name and be done with it. There should be a discussion and process that's adhered to but what did I know. Maybe someone can change their mind that quickly, especially if they feel they have good reason to do so. *Just try at least*, Cleft said. Maybe he was right.

"I'm not ready." I said as I put the pen down.

"Suit yourself, man." he said as the door to the motel room flew open.

"Turn on the television." Marie said to Cleft as she burst through the door and tossed three prescription bags on the bed.

"What's going on?" I asked as Cleft pointed to the remote on the end table not sensing the haste in Marie's voice.

"They found you. That's what's going on." She grabbed the remote and flipped through the channels and stopped on KVAN. It was an aerial shot of local police and various members of the sheriff's department surrounding a dark blue Tesla outside a seedy motel off the interstate.

"Are you sure that's here?" Cleft asked Marie.

"Yes, they're right outside – in the sky."

"Whose car is that?"

"It's David Prescott's car," I said. Cleft turned his head towards me. "His wife loaned it to me. She must have tipped them off – reported it stolen. I should have known."

"Holy mother of God." Cleft said. "We are fucked. Marie, did anyone see you come into the room?"

"I don't think so." she said apprehensively.

"Doesn't matter." I said "They are going to search all the rooms anyway. Give me your car keys."

"What?" she said "I'm not giving you my car keys. You're crazy if you think–"

"Where do you think you're going?" Cleft asked.

"Going to see someone in Houston." I said. I was thinking ahead. Cleft was a soft man. I know the type. I was the type. He was going to give me up so I might as well buy some time with an obvious misdirection.

"Jesus. Be a man, Peter." Cleft added. "They're going to catch you eventually."

"Doesn't matter." I said again. "There's a record of my prescriptions being picked up. Skelly probably already has a warrant to search the video surveillance of whatever corner store you went to. Give me your keys and when you hear the cops outside you are going to yell for help."

"I'm gonna walk out that door and tell them what you did. I ain't going to wait until they start banging on doors." Marie said.

"Yes you will. Because when they get here you and Cleft will be tied up. So they are going to break the door down and untie you and then you tell them that I took you hostage and forced you to pick up my medicine – "

"You pretty much did force me to, you sack of shit."

"That's fine. Then tell them." I said "But if you were complacent, and you aided a criminal, then you'll both go to jail."

"But I thought you said you were innocent."

"That's right. Innocent until proven guilty, that's the American way, but I'm sure you don't want to sit around a jail cell for ten years waiting for the justice system you love and trust to figure it out. Do you?"

It was rhetorical but Marie said "No." anyway just to let me know she understood.

"This is a real crummy way to treat your friends, Peter." Cleft blurted out.

"I don't have much choice and you know it." I said as I grabbed the rope from the bed that Marie was entangled with earlier. "Plus, you can tell them that I brought you here against your will and I didn't stumble across you having an affair. Anyway, I need to get to Houston." In case they missed it the first time. "Figure out the details."

Cleft looked over at Marie and nodded his approval. They didn't have much choice so the resignation was inevitable. I went over and pulled both of the chairs out from the desk near the television and placed them back to back. I signaled for Cleft and Marie to come over and sit down and then I tied them up. Pretty tight too. I didn't want Marie getting any second thoughts about this, and I think, her being pissed at me was going to make the story more believable.

"They won't believe us, Peter." Cleft said.

"Does your phone record audio?" I interjected.

"Yes, why?"

"No reason. Just a random survey." I said. "Anyway, I'm sure you can find a way to make it convincing." I said as I reached into Marie's pocket and pulled out her car keys. She drove an old compact car that ran like a golf cart and looked no better. It was a piece of junk but it would do.

"Good luck with your heart, asshole." Marie added.

"Marie – that's not necessary." Cleft said.

"Shut-up, Cleft." She looked back at me. "I hope you drop dead in front of the cops as soon as you leave this room. That'll teach you something."

"Well, I did it once so maybe you'll get lucky."

"That's right. I forgot you were an enigma, Peter." she said

"Jesus, Marie."

"Shut the fuck up, Cleft." Marie said and that was my cue. I reached into Cleft's jacket pocket and pulled out his phone and then grabbed the prescription bags off the bed and looked out the window. Other than the soft hum of traffic on the interstate it was silent. The cops hadn't made their way over to this side of the motel yet so I still had some time. I opened the door and went down the stairs. Marie's car was parked right at the bottom so I got in and started the engine. I backed out and took a right on to the service road that ran behind the motel and then passed a series of police cars. An officer was nice enough to wave at me right before I turned on to the freeway and headed north to visit Darren Bales.

21

Darren Bales failed the Texas State Police written exam. Twice. There were fifty questions total including two essay questions. He got thirty answers correct the first time and twenty nine correct the second time. He said he was putting too much pressure on himself. It wasn't until the third time, months later, that he got a whopping forty-two questions correct and passed the threshold to move on to the physical examination. Darren grew up watching Kojak and CHiPS and wanted to fulfill his boyhood dream of being a fully credible police detective. When he was a freshman in high school he told his parents that he didn't want to go to college, instead he enrolled in the military and his parents put their hard earned savings towards a month long vacation in the Bahamas while he was away at basic training. Once he finished basic training he was stationed at Andrews Air Force base as a reserve and then retired and did some freelance security work. You can't quit the military, or get laid off, or even be fired. You either resign, go AWOL or get discharged, that is unless you don't die first. Darren decided to resign, move back in with his well-rested parents and apply to be a fully certified police detective. He didn't care about the military anyway, it was just something to put on his resume when he applied to be a Texas State Trooper. He was only in the military for six months, including basic training, but he didn't think the people reading the resumes would pick up on that. In fact, he submitted the resume online specifically because he thought no one was going to read it and that it was going to be accepted by some automated process. Nonetheless, he was accepted, passed all the necessary milestones, see above, and started his first year as a Texas State Trooper guarding the State prison in Dallas from seven p.m. to seven a.m. seven days a week for three hundred and sixty five straight days. A few days after he started, he went home and complained to his dad that this wasn't what he had pictured for himself. His dad said to suck it up and that life isn't going to be handed to you on a silver platter and if you want to be a gold class detective you have to work for it and show people you deserve it. So he did just that. He stuck it out at the prison and then moved on to traffic duty pulling over sports cars going a few miles over the speed limit so he could hit his monthly quota and move seamlessly through the system. A few years after that, he got put on a night shift riding around south Dallas picking up prostitutes with Leroy McReynolds, who was also a newbie. No one wanted to work with the new guys, so command just put the new guys together and let them sort it out. He and Leroy didn't care for each other all that much. He thought Leroy was scum and Leroy picked on him for still living at home and listening to film scores as they drove around which was a big offense as far as command was concerned, but Darren said it helped him focus. Having some Bernard Herrmann playing in the background made him feel invincible. It also muffled the sound of Leroy negotiating a treaty with the hookers so they didn't have to bring them in and charge them. Leroy liked hookers and hated paperwork.

It was getting late and Darren was irritated that Leroy wasn't in yet. He wasn't back from his trip yet and Darren was catching up on all the paperwork that Leroy didn't like doing. It was burning into the hours that he could do actual police work.

They worked eight to eight for six straight days and then took three days off. The twelve hour shifts didn't include overtime and they were strongly discouraged from taking overtime. If a case needed extra special attention, that's what corporate likes to call it, then they need to submit a K91-v form for overtime or formally pass the case over to the on duty detective which also required a paper trail. Sometimes it was just easier to work overtime and not bother with the paperwork. Besides, getting the bad guy was rewarding whether you were getting paid for it or not. That's what Darren liked to think anyway. Leroy didn't give a shit and always tried to find a reason to pass their cases over to other officers. He called it delegating. Something he was practicing for when he became a sergeant.

Leroy was asked to drive a colleague, Detective Fritz, out to a possible crime scene and that turned into a road trip to the place where they won't shut up about how good their breakfast tacos are. They were gone for about two day's and got back late the night before last. Darren idolized him and had been trying to get on his good side for a few months now. The word was, if you wanted on his good side you didn't talk about Kennedy. Want in – don't talk about Kennedy. Fritz, according to reliable sources, worked the Kennedy assassination and knew who killed him and everyone wanted to fucking talk about it with him, despite him having tight lips in regards to the matter. But Darren knew the drill, play it cool and he'll warm up to you. But it was Leroy who got to drive him around and they certainly talked about Kennedy and they probably ate some pretty tasty breakfast tacos. It was all Darren wanted: to get in a car, drive Fritz around and not talk about Kennedy.

He looked up at the clock, it was almost two. He opened his desk drawer and pulled out the lunch sack his mom made for him. It was the same thing every day: two tuna fish sandwiches with fresh celery and chipotle mayo, sliced cucumbers, wheat thins and a honey crisp apple. He had the first sandwich at eleven and saved the second sandwich and sundries for later. He got up at 4 each morning to go running, or at least that was his intention each morning, so he was famished by 10 and was able to wane his hunger until 11. He could usually hold out until 3 for the second round but he was more ravenous than normal so he set the second sandwich on his desk and slowly unwrapped it as he looked out over the squad room, unaware that he was about to hit the jackpot. His desk was up against Leroy's and they both looked out towards the command floor. In the center was a war room like area set up for department meetings and to the right was the entrance with a tall desk like you see on television sans the bullet proof windows. Madge was behind the desk. She had been with the State Police department for almost fifty years. She was a glorified secretary but knew where to send people when they came in. No one came in though. People usually go to the local police first, mostly because they really have no idea what the State Police does other than sit on the freeway looking for speeders. The Texas State Police is also called Texas Highway Patrol which is part of the Department of Public Safety which is responsible for traffic supervision as well as criminal law in rural parts of the state, and assisting other police agencies as needed. That's how they know Detective Fritz. He's with the Dallas Police department and routinely works with the Department of Public Safety in a handful of various matters, mostly it's running down drug traffickers from Mexico. He usually sits in the conference room and drinks their coffee and eats their food and doesn't talk about Kennedy.

Darren finished the first half of his tuna fish sandwich as one side of the double glass doors opened up. A man walked through the door and up to the desk and spoke softly to Madge. He was about fifty feet away but appeared tall and looked like he needed a nice long nap and a good shave. He was carrying a banker's box and set it next to Madge as she said "You have the wrong place, sir. We're the Department of Public Safety." She had it down perfectly and mastered the intonation just enough to let people know they made a simple mistake and that it happens all the time but they're still stupid for making it. It's probably the same tone she uses when people ask her if she knows who killed Kennedy. Madge understood layers. The man leaned in closer to Madge and whispered something. Madge looked over at Darren and pointed. "Darren, this man is here. He says he wants to make a confession. I told him we don't do confessions here but he insisted on speaking with you."

22

To be perfectly honest, I expected Darren Bales to look somewhat different than his 5'6" wee figure. His shoulders were bulky but any man can do that if they lift a few weights. The rest of him was slender and weak and his breath stunk of dead fish. This man-boy was no killer but I was here and I had to get down to business.

"What did you say your name was?" Bales asked me.

"I told you. Peter Richards. I'm turning myself in." I said as I looked out at Madge through a small window behind Bales. She was filing her nails. Such a Madge thing to do. I was in an interrogation room. Bales said it was a waiting room but I know what's what.

"One second." Bales said as he opened up a small notepad and pulled out a Highway Patrol issued pen and clicked on it. He pronounced each letter in my name as he wrote it down and then turned the notepad around to show me. "Is that it?"

"Ya, Peter Richards."

"OK, just making sure. You get the name wrong and the lawyers have a field day with you."

"I understand." I said as I adjusted the lid to the banker's box on the table next to me.

"Madge, out front, can watch that for you if you like." he offered.

"Do you want my address?" I said.

"Sure."

"It's-"

"One second." In the time I fixed the lid on the banker's box he managed to put the pen away. He pulled it out again and clicked it again. "OK – go. "

"1112 Candida Circle." I said slowly so he could catch it, let it sink in. "Austin, Texas." I added.

"Huh." he said.

"What is it?"

"They got those tacos down there. With breakfast in them, right?"

"Right. You know the address?" I asked. "It's right across the street from 1109 Candida Circle."

"No, can't say that I do. The military base is down there though, right? You near that?"

"Not really. You've been down there though, right? When you worked for Mach 10?"

"How'd you know about that? You a Svengali or something?"

"Something like that. What did you do for Mach 10?"

"Nothing really, I was only there for a couple of weeks before they – fired me." he said softly as if someone was listening in. "They said I was a non-performer, as if that's a thing."

La dee da.

"So, what are you confessing to?" he asked.

"I'm not confessing, I'm turning myself in."

"For what?"

"Nothing. I mean, there's a manhunt out for me. Don't you turn on the television - ?"

"Not really, bunch of shit on – "

"I'm wanted for the murder of Janice – "

"Oh, murder." he said as if he were learning a new language. "We don't deal with that sort of stuff here much. We're the State Police, also known as the Highway Patrol. We're part of the Department of Public Safety and we're mostly responsible for traffic supervision and management, some criminal stuff but mostly rural, we also work with other agencies as needed but that's about it. No murder really. To be honest with you, it's mostly running down drug traffickers who hop the border. If you want to talk murder you should talk to Detective Fritz with the Dallas police – he knows who killed Kennedy."

I leaned into him and put my hands on the table for full affect. I looked him in the eye and said "I don't give a shit who killed Kennedy."

"Well, alright, that's fine. Most people are at least a little bit curious, but that's your choice."

"I know what you did." I added.

"Excuse me?"

"I saw your car at my neighbor's house the night she was killed. I saw you get out of the car and go inside and kill her."

"Excuse me? When was this?" The levity in his voice was gone. He could play dumb but I had the facts.

"What day is today?" I asked.

"Tuesday, the second."

"It was Thursday morning. Department of Public Safety license plate 234 ZH1." BAM, asshole.

"In Austin, you said?" He sounded concerned but kept his cool as he wrote the plate number down. I didn't need to repeat it for him.

"If you could wait a second. I'm going to go check on something." he said and started to slide the pen back into his pocket.

"No, I'm not going to wait a second. I'm not going to let you go out there and walk away from this." I took Cleft's phone out of my pocket and set it on the table. "I've been recording this whole conversation."

"I'm just going to check something on the car. That's it, I promise." he said.

"Over my dead body, asshole." I said as I opened the banker's box and pulled out the first file. "Tell me about Carol French," I said as I set 001 in front of him.

"Who is that?" he asked as he stared at Carol French's picture. I was getting nowhere. I looked out into the main area of the station. It was quiet. Madge was finishing her nails as the double glass doors opened. Two men came through and said hi to her. One was bulky and sweaty, looked like he needed some kale in his life. It was the other one who caught my eye. Six feet tall, dark hair with a slender face. So generic looking he just blended in but he stood out. His plainness was what was so unique about him. Most people stick out because of a tattoo or a scar or blemish, some strange idiosyncratic trait, but this guy was seamless and straight from the factory.

"Who's that?" I said to Bales and pointed to the guy I was sure was at Janice Walton's house the morning she was killed. I was wrong. I had the license plate and knew that tied back to Darren Bales so I was confident I had my man but I was dead wrong. It didn't occur to me that Darren didn't fit the description. I didn't even think about it.

"That's Leroy." Darren said. "He's my partner. Why?" He turned back around and looked at me. Our eyes locked and we had a moment because I hadn't been in this room for more than a minute but Darren and I, fast friends, both knew what I was going to say next.

"He's the person who killed my neighbor."

23

"I'll be right back," he said. "All the patrol cars have GPS in them. I'm going to ask Madge to run the location on where the car was Thursday evening."

"Alright but be careful."

"It's fine. He's a terrible partner."

"Can I use the phone?" I asked. There was a dilapidated rotary phone on the far end of the table. If suspects were allotted one phone call this was the antique they were fortunate enough to use.

"Dial nine," he said as he stepped out and let the door close behind him. I reached over and grabbed Carol French's file. The upper-left corner listed her address and telephone number. I dialed the Austin local number and waited a few rings before someone picked up.

"Hello?" a woman's voice said. It sounded like I woke her up.

"Is this Carol French?" I asked.

"Who is this?"

"My name is Peter Richards. I was wondering if I could speak with you — "

"Look. She isn't here. We're not interested. Don't call again. Put the number on your list. Whatever that list is called, just don't call us." Then she hung up.

The door opened and Bales came back in. He set a sheet of printed paper down in front of me. It had a list of latitudinal and longitudinal coordinates on it. "Turn it over," he said. I flipped the paper over. On the back was a map with a police car icon on it. It was parked in front of Janice's house. "Looks like he was there. The car you said you saw, the numbers you saw, you were right. That's our car."

"I know I'm right."

"Why don't you hold tight. I'm going to talk to my boss about this when he gets back from lunch."

"And what? Tell on your partner? Your partner buried my neighbor's body in my backyard. In my daughter's sandbox. You're going to talk to your boss and then what - call your partner in for a little heart to heart?"

"I don't know, I have to take this up the chain."

"For fuck's sake."

"What do you want me to do?" he said, exasperated with me.

"I need your help. I need you to call a detective in Austin. Detective Skelly. He thinks I did it, everyone does, but if only he could listen to reason."

"I am helping you – you came in here, you found me."

"What do you think your partner is going to say? 'Oh, yeah, I killed her, and framed this asshole, sorry about that.' "

"Why do you think they framed you?"

"Well, I didn't do it so therefore I was framed."

"Right but why?" he asked like I had the answer at hand ready for such a specific question. I hadn't thought about it and his asking me unnerved me. "I don't know. Maybe they just needed a place to hide the body."

"Maybe it's not about you. You were just in the wrong place at the wrong time."

"My house doesn't seem like the wrong place, if we're sticking with the metaphor." I said. "Besides, there's other stuff."

"What other stuff?"

"The police said they found love letters from me in her house."

"Who's house?"

"Her house. Janice's house."

"Who's Janice?"

"The woman who they're saying I killed."

"Oh right. Were you two intimate?"

"No, that's what I'm saying. I've hardly said more than two words to her and now the police claim that I was having an affair with her."

"Were you?"

"Jesus, no."

"People lie about that stuff all the time. Married, kids, lots of assets to protect, so I am sure you can understand my apprehension on taking your word for it."

"I wasn't sleeping with her. I swear."

"You married?"

"Going through a divorce, I guess. It's complicated."

"I can imagine."

"The guy – that guy – your partner. He was looking for these fold-ers. They were in my neighbor's house and that's why he killed her." I said as I waved my hands out over the table and the banker's box like a magician doing his big reveal.

"How do you know?"

"Because the day before someone came and picked them up and brought them to David Prescott's office, and the night Janice was shot, he was looking for something. This is the only thing I can think of. It makes sense." He looked down over the folders. I can tell he was think-ing this over in his head but he wasn't saying anything. "Don't you want to know who David Prescott is?" I asked.

"No," Darren said. "I know who David Prescott is."

"You do?"

"Yes. He's awesome."

"You've met him?"

"No. I haven't met him. But Leroy, my partner, the guy you said killed your lover – "

"We weren't lovers – "

"Right, right." He jotted a note down on his notepad. "Leroy and Fritz, the one I told you about, they took the cruiser and went to Austin a few days ago to pick up David Prescott. I guess he shot some guy –"

"Harvey Marcona." I said. The name wheezed out of my mouth.

"Huh?"

"David Prescott shot Harvey Marcona."

"Ya, right. Leroy said he'll get time served. I guess Marcona was the scum of the earth. Anyway, Prescott shot this Marcona guy and had his assistant toss the gun for him. Leroy said he's a real classy guy."

"Why are two cops from Dallas going down to Austin to pick a guy up?"

"Not sure on that one. All I know is that Fritz made a formal re-quest for Leroy. Said he needed a guy to drive him around."

"When did they leave?" I asked.

"A few days ago – Monday – I think."

"When was Marcona shot?"

"The day before."

There was a loud banging noise on the door "Hey, shit for brains. Let me in."

"It's all in here." Bales said as he set a folded newspaper down in front of me and tapped his finger on a short article near the bottom. He got up and opened the door and peaked his head out. He said a few words with someone I suspected was Leroy and then stepped out. I looked down at the article.

FRIDAY, DECEMBER 6TH

Endochrone, headquartered in Northwest Austin, develops proprietary technologies which target the genetic basis of human diseases and the role these genes play in the onset, progression and treatment of the respective diseases.

On December 2nd, Dallas Police arrested David Prescott, financial backer of Endochrone, in connection with the murder of Harvey Marcona, CEO of Endochrone. Marcona was said to have called 911 when a fire broke out in the Endochrone research facility the evening of Sunday, December 1st. When officials arrived on the scene they discovered Marcona's body and determined the cause of death was from gunshots.

The cause of the fire is under investigation and no ongoing research was harmed.

On December 2nd, a Texas Park Ranger reported a man identified as Jack F. disposing of a gun in Lake Shelton just outside of Waco to Dallas Police. Upon questioning Jack F. said he was disposing of the gun for his boss, David Prescott. The gun was licensed to Harvey Marcona.

Last quarter, Endochrone announced publicly its long rumored partnership with Green Pharmaceuticals and the development of Memoton which fights the onset of Alzheimer's Disease, the result of years of testing of Chromosome 16 which Endochrone owns the exclusive rights to in perpetuity.

On November 1st, Endochrone announced that Memoton will be available to the consumer market January 1 with an average selling price in the range of $2,200. The product has an expected estimated gross margin of 92%, unprece-

dented in current market conditions. Green Pharmaceuticals is launching Memoton in a phased approach, starting from an early-access, clinical experience program to a specific number of medical and scientific outlets. Endochrone will then begin an expanded access program later in the year.

When asked for comment, a rep for Green Pharmaceuticals said they are "very excited about this game changer to the drug market." and "They are deeply saddened by the loss of a great man."

The IPO is scheduled for Tuesday, December 10th."

I set the newspaper down and pulled 002 out from the banker's box and set it next to Carol French.

Paula explained to me once that pharmaceutical companies are known to use two labs simultaneously. One lab is where all the work and research is done and the second lab is purely a showroom for investors. It's very possible that the fire took place at a dummy lab and the real lab, where the research was performed, was somewhere else entirely. That's why no ongoing research suffered, because nothing was actually happening there. Sure, there may have been chemicals and lab coats, but someone with a twenty million dollar check book wasn't going to discriminate. The dummy lab can also be used to deter genetic theft. If Endochrone wanted to hire the next great science whiz kid they could very well put him in the dummy lab for a few months, or even years, to determine that he wasn't selling trade secrets to competitors or the black market. A conglomerate like Green Pharmaceuticals also has labs where all they produce is faulty information and they hire people they suspect are moles and feed them bad information five days a week ad nauseam with the hopes they go back to their true employer and share the information. The hope is that the false information could delay a competitor's product by a few months, or even years depending on how much money and resources the competitor dedicates to the information they receive. 21st century corporate espionage.

With the exception of personalized patient data, the info on 001 and 002 was the same. They were both accepted applicants to participate in the trial of P39i, the code name for Memoton. I put Carol French back in the box and pulled out 029, David Closter. He was also in fairly good health and appeared to be an above average person both intellectually and financially. On the backside of his, as with the others, there was a space at the bottom where a doctor, or administrator, could make notes on side effects and progress. David Closter suffered from weight loss, and moderate to severe headaches. There was a note to prescribe David 900 mg of Eflixer. Carol French didn't suffer any side effects and wasn't prescribed anything yet the person who answered her phone was very unhappy.

The door opened and Darren came back in. "You OK in here, boss?" he asked.

"Sure. What's going on?"

"Nothing," he said. "Just a few things. Hold tight, OK?" he said as he tossed me a bottle of water and shut the door. Then I heard him lock the door. I got up and grabbed the handled – locked.

"Hey – Darren, you locked the door!"

"Hold tight amigo, you'll be OK in there." he said from the other side. "Just trust me."

"Let me outta here!" I shouted at him as I listened to him walk away. *What an asshole.* I stepped back to the table and looked over the files. They were splayed out in front of me like a deck of playing cards: the names and faces of people who donated themselves to science. Maybe it was for money, maybe it was to help the progression of science. Whatever it was, they had their reasons and Harvey Marcona chose to isolate them. He took them out of the bunch and put them aside, maybe it was so they could be reviewed at a later time or maybe it was so they were forgotten about entirely. There was a connection but I couldn't tell. All I had was unexplained information – a black hole of possibility. I let what I thought was a few hours pass before I picked up the phone and dialed 9 plus 411.

"Information."

"What time is it?" I asked

"6:17 p.m., central time – "

"Thanks." and hung up. Paula was probably just finishing dinner with Joyce. I picked up the phone dialed 9 and then our home number. It rang a few times before Paula picked up. She sounded rushed, maybe this wasn't the best idea.

"Hey. It's me." I said in the best nonchalant voice I could come up with. Just calling to check in, see how things are, no big deal.

"What do you want, Peter?" Paula said in a tone that suggested I was a telemarketer who just could not leave her alone. *Take my name off your list.*

"How's Joyce?" I asked skipping the formalities.

"She's good. Joyce, do you want to say hi to daddy?" she asked Joyce which was followed by a faint no. I don't take it personally. Joyce doesn't want to talk to me because she's a toddler and doesn't understand her dad's voice coming out of a machine. It isn't because I allegedly killed her neighbor and she's holding a grudge against me.

"Thanks for calling, Peter." Paula said quickly. Talk to the kid and say bye was the routine these days.

"Wait – wait – one second."

"What is it?"

"Have you heard of a drug called Eflixer?" I asked.

"Is the internet broken?"

"Nothing came up." Thinking on my feet here.

"I think it's new. Something about cancer maybe," she said. "I remember seeing some article about it in Pharma Exec." That was short for Pharmaceutical Executive News and Information, a bi-monthly publication that Paula reads religiously.

"Can you check for me please?"

"What? Now?" she said as if it was the most outlandish thing I could ask for.

"Yes, that would be great actually. Time is of the essence."

"God, you're so weird, Peter." she said as she set the phone down. It's good to know that we can still be civil to each other despite the potential divorce. That's how I'm referring to it these days, until everything is sorted out. She came back. "OK, here you go. FDA approves Eflixer for common use in cancer treatment and management. The brainchild of Green Pharmaceuticals in conjunction with – blah blah blah - Eflixer is the revolutionary anti-cancer drug which will be used to governor the evolution of dangerous-" She trailed off.

"What was the blah blah blah?" I asked.

"Huh?"

"You blah blah blah'd something – what did you skip over? In conjunction with what?"

"The brainchild of Green Pharmaceuticals in conjunction with Endochrone." she said. "Happy?" Huh.

"Is it out yet?" I asked.

"Not until the spring but the article, it's short, says there has been a huge push by the federal government. I guess it's a cancer killer."

"Cure?"

"Killer. Someone cures cancer it's not going to be a byline in the Pharma Exec. See I used a term you'd understand."

"That's actually a newspaper term. Television investigative journalists don't use bylines."

"I get it, you were a television journalist. You don't have to say the whole title every time you tell me what you did. Past tense." I think this conversation was about over. "I heard you got the divorce papers from Cleft." she added.

"No secrets these days, huh?"

"You tell me."

"He just wanted me to know that it wasn't his responsibility anymore." I said wondering what Cleft had told her. Did he say he just happened to run into me on the street while I was evading the law or did he tell her about my serendipitous appearance at the hotel. Paula suspected for a while that Cleft was having an affair, he's the type she would always tell me, but I can't imagine that he would actually tell her. Did she know I was on the run but now in custody? Pseudo-custody.

"Do you want to know where I am?" I asked.

"No and I don't particularly care where you are. Maybe the police caught you by now or you're still on the lamb." she said, the words forced out of her mouth. "If it's the latter of the two, I'm sure they'll get you any minute now."

"Such confidence."

"Always and forever," she said. "Anyway, did you sign them?"

"Not yet. No."

"Are you going to?" With everything going on it was the least burdensome question she could ask. She wasn't concerned about where I was or me killing the neighbor or the affair even. She was just checking to make sure that I got the divorce papers and if I was going to sign them. It was housekeeping really. Just a husband and wife talking to each other about things that needed to get taken care of. Pick up the laundry, take out the trash and sign the divorce papers so we can both move on.

"I'm thinking about it." Was the best response that I could come up with.

"Well, you either sign them willingly or you sign them unwillingly. The choice is entirely yours and I don't particularly care what you choose." Very eloquent.

"Nice to hear those ESL classes are paying off."

"Fuck you, Peter."

"No, you're right. Where did we go so wrong, Paula?"

"I didn't do anything, Peter. This is all on you."

"Right, sure, I shouldn't have said that. I was wrong. Don't you want to talk about this?"

"Not really – one second, honey" she said to Joyce. "I gotta go – make sure you take your meds so I don't have to deal with your corpse. Again." and hung up the phone.

You're such an idiot, Peter. You want to make things right.

I pulled one of my prescriptions out of my bag and rolled it around in my fingers. Baker Family Pharmacy.

Sounded friendly enough even if it was in a seedy part of town.

I dialed the number and waited until someone picked up.

"Baker Family." an older man's voice said on the other end.

"Uh, yes, I had a question about one of my prescriptions."

"Are you ordering one?"

"No, I already have it I just needed some more information." I said as I flipped the bottle around.

"OK."

"I have a question about my Ciclosporin."

"What's the question?"

"How often do I need to take it? It doesn't say anything on the bottle." I flipped the bottle around a few more times – nothing.

"Did you recently get a transplant of some sort?"

"Yes, my heart. I got a new heart. Well, half a heart."

"Did you get one of those mechanical ones?"

"Yes, half real, half fake."

"You should probably have a conversation with your doctor but usually people take it twice a day with meals. Take it every day."

"Until the bottle runs out?"

"When the bottle runs out you get a new bottle."

"Bonus, huh?" I said and cracked a small smile.

"You take it for the rest of your life. Ciclosporin is an Immunosuppressive which keeps your body running. Your immune system rejects anything foreign in your body, including transplanted organs – real or imitation. To prevent rejection of your new heart, this system is suppressed, or slowed down, with immunosuppressive's. After your transplant, you must take these drugs *exactly* at your prescribed dosages for the *rest of your life*. If you take too little medication, your immune system will destroy your new heart. If you take too much, your body will be less able to fight off infection and you will be more likely to develop side effects. In the future people won't need them. But today they do. You do."

"The future, huh?"

"That's right. Surely they explained this to you."

Surely.

"What's your name, sir?" he asked.

"I don't know." I said and then slammed the phone down.

About a half second after that the door to the interrogation room opened. Darren stood at the precipice of the door holding a bag of food from a local burger joint. Behind him was the guy they called Fritz.

"Hungry?" Fritz asked.

24

"No pickles, right?" Fritz said to me.

"Is it that obvious?" I said as I extended my hand to him. "Peter Richards, don't believe we've met." I let my hand hang out there for a few seconds but he didn't return the gesture. Instead he leaned into the hallway. "Madge, you can go home now. We're just getting started on this guy," he shouted at her.

"Oh, OK." she sighed. "You guys are really dedicated policemen. Your parents would be very proud." She gave him a small wave and he reciprocated.

Fritz came into the room and slammed the door. Darren set the food on the table as Fritz took the chair across from me and spun it around. It was an interesting choice and said a lot about him. He was trying to tell me that he had no respect for the integrity of the chair, how one is supposed to sit in the chair and, therefore, he had no respect for me and could do whatever he wanted to me, consequences pending. At least, that's what I think he was getting at. Hard to tell these days. Fritz pulled two burgers out of the bag and tossed one to Darren.

"Thank you, sir, but I'm stuffed from-" Darren started to say.

"Eat it." Fritz said to him.

"Sure, sure." Darren said as he fumbled with the foil wrapper.

"Pack this stuff up to while you're at it." Fritz said and extended his index finger towards the files on the table.

"Yes, sir." Darren said and started putting the folders back into the banker's box with one hand while munching on the burger with the other. He made these very pronounced chewing noises, probably so Fritz was aware that he was doing as he was told. It was tough to tell which was more vexing to me, the grinding of the teeth or the smacking of the gums.

"Those are mine." I said about the files. Darren stopped putting them in the box but his lips kept smacking.

"No they aren't." Fritz retorted. "They don't belong to you."

"Am I under arrest?"

"Answer the question!"

"They were given to me so, yes, I believe they are mine. There was a very clear transfer of ownership."

"Incorrectly so, actually. They shouldn't have been given to you. Adrienne made a mistake."

"That's up for debate and you weren't there." I said.

"It's unfortunate, the situation you're in. Sounds like you and Janice, your neighbor, had some rich history. An affair, love notes. You even had a trip planned together, right? Cabo? The local police saw the tickets on her refrigerator. You were going to skip out on your wife and your kid."

"None of that's true." I said. "Darren ran the tag on the cruiser I saw outside of Janice's house, he can confirm that his partner was there the night of the killing – and he said you were with him."

"That's what I was told." Fritz said. "You see though, Darren isn't that smart. Obtuse, if you will. He doesn't really see the big picture. He ran the tag on the car and, you're right, the car was there. But he also asked Madge to run it for him and Madge well, she's also obtuse so she came and asked Leroy to confirm the tag number. Leroy panicked - freaked out, if you will - and called me and well, here we are now."

"What's your involvement with all of this again?" I asked "Just want to make sure I know the roles of all the suspicious people."

"I make sure Darren and Leroy follow protocol."

"Right and who killed Kennedy again? I can't remember."

"What?" He looked over at Darren.

"What?" Darren asked. "Are you going to tell him?"

"You're such a piece of shit, Darren." he said.

"It's true, though, you do know." Darren said.

"I want to talk to my lawyer." I said.

"Sure, and you can and we want to help you." Fritz said.

"I'm really sorry, Peter." Darren said apologizing for the confusion with the license plate. A piece of lettuce fell out of his mouth.

"It's fine. You didn't know." *What a fucking idiot.* "Can I talk with Detective Skelly with the Austin Police Department?"

"There's just one issue and it's your word against Leroy's," Fritz added "and Leroy was with me that night. I can vouch for him."

"Who can vouch for you though?" I asked.

"I don't think it matters who can vouch for me because I'm pretty sure no one is going to believe whatever you say."

"I got Darren here." I said as I leaned back in the chair and put my feet up on the desk. I made sure they got right near Fritz's hands and his burger. Stink it up real good.

"He's got a point, Fritz." Darren added. "Whatever Leroy did, I don't know, but this guy here – he's on to him."

"Shut up, Darren." Fritz snapped. He looked back at me. "You have two choices here, Peter. We can call detective Skelly up and you turn yourself in for this heinous crime."

"What are you talking about?"

"Confess to killing Janice Walton. Confess to what you did."

"Come on…"

"You had a change of heart after all, a renewed moral guidance, if you will. Or, better yet-" he unlocked his pistol holster and set his firearm on the table. "We can end it right here. Bullet in the mouth. Your choice."

I looked over at Darren, he looked at Fritz for a second and then went back to filing the folders back into the banker's box. "You're bluffing." I said as I forced out a small smile. Fritz slid the gun closer to me and turned it so the barrel was facing him.

"Go ahead," he said. "Your choice."

"That's it?"

"That's it. Choose wisely, Peter."

"Can I just ask a question?" I said. "It will help me in my – decision making process."

"What's your question?" he asked as he leaned back.

"When I went into Janice's house, after Leroy killed her. Why was there a plane ticket for me on her fridge?"

"Because you were having an affair. You were going to leave your wife and go to Cabo with her." he said like it was plain as day.

"You know that's not true so tell me why it was there. You and I both know I'm not getting out of here alive, even if I do agree to confess to the crime. There's no way that Leroy saw me across the street and then decided to print a fake plane ticket in order to frame me with the hopes the police would find it."

"You wouldn't understand." Fritz said.

"Love letters too, I forgot to mention those."

"Peter, can I call you that? Peter, things are complicated. It's a complicated world and there a lot of moving pieces. You're just a very small piece of that puzzle and you are expendable whether you like it or not. Got it? So tread carefully here. You are right. There was a plane ticket for you on her fridge but it wasn't fake. It was real and it was purchased with your credit card two weeks before Janice was killed. Why, you may ask. Because Janice Walton was a liability and needed to be eliminated and you were the person who was going to do it for us." Then he stopped.

"Context?" I asked.

"Exactly."

"Because she found these?" I asked and looked at the banker's box.

"That's part of it. About six months ago Janice made a very unfortunate discovery and we decided that she needed to go."

"She found these six months ago?"

"Yes."

"That's a pretty shitty turnaround time if you ask me." I said. "Six months to kill a poor helpless lady. You need to work on your –"

"Doesn't matter how long it took. The point is it's done."

"Touché."

"It gave us time to build an insurance policy. We couldn't just kill her in a car accident or a fall down the stairs, we needed to know what she knew and who she told."

"Sounds like it's just more time for her to go and share the information."

"Sure, but we aren't reactionary."

"You didn't know, did you? You didn't know she had the files. When did you find out?" I asked but he didn't say anything. He stared at me so I continued. "What's to stop me from agreeing to play along and then I go to detective Skelly and my attorney and the news and tell everyone about this conversation?" I said. "What if I'm wearing a wire and I'm recording this whole conversation. I can send it over to my friend at KROQ and have him put it on the evening news."

"No one will care," he said. "Your friend will think it's a sad attempt to save your tarnished reputation. He would never put his career on the line. It's too much of an amazing story, isn't it? Just like Louis Kleiner, airline ticket man mob boss man, right? Remember him? The tonic for your career right there, except no one believed you and you couldn't prove it. You looked like a looney." *Such an asshole.*

"What about Darren? What's to stop him from telling his friends about this conversation?"

"Because Darren thinks you're a lunatic who killed his neighbor. He will also be compensated for his assistance in the matter."

"Hey, boss." Darren said.

"What?" Fritz said and looked up at him.

"There are five missing." Darren said as he flipped his fingers through the banker's box. "Zero twenty-one through zero twenty-five are missing."

Fritz looked at me and I smiled. When I was in the hotel room with Cleft and Marie, I pulled a few of the files out of the box and put them in Cleft's briefcase. I also scribbled a small note on the motel's fine stationary asking Cleft to look into it. I didn't really have a plan, or know what I was asking him to do, but I knew whatever was in the box was valuable and it was a wrong place, right time sort of decision. I guess it's possible that Cleft still hasn't found the files or the note but that was a risk I was willing to take.

"What do you want?" Fritz asked.

"Let me go. Let me walk out that door and back to my house. Tell them you were wrong. I didn't do anything." I said but Fritz wasn't buying it. He reached out grabbed the gun and pulled the hammer back.

"Alright, alright, fine." I said. "I want to talk to your boss. Let me talk to him and then I'll say whatever it is you want me to say. OK?"

Fritz removed his finger from the trigger and set the gun down.

25

It was nearing the end of the day and Cleft hadn't eaten anything since dinner the night before. Fact was, he wasn't hungry and hadn't been hungry since last night. He didn't make a habit of indulging in breakfast and the events at the motel with Peter set him off. It wasn't so much the charade with Marie, he could manage that, it was the five files that Peter left sitting in his briefcase along with a rather imprecise note – *LOOK INTO THIS ASAP* – that caught his attention and sent his stomach into a tailspin. The files looked like medical reports that a hospital or doctor's office would issue on patients, the front and back were littered with information but he couldn't tell for sure what it all meant.

Cleft was pissed.

He was pissed at Peter for putting him in this situation. Maybe things would be better if Peter just died when he had the heart attack. He had enough pressures in his own life he didn't need to be immersed in Peter's troubles as well. There were some people who take your favors and generosity too far and he was beginning to think that Peter was one of those people. Maybe not intentionally, but Peter was certainly taking advantage of Cleft's seemingly unending bounty. He sat back in his chair and recounted when he first hired Peter, fresh out of Boston and trying to leave behind an uncomfortable past. Peter was honest about the events in Boston and Cleft found his self-deprecating sense of humor disarming. He hadn't seen that side of Peter in a while. About six months ago, Peter came into his office and said that he was admitting himself into rehab for a substance abuse problem. He didn't ask, but he knew that Peter had been taking a wide variety of pills on a pretty regular basis. He never asked, but one day at Peter's house he was helping Peter make cocktails and found a tray of prescription pills stashed in the pantry behind the cocktail olives and the assorted crackers. Hydrocodone, Oxytocin and Vicodin. Triple threat. He knew Peter had his wisdom teeth taken out a few years ago and along with that came a series of prescription meds that you could nurse for a few days or weeks depending on the pain but Peter had let it get out of hand. Cleft looked the other way, he knew Peter would have done the same for him. Besides, Peter was a grown man and could take care of himself and make his own decisions. Peter also had Paula, and as strange as that union was, she would help steer him in the right direction when the time came. In addition to Paula, Peter had the guidance of his drug counselor, or support buddy, or whatever they call it, Brad. Cleft had met Brad a few times and thought he was an OK guy doing a tough job. Cleft had also liked that Brad was connected, even if peripherally, to the police force. It gave him a contact and someone to call should he need any info on current crimes or cases they were doing a story on. He liked the idea that he could pick up the phone at a moment's notice and have an artery into the police station. It was unfortunate that Brad was never helpful. He always responded with 'no comment' or said he didn't know about the cases Cleft was calling about. Brad worked the interstate, six days a week. Brad and his crew would run routine traffic stops in the hope of catching smugglers running drugs up the interstate which was a huge artery into Texas and, by design, North America. It has been estimated that two point five billions dollars worth of narcotics is transported into the United States each year, a third of which is driven through Austin by middle aged white guys in minivans. The cartels have it figured out and Brad was the frontline of defense. Too bad he wasn't helpful and could never point Cleft in the right direction or help him in anyway whatsoever.

"Marie," Cleft said into the intercom "can you get me Vanessa Snowdin on the phone please?" His stomach did an involuntary somersault at the very mention of her name.

"Snowdin?" Marie repeated.

"That's the one."

"One second, sir." she said and put the line on hold. Cleft laid the five files out on the desk in chronological order based on the number on the file tab. 021, 022 and so on. He opened them up and folded them over so he could see the picture and information of each person.

021 – ADAM STARR, ISSUED 10/2/2003 x
022 – DEBORAH LEE, ISSUED 11/1/2003 x
023 – STANLEY ADKINS, ISSUED 1/3/2004
024 – ART ARTHURS, ISSUED 1/5/2004 x
025 – JOHN WALSH, ISSUED 1/5/2004

They were all between the ages of 27 and 40. Adam Starr turned thirty last week and Stanley Adkins was about to turn 40 next week and everyone else fell somewhere in-between. Cleft couldn't see any noticeable similarities between them other than the fact they had all been approved for Memoton and they had all signed away their life to Endochrone.

On the opposing page he found a section where the doctor in charge made a few notations. 021, 022 and 024 all had a note requesting that they be prescribed 900 mg of something called Eflixer. Cleft dialed the number below Adam Starr's name. After a few rings someone picked up. It was a young man. "Adam Starr?" Cleft asked.

"Who is this?"

"Cleft Duvall with KROQ. I'm the news director. Am I speaking with Adam?"

"Adam's no longer here."

"Do you have any forwarding information for him?"

"No, I mean, he's dead," the young man on the phone said. "He died of cancer last year."

"Oh, I'm sorry." Cleft said and hung up. He dialed the number under Deborah Lee's name.

"Hello?" a voice said. He couldn't have been older than ten.

"Hi. Is your mom there?" Cleft asked. There isn't a handbook that outlines the protocol of calling the deceased.

"Daddy!" the boy screamed. A half second passed and the dad barked into the phone. *Who is this?* Cleft hung up and looked at the next name on the list: Stanley Adkins. He dialed.

"Hello?"

"Hi. Mr. Adkins?" Cleft asked. The lump in his throat got in the way of the words.

"Speaking." *Phew.*

"Hi. This is Cleft Duvall with KROQ. I'm doing a story on – *man, what was he doing a story on?* – I'm doing a story on Alzheimer's for a non-profit we work with. I'd like to ask you a few questions.

"Sure." Stanley Adkins said. "I'd be happy to help." Add non-profit to the end of sentence and watch what happens.

"First, do you have Alzheimer's?" Cleft asked.

"No. Not anymore."

"Were you cured?"

"Oh no, no, it's not something you can be cured of, but I've been taking medication and the medication helps with the conditions."

"Vanessa Snowdin is on line one." Marie busted in over the intercom.

"Yes – one second, Marie." Cleft said.

"Excuse me?"

"Not you, sir. Sorry." Cleft said. "Would you say your Alzheimer's is manageable and you're alive and well, correct?"

"You are speaking with me, aren't you?"

"Yes, that's right. Thanks for your time." Cleft said and hung up. Two dead and one still living and breathing. He could only assume that the names with the other x's next to them were also deceased.

"Vanessa, Cleft." Marie said.

"I'm coming." He pressed a button on his phone.

"Are you ready to put something on the record about that intern you gave syphilis to?" Vanessa's voice echoed through his office.

"That was over five years ago."

"Four."

"It was herpes."

"Who's counting, right?"

"I need your help." Cleft said, beaten down by her frontal attack.

"If you give me a quote on the whore, I can help you."

"She wasn't a whore, she didn't know any better."

"Who can resist your good looks and charming ways, right?"

"Do you still have that contact at Gracie Smith Klein?" He listened as she tapped a pen on her desk and thought about how to best answer the question. A faint breeze came through his office. It was an old building and poorly insulated especially when it got cold outside. He couldn't stand it. Moving to Texas and suffering through a cold winter. What was the point? Was Vanessa going to say something he wondered, maybe she put him on hold so she could flip through her rolodex of easily accessible contacts.

"Depends." she finally said.

"Look, if you don't help me, I'll call Travis and he'll tell me and I'll call them and still said you referred me. People will think we're friends." Vanessa didn't care for Cleft and, better yet, Cleft despised her so he felt like this was the best approach.

"Hardball, I like it. His name is Ronald Wexler. Do you want his number?"

"I have a computer." Cleft said as he hit the release button on the phone. Ronald Wexler held various teaching positions at numerous central Texas colleges, and is the current chairman of the safety committee at Gracie Smith Klein which works as a middleman between drug companies and the FDA's Center for Drug Evaluation and Research which evaluates new drugs before they can be sold to consumers. It ensures that drugs, both brand-name and generic, work the way they should and that the health benefits outweigh the risks. If a drug company wants to sell a drug in the United States they must first test it and navigate their way through a demanding bureaucratic system, this is where Gracie Smith Klein can step in and help drug companies. They work on a hefty monthly or quarterly retainer and don't guarantee a drugs approval, they just guarantee that they will be able to assist in the approval process. Cleft thought if anyone was going to be able to find out anything about Memoton it would be Ronald Wexler. It was a good a place as any to start.

Cleft pulled up the homepage for Gracie Smith Klein and punched their main number into his phone. He didn't need Marie's help with this one. A receptionist answered the phone and put him through to the office of Ronald Wexler. A man's voice answered. "Hello?"

"Uh, yes, Ronald Wexler please." Cleft said into the phone.

"Speaking."

"Oh, hi, this is Cleft Duvall with KROQ news-"

"What's this in regard to?"

"I got your number from my friend Vanessa Snowdin. She said you could help me with a matter I am working on."

"You have two minutes."

"Memoton. Have you heard of it?"

"Yes, Alzheimer's. Next question."

"Are you aware of any complications or roadblocks during the approval process with the FDA?"

"It wasn't something we consulted on so I can't answer that question."

"Can a drug company prescribe a secondary drug for treatment of a side effect or condition they discover in the trial period of another drug?"

"What do you mean?"

"Some of the people who were part of the trial for P39i, aka Memoton, were prescribed 900 mg of Eflixer."

"What was that drug?"

"Eflixer?" There was a pause. Ronald's hasty momentum was broken. "Do I need to say the - ?"

"No comment."

"I didn't ask you anything."

"You're running short on time and you're talking nonsense."

"Have you heard of Eflixer?"

"I said no comment."

"I just asked if you heard of something – "

"Yes, I've heard of it."

"Is your company working with Endochrone on the FDA approval process for Eflixer?"

"No comment."

"Can you tell me what Eflixer treats? What's the primary condition?" Cleft asked as he typed Eflixer into his search engine.

"I am under a binding contract with Endochrone and I don't make a habit of speaking about what a client may or may not be working on even to people in your profession." He let those last two words stick.

"Maybe you should stop answering your phone."

"Did you know you were out of time?"

"Just another question?"

"What is it?" Ronald wheezed as Cleft watched his computer screen fill with search results. He clicked the first one. It opened to a page hosted by Green Pharmaceuticals with a general overview of Eflixer. The headline read: *GREEN PHARMACEUTICALS DEVELOPS NEW CANCER DRUG.*

"Are you still there?" Ronald asked. Cleft had to think about it this and get his next question right. He wasn't going to get this opportunity again and he already pushed Ronald Wexler far enough.

"Why would the FDA approve a drug if it knew or even suspected that it could cause cancer in some of its test patients?"

Click.

"Hey Marie." Cleft said so she could hear him through the door. He waited a second until she came in.

"What is it?"

"I need you to find Peter for me. It's important."

"Right. And how would I do that?"

"Get Brad on the phone."

"Who?"

"Brad. He was Peter's sponsor. He works for the highway patrol. I need his help."

"He got a last name?"

Cleft shrugged. He didn't know but figured that if Marie used her head for half a second she could find a way to figure it out. He looked up at her and she was still staring at him. "Anything else?" he asked.

"Your fly is open."

26

Fritz let me hangout in the interrogation room with the aroma of burgers for what I suspected was another two to three hours before he came for me. When I told him I wanted to speak with his boss, he said that wouldn't be a problem with a tone that had a slight nuance of panic. I ordered Coquilles Saint-Jacques but the waiter misheard me and brought me dried toast so I had to complain. Fritz said he needed to make a few phone calls before we could leave. I guess that meant his boss wasn't coming here. He carried a certain calmness during our exchange that suggested confidence but the coolness came with a dose of apprehension. I don't blame him, people rarely like it when you decide to go above them and ask for a meet and greet with their boss. I guess it's possible Fritz thought I was going to complain about him. He didn't let me take enough bathroom breaks, he was imprecise in his interrogation methods and wouldn't let me take my medicine which was actually pretty important. There could very well be a long list. I understood, he didn't want to take me to his boss but he couldn't contain whatever this situation was and I had the upper hand. I gave the folders to Cleft with the hope he could figure out something that I couldn't. I didn't realize doing so was going to give me so much leverage.

But with who? *I mean, with whom?*

Fritz was smart, he had lots of experience and knew about the Kennedy thing which had to account for something, but when it came down to it, he was just another body in a room and someone to tell Leroy and Darren what to do and there was someone who inevitably told Fritz what to do. That's who I needed to get to. If there was any hope of salvation it was the expectation that Fritz could convince his boss to an old fashion sit down with me and not the alternative which was him blowing my brains out over the interrogation room. From the two hours Fritz spent away from the interrogation room I knew he was making some headway. He wasn't going to convince me to confess to killing Janice and if he did in fact decide to blow my brains out he was never going to get the files back, at least not easily, and that's all they seemed to care about. Paper plus information. Granted he could probably figure out who I gave them to inside an hour and Cleft was probably pretty easy to break. But Fritz was just going to have to figure that out on his own.

I pushed the chair back and stood up and paced around the room. I was starting to feel trapped and anxious and needed a release. This happens every now and then but not nearly as much as it used to. The first few days of rehab I wanted to jump off a cliff into a pool of prescription meds. But treatment and counseling helped me manage my feelings and desires. When I stopped taking pills, all I could think about was taking pills. Every second of every minute for days on end. I didn't sleep, I just laid in bed and strategized how I could get a fix. It didn't matter. I would try to bribe the nurse for the sleeping pills I was convinced she had just so I could get something into my system. I even tried to get people to smuggle drugs to me. But with counseling and treatment those minutes turned into hours and after a few months the hours turned into days. Sure, it still happens. I find myself in situations where I convince myself that the only solution was two pills of hydroc-odone. Problem solved. That's how I was starting to feel now. Fritz was taking his time and I thought, *maybe if I just take a few pain killers, this will all go away. Fritz will vanish into thin air and I'll be back at home with Paula and Joyce and one on the way.* But nope, there were no drugs in here. The old version of me may have gone crazy, scratching the walls like a cat in heat with the hope that 800 mgs of oxytocin would fall out. But not now. The new refined, post-pill-popping, heart transplant Peter wasn't like that. Sure, I had my heart meds and could take a few of those but that wouldn't do much and I needed to think and focus on something. Then Fritz would come back and we'd be on our way. Maybe he would be nice enough to let me roll the window down in the car, let me feel some fresh air, maybe he would blast the music for me.

Janice worked for Harvey Marcona for a long time. Years. At some point, recently, she discovered the files. All fifty of them tucked away nicely in a banker's box. Maybe it had to do with the upcoming IPO.

Endochrone was going to be audited and Janice was starting to put files and statements together, anything timely and appropriate. Then she found it. A banker's box, standard size, tucked away in some back corner of the archives. Somewhere Marcona knew it was safe and forgotten about -- but also a place where he could find it if he needed it. Janice told Adrienne, maybe over a glass of white wine, that something didn't add up. She was only Marcona's secretary but she knew the drill and had at least a peripheral understanding of how the testing phase of drug research went. Everything was above board and duplicated and triplicated. But this was different. Out of the thousands of people who volunteered for a study of Memoton here were fifty hiding in a back corner, half of whom were getting prescribed something else. Adrienne then told her husband and he confronted Marcona and here we are now. Besides, David Prescott managed hundreds of millions of dollars for Endochrone and a sea of investors. If he found out that Marcona was fixing the books, rigging a trial, he needed to take action. Maybe killing Marcona was the only solution that made sense to David Prescott. Maybe David Prescott didn't have faith in the legal system. *I need to buy him a drink.*

I pulled the chair out again and sat back down. Something didn't add up. If Janice had the files for six months and Prescott found out about it then why did it take him six months to confront and kill Marcona? And, come to think of it, why would they invest so much time and energy to make me the fall guy for killing Janice? Were they that concerned the FDA would discover they were testing two drugs in the same trial. What's the penalty for that? A couple thousand dollars? Maybe. Who cares if you're testing two drugs in the same trial, I am sure it happens all the time. I'm sure nobody cares.

Huh.

Well, it's also possible Janice found the files and told Harvey Marcona about them. He panicked, told his partner in crime, to be introduced later, hopefully, and they devised a scheme to get the files back, eliminate Janice and the problem in its entirety. But all for one small offense? It was too much, it was giving me a headache and I didn't have a solution. The more time I spent in this room, letting my mind run around itself, the less I thought I knew.

Just as my mind was about to fold into itself I heard the deadbolt on the door open. Fritz opened the door and peaked his head in.

"Where's your buddy?" I asked.

"His shift was over." Fritz said as he took my heart medication and put a black ski mask over my face. The eye sockets on the ski mask were cleverly covered with black tape so all I could see was a piece of dust stuck between my eyeball and the back of the tape. He pulled me out of the chair and handcuffed me and led me through the squad room and out through a door and into the back of a car. It was just him and me this time, Darren was a fly in the wind at this point. Fritz was probably right not involving him in this part of it. He seemed like he had the best of intentions, but as Fritz said himself, he was a bit obtuse. The car ride was nice. He wouldn't roll the window down for me but he did turn on the radio and even asked me what station I preferred. I didn't really have a preference but it was considerate of him to ask. Fritz picked a nice classical jazz station but all I could hear were the small bumps in the road and the sounds of trucks whizzing past us outside. My guess was that we were on interstate 35 which meant we were either headed north to Oklahoma City or south to Austin or San Antonio. The radio was soothing and they did weather and traffic updates every thirty minutes which was kind of pleasant. The last update was just before 10 p.m. and then the reception cut out. Fritz played with the radio dial a bit and stopped on an Austin Public Radio station. The commentator was talking about the below freezing conditions expected in the next few days when we pulled off the freeway and drove around what I expected was downtown and parked the car and killed the ignition. He sat there for a few minutes before he came around and opened my door and pulled me out.

"I need to take my meds." I said as he pushed me away from the car. "You stole my meds."

"You can take them when we get downstairs," he said.

We walked through the garage and onto the elevator which took us down a few levels to what I imagined was the basement. When the elevator doors opened he took off my blindfold and gave me a light shove. I stepped off the elevator into what looked like an abandoned warehouse. About a hundred feet in front of me was a small room with a single incandescent light bulb hanging from the ceiling. I knew this place. It was the basement to an old office building across from the Intercontinental hotel in downtown Austin. The basement and backroom used to be a television news studio back in the early 1970's but was shut down due to lack of funding. I asked Cleft once if he would ever consider moving here but he laughed at the idea and said I had too much sentiment. Besides, Kingsman was fully aware of the dwindling state of local news and would never spring for such accommodations even if they were novel. Rumor was that Kingsman even came to look at the place but then scoffed at the idea.

I followed Fritz as he walked towards the back room. Once we reached the room he asked me to take a seat across from a large legal desk under the light. He even pulled the chair out for me. There had been a few updates since the last time I was here. The cement walls had been covered with an expensive looking geo flower scroll wallpaper and the formally cold floors had been covered with the thickest and softest carpeting a man could find. But just in this room, the rest of the floor was still dilapidated and forgotten about.

Once I sat down, Fritz pulled my arms around the back of the chair and put the handcuffs back on me and left. A few minutes passed and a door opened and a gentleman, older and more refined than before, sat down across from me.

"Hello, Peter." he said.

"Hi, Hector." I said.

27

"I'm sorry that things have come to this and that you're in this situation." Hector said to me. His voice was calm and he sounded more polished than when I saw him at the hospital. "But you have something that I need and it's very important that you give it to me."

"You should have been more careful," I said. "If the files were so important you should have done more to protect them." He looked down at his desk for half a second and furrowed his eyebrows at a paperweight. He knew that I was right and he knew there was very little he could do about it now.

"You think you know what's going on, don't you, Mr. Richards?"

"Yes, I do, I think I do."

"Why don't you explain it to us then," he said. "Go ahead, we're listening."

"Well, a few months ago, Endochrone decided that it was going to go public and ride the coattails of this new drug it was developing with Green Pharmaceuticals. It's an Alzheimer's drug, something that was the result of years of testing on a gene it bought the – rights to, if you will. However the fuck that works. But, and probably in order to save money, Endochrone decided that it was going to also test a separate drug during the trials for Endochrone. Not immoral, really, but not the best decision a company could make right before its IPO. Cross contamination, if you will. In preparation for the IPO, Janice was collecting files and records for the investment bank and came across fifty medical files that proved Endochrone was piggy backing one drug onto the test of another. Then she told Adrienne who in turn went and told her husband, David Prescott, who then confronted Harvey Marcona and killed him in a fit of rage and confusion. I'm still working on how you fit in." I leaned back in the chair and gave Hector a small Peter Richards issued grin. I may have been down on my luck but my skills as an investigative journalist had stayed sharp.

Hector smiled back at me. "Very interesting deduction, Mr. Richards," he said. "Too bad you are only half right."

"Well, it's a start." He could stonewall me as much as he wanted to, I didn't care. "I still have a few things I'm thinking over in my head."

"That's OK, take your time. If you knew I would have to kill you."

"How do you know that I'm not lying about what I know? Maybe I did figure it out. Maybe Janice and I were really lovers and she told me all about the files."

"You didn't and you weren't," he said.

"That's not fair. Give me some credit."

"You are correct about the fact that Janice found the files though. But that's about it. Janice discovered the files when she was over at David and Adrienne's house six months ago. She had a fundraiser to attend and Adrienne offered to let her try on some clothes. She and Adrienne were in the master bedroom and Adrienne told her that she found this box that looked like it belonged in the office. It must have been misplaced after all. Janice told Adrienne that she would take them back to the office. David always had a habit of misplacing stuff anyway. That night she went home and looked through them. The next day she told her boss, Harvey Marcona about them. He shrugged her off at first but she brought it up again and pressed him. Finally, Marcona sat down and looked at the files. Janice was right, there was something there but he wasn't sure what. It was inconsistent with the way they kept any of their records. Totally out of FDA protocol. So Marcona decided to go and confront Prescott."

Prescott had them?

But he was the good guy and had enriched moral fiber. Everyone said so. His do-gooder-ness was ubiquitous and unquestionable. It was Marcona who was scum and the threat that had to be eliminated.

"But Marcona was corrupt, he was the one who was cheating the system," I said.

"That's what you wanted to believe and just because you believe something doesn't make it true. You of all people should understand that."

"Vanessa Snowdin was writing a piece on how Harvey Marcona was guilty of tax fraud."

"That's right, I'm familiar with that. We provided her with that completely fabricated information and paid her a generous sum of money to write the story."

"But why?"

"Perception. We wanted Marcona to come across a certain way so we took the appropriate steps to make that happen and Vanessa, well, everyone has a price. You see, if people think Marcona is a bad guy and David Prescott is a good guy they rationalize him shooting Harvey Marcona. He must of had a good reason, since he's such a decent guy. People don't feel bad for supporting him. They rationalize his actions even though they don't really know anything about him. David Prescott, in fact, is a very bad person and manages money for some very bad people but that's his job and he was very, very good at it until he killed Marcona."

"See – you're telling me now."

"But only a small part, Peter, and mostly so you'll understand what you're up against here and how weak you are in comparison. Has anyone ever called you that before – weak?"

"No."

"Well, you are. You're very weak, I'm surprised you made it this far. I'm surprised they even gave you a new heart."

"You know nothing about me."

"You'd be surprised what I know about you," Hector said. "I know about your family, your marriage, your wife and even how much you paid for your house. I know about your drug addiction. I know about Boston. All of it." He pulled a binder out of his desk drawer and set it on the table. "Everything about you is in here." He ran his hand over the binder like he was petting a rabid dog. The binder was thick and had at least a hundred pages filled with - *God knows what* - maybe bank statements, tax returns, report cards from elementary school and commentary from various ex-girlfriends. He had a robust profile on Peter Richards and probably knew more about me than I did.

"What do you want?" I asked.

"I need you to turn yourself in for the murder of Janice Walton, your neighbor and lover. I'll work with you as your attorney to make sure you get some leniency with the court but you should expect to do some time. We need you to toe the line, as they say."

"What makes you think I would do that?"

"To be honest, it's because you are very good at it. You're safe and predictable, that's just who you are." he said as he stared at me. I flinched and looked down at the floor. Maybe he had a point. "We need you on our side, Peter."

"Why would you think I would ever turn myself in?"

"Because if you don't, I'll kill you and make it look like a suicide. Fuck, I don't even need to do that, they'll just think your new heart gave out again. Then I'll dump your body in Janice's house and Skelly will have a closed case and we'll go on our way like nothing happened."

"So I confess to killing Janice, confess to a love affair with a woman I hardly knew, go to jail and that's it?"

"Yes."

"This is insane." I said.

"You are welcome to believe that but as far as we're concerned it's a rather economical proposition."

"Who's we?"

"Just people running a business is all. No different than anyone else in the world. We're just trying to make money and manage the money we have and keep a relatively low body count. I'm sure you can understand the practicality of that. Maybe our methods are a little different than yours. Blackmail, murder, coercion, but the results are all the same. Protect the investment and uphold the brand. Take your heart, for instance."

"My heart?"

"Yes. Part of it is a machine that was manufactured by a company, right?"

"Right."

"That company – Ə-zero, in this instance – has a certain level of excellence that it needs to live up to. A brand standard, if you will. That's all we're trying to do here."

"Mob?"

"We don't like that term. It has a thuggish vibe to it that doesn't resonate well."

"What do you prefer?"

162

He shrugged. "Eh. Doesn't really matter but the words mob and mafia are so antiquated and have such bad associations."

"But the principals are the same – money and profit at all cost no matter what?"

"Sure, I guess so. Fact is, Harvey Marcona was a threat but not for the reasons you suspect. He did need to be eliminated but only because he found out about the files and was starting to put the pieces together. He probably shouldn't have been killed by David Prescott in a crime so heated but that's the way things went down and we can't undo the past and David Prescott will suffer for his choices. In fact, the plan was to have you kill Janice and Marcona together. It was going to be a lover's tryst gone wrong at her house, of course. You were having an affair, got jealous and against your better judgment killed them."

I looked past Hector's head. A large red circle was mounted on the wall behind him. It had a small black circle in the center like a tiny bull's-eye.

"So you found out that she had the files and then what – decided to frame me? Is that it?"

"More or less."

"Why don't you just kill me? I know everything – you're telling me everything. This is what you're not supposed to do. You should kill me and put my worthless body in her house, like you said."

"Have some confidence, Peter."

"I'm confident that you won't kill me."

"You don't know shit, Peter." Hector snapped at me. "Marcona and Janice can't die and then you die. It's too messy."

"No one knows where I am though. I am officially on the run. You could kill me and no one would ever know. Or is there something else?" I asked but he didn't respond. For the first time he looked down. I don't know what he needed from me or how I was an asset but he wasn't going to tell me, at least not now.

"Do you even know what was in those files, Peter?" he asked.

"From what I could tell Marcona was doubling down, if you will. He was using one drug trial but secretly testing a secondary drug along with a primary drug – Memo – something."

"Memoton." he corrected.

"Right. That. Am I close?"

"Hardly." he smirked.

"Well, it was worth a shot, right?"

"It's cancer, man." Fritz said.

"Could you shut-up, Fritz?" Hector said to him.

"What man? You asked and he didn't know. What's the point? He's right you know, we should blow his brains out. He wasn't supposed to make it this far." Fritz had a point.

They should kill me.

"You can't do it, can you?" I said. "You can't kill me because if you kill me then you won't have those files."

"Fritz?" Hector said. "Come here for a second." He reached his hand out and signaled for him to come over to the desk. Fritz walked around me and stood in front of Hector's desk with his back towards me. I tried to arch my head around to see Hector but I could only get a glimpse of a baseball bat heading straight for Fritz's torso. Hector must have had it on standby for when we came in, or maybe it's always on standby. Just before the bat made impact with his ribcage Hector locked his eyes on me: *you're next, asshole* is what I think he was trying to tell me. There was a loud crackling noise as the bat made impact with Fritz and he crumpled over on to the floor into the fetal position. Hector pushed his chair back and walked around the desk and slammed the baseball bat into his neck. Fritz let out a loud whelp and Hector let the bat fall to the floor.

"Get up, you piece of shit." he said as he went back and sat down in his chair. He corrected his jacket and looked at me. "I want to talk about the files." he said.

"That's fine and I am sure that we can work out an agreement that is mutually beneficial." I said trying to look nonplussed that my hospital appointed attorney was sitting across from me and had just beaten a police officer with a baseball bat.

"What do you want?" Hector asked me.

"I want my life back," I said. "I want my job back and my house back and my credibility back. Can you do that for me?"

"You didn't have credibility to begin with that's why we picked you. You're just a worthless law-abiding yes man." Hector said. "You give us the files, go to jail for a few years, legitimize this shit then you get your life back. Can you do that for us?"

"Go to hell," I said.

"OK, if that's how you want to do it, we'll renegotiate," he said as he swiveled his chair around and opened one of his drawers. He pulled out a remote control and clicked a button. A few seconds passed and a projector screen lowered itself from the ceiling.

"Hit the lights," he said to Fritz when then stumbled over and killed the lights so we were just floating in the blue light from the screen. Hector pressed another button and an image appeared on the screen. It was an image of Paula. She was spread eagle on a mattress with each limb tied to a bed post. She had a rope around her mouth and was looking up at a camera. She blinked a few times and I could tell it was live.

"Where's my daughter?" I asked.

"Your soon to-be-adoptive daughter."

"Where is she?"

"Give me the files, Peter."

"No – I want to know where she is – now!"

"Ah – there is some man in you after all. I'm surprised."

"Go fuck yourself. I want to see my family."

"You don't have any leverage to negotiate with us, you understand? You give me those files or we're going to kill your family." The way he said it was plain as day. He was just someone reading a list and pointing out facts. Do this and this happens or do this and this happens. The choice was entirely up to me and as much as he needed the files, he didn't care what I chose.

"I don't know – I gave them to Cleft – "

"I need to know where the files are, Peter. Tell me and we'll make you a deal, understand? Give me the files and this will all go away."

"You get the files and then you'll kill me and my family," I said.

"You tell me where the files are we'll work out a deal." Hector said. "I have something you want and you have something I want so if you tell me where they are I think we can find something that works for the both of us."

"I just told you – I gave them to Cleft."

"That wasn't very smart. You gave up any control you had and now we'll probably have to kill Cleft too."

"I thought you didn't want to be messy."

"I'll figure something out."

"I need my family."

"That's fine, Peter." He turned off the television. "But I need you to focus on the task at hand. I spoke with the DA and they said they can get you three to five. If you get me the files I say take the deal and you can have your family back too, OK?"

"OK."

"Where is Cleft?"

"He's at work — the studio is on MLK just past the stadium."

"OK — thank you, that's a start and we'll look into it. Once we have the files back, me and you, me - acting as your attorney and you - acting as a guilty murderer, will sort out your plea."

"And my family?"

"Yes, them too. Don't you worry yourself, Peter. You're doing a good thing here. Path of least resistance."

"The night Janice was killed, how were you going to frame me — just hope the cops would see the plane tickets and come across the street and knock on our door?"

"No, actually, the night Janice was killed, the same night you had your heart attack, you were given a medical grade roofie."

"How?"

"It was in your food. It was supposed to put you under for a few hours but — I don't know — it didn't kick in, it didn't stick. I told them a hundred milligrams because you have a tolerance built up but they didn't listen. They thought they knew better."

"How did you get a roofie into my food?" It was just me, Paula, and Joyce. "You're making this up."

"Someone put it there." Then I thought of the food that Brad brought over for us. He was picking up a swing shift at work and wanted to see Joyce and Paula before heading in. I attributed the visit to a little sober buddy check in session and didn't think anything of it. There's no way Brad would have put a roofie in my food despite all his connections. Come to think of it, Paula and I had secrets, so maybe they leveraged her citizenship status to get her to pop a pill in my Blue Plate Special and asked her to pretend to play hostage to drive the point home. But Joyce did have a crummy day at school that day. Maybe it was because someone approached her and asked her to put something in her dad's food when she got home. Anything's possible at this point.

"Who?"

"Do you really want to know?" he asked. He was positioning himself to tell me that Santa Claus wasn't real and he was enjoying himself.

"I died. I went to heaven or what I thought was heaven. I met people there – I saw the gates."

"That's a known side effect."

"What does that mean?!" I screamed at him. I pushed my body out of the chair and leaned over his desk and slammed my fists down in front of him. "What do you mean, a known side effect?" Fritz started to approach me but Hector waved him off. He wasn't a big guy but he looked like he could take care of himself.

"The roofie we gave you, allusions of death is a known side effect," Hector said. "Sit back down." He stared at me for a second and then moved his hand towards the baseball bat.

"Do it." Fritz said. "Get rid of him."

'Not yet." Hector said and nodded towards my chair. I took a few steps back and sat down. In my place.

"So again, why me?"

"You're the perfect candidate, Peter. You have a sordid past. Drug addiction, questionable activities in Boston and possible murder rap all tied together. Your word isn't good for anything so no one would believe you, no matter what. We tarnished the reputation of one of the most well respected people in the medical field, imagine what we could do to you. That's what makes this so perfect."

"But that's a stretch, isn't it. If Dick Van Dyke lived across the street from Janice it wouldn't work."

"Very good point and whoever killed Janice had to live next to her. I won't lie to you, Peter, you're a questionable person. You're nice and probably mean well, but drugs and some less than wise careers choices don't add up to much if you didn't live near her. It would have been too much work for Skelly and his crew to put the pieces together so we did it for them. They like it when crimes come in a neat package, makes them feel like they did something."

"But – "

"But nothing. I know your friend Cleft has been helping you and that's great. That's what friends are for. Do you know how easily it would be for Cleft to find out that his son, Avery, was the one selling you drugs?"

"That's not true."

"Fine, whatever, it's not true, but if Cleft got wind of that he would never speak to you ever again. Not because of that one thing necessarily but because of that one thing in addition to all the other weird questionable stuff you have done."

"We were in that house for a few weeks, we were just getting settled."

"Unfortunate too really. When we first made contact we weren't sure, it was such a tight timeline. I thought it was a little crazy myself but the boss gets what the boss wants."

"Made contact?"

"Yes, that's right. During your recovery sessions. Brad picked you out actually."

"Brad?"

"That's right. Are you surprised?" I nodded but I wasn't sure. "I thought you might be. He said to leave him out of it, since he was a significant contributor to your recovery but a job is a job. He was assigned as your sober buddy and set you up with that realtor. I thought it was going to come off as eager and premature but he really sold it. Besides, you were looking for a house anyway and Brad was helpful so you couldn't say no. The financing was approved and you moved in. We just needed to make sure that Janice didn't do anything with the information she had. That was the hard part. You were easy. Once we knew that she didn't tell anyone we pulled the trigger." He stopped and took a breath and looked over a Fritz and said something to him but I stopped listening. There was a soft haze growing around my eyes and all I could see was the large red circle above Hector's small head. *Brad set me up?* We were so close, but maybe that was the idea. They just pick someone vulnerable in recovery and make him the fall guy. Seems like a lot of work to protect some unethical drug testing but who am I to judge. It sounded like Hector was just taking orders though. He had this nice palatial office and certainly talked like he was in charge but maybe he wasn't."

I lifted my head up and started to say something – "Who?" *Who do you work for, who is your – why is this – what about my family* - and so on, but the phone rang. It was a black standard issued Bell Atlantic rotary phone hard wired into the wall. It rang once and Hector picked it up.

"What is it?" he said and then hung up the phone and looked over a Fritz. "Get up, they found the files. Kill him but make the wife and child watch."

If I didn't die before, I was dead now.

168

28

Traffic was unusually light for afternoon rush hour on interstate 35. Brad and his partner, Roy, were positioned just south of downtown under an overpass. This was their spot and had been for the past few weeks. It was the perfect location and allowed them line of sight down the interstate to oncoming traffic while not sticking out like a sore thumb. Also, it was just past the exit for 290 and 71, so potential suspects didn't have an immediate escape route. They would have to push up past downtown, or get off at the next exit and shuffle through traffic ,before they had any chance of getting away and that wasn't an option. Brad and Roy spent weeks driving up and down the interstate and testing out various locations and this one seemed to work better than the prior ones. Maybe one day they'll find something more strategic and thought-out but for now this would do. As part of their DPS protocol they each had a state issued cell phone along with a police radio that was part of the infrastructure of their vehicle, a refurbished Ford Explorer. The department buys the vehicles on the cheap from vehicle auctions. A late model Explorer, nearing a hundred thousand miles, can set the department back a meager few thousand dollars. They paint it, tweak some things in the engine and put all-terrain tires on. Not to mention, a state of the art siren package for the roof. Brad liked driving around in it. He was high off the ground and felt invincible to oncoming traffic. Other than the radio and Explorer they each had a state mandated taser, for the left hip, and a state issued handgun for the right, and a collection of plastic wrist ties instead of handcuffs. The idea was to keep them light on their feet and not held down. They were instructed, almost weekly, to use the taser first and only resort to deadly force when their lives were in imminent danger. The situations were always subjective, and never the same, so it was up to them to decide what constituted imminent danger. They were pulling over suspicious vehicles on their gut assessment of the vehicle having drugs and that, by general rule and principal, brought them a shady cast of characters.

Brad and Roy had spent years building profiles of suspected drug traffickers. It was a science for them and Roy liked to joke that Brad was the Sherlock Holmes of international manhandling. They would make assessments based on the make and model of the car and the profile of the driver and whether or not they could see the driver. Then they would factor in speed, which lane the person was in and driving habits. Then they factored in environmental conditions like time of day and weather. Their shift was early in the morning but it didn't matter, drugs were drugs and they needed to be sold and according to a rigorous metric system in the department, there were at least two vehicles a day carrying weapons-grade narcotics that passed through the Austin corridor. This didn't mean some guy getting off his shift at Blockbuster with a bag of weed in his pocket, this meant enough weed, crack and heroin to put someone away for a very long time. On average, the DPS only has ten or eleven guys who do this sort of work. It is considered a pay grade above entry level and a way to get experience and your foot in the door, but Brad and Roy loved it and were exceptionally good at it. When they first met during training a few years ago, they were told only one in every fifty vehicles will provide enough circumstance and evidence to warrant a full search and out of the vehicles you search one in twenty will have narcotics and half of those are worth brining in and are considered connected, which is the term Brad likes to use when he thinks someone is running drugs for a cartel.

There are twenty six border crossings between Mexico and Texas, twenty-three of which are bridges, two are dam crossings and one is a hand-drawn ferry. There are two additional ones, The La Linda Bridge and Roma International Suspension Bridge, but they are closed indefinitely. Over three million cars and trucks go between Mexico and Texas annually and a majority of those vehicles end up on the interstate headed towards Austin, Dallas and points farther north. Factor those in with the rising commuting population of Austin and the odds of catching a cartel runner are next to impossible.

Brad and Roy had a solution though.

Roy's cousin, Harold, worked part-time for the United State Border Patrol which operates a dozen or so checkpoints around and near the Texas-Mexican border. The sole purpose of these checkpoints is to discourage illegal immigration and drug smuggling. After 9/11 the Border Patrol also took on the responsibility of terrorism dissuasion. Their agents are on average leftovers from the military that came home from fighting overseas and unable to get high priority jobs in the private security sector. They live on ranches, drive around in pickup trucks and are habitually overworked eight hours a day, six days a week all while protecting the country from whatever filth that is coming over the border.

Roy and Harold play fantasy football together and Harold would usually come over on Sunday and watch the games with him. Roy agreed to pay his cousin five hundred dollars a week cash for information on Roy's colleagues. Harold would brag about how he and his colleagues would allow certain people to cross the border for a fee. Depending on the arrangement, they would overlook an out of date inspection sticker or expired license for a thousand dollars, for two thousand dollars they would ignore errors in documentation and for five thousand dollars they would let vehicles pass through with no questions asked. One day, Harold was approached by a handler for a large Mexican drug conglomerate, The Juárez Cartel. The Juárez Cartel controls billions of dollars of drug shipments annually into the United States from Mexico and they needed a pass through and wanted to cut a deal with Harold. They would pay Harold and his colleagues ten thousand dollars every time they needed to cross the border, twice the going rate. They threatened to kill Harold's family if he refused and then they would decapitate him and just find someone else to do the job.

Harold took the deal.

It was only a few times a month and was usually SUV's or mid-sized cars, manageable. Every now and then a large shipment would come through in a U-Haul or eighteen-wheeler, but that was the exception to the rule. Harold didn't make more than thirty-six thousand dollars a year. He served two tours in Afghanistan and felt like he was entitled to more. This was a chance to put his son through college, maybe go on vacation and do something with his life.

When Harold bragged about this to Roy, Roy went and told Brad and they saw opportunity. Harold would make more money and they would catch the bad guys. Every time a shipment came through, Harold would take the cash and then send a message to Roy through an app that each of them had on their phones that tracked sports scores.

Roy's phone beeped and he looked down at it.

"What is it?" Brad asked.

"Patriots 19, Cardinals 07."

Brad looked down at the mutually agreed upon cheat sheet to decipher. Football teams were vehicle types and baseball teams were colors. The scores indicated the first and last digits of the license plate. Patriots 19, Cardinals 07 was a red Dodge Charger license plate 19 --- 07. Brad and Roy could fill in the blanks.

"They'll probably be here right around sunset."

"Perfect," Brad said and closed his eyes. He liked the sound of the cars running up and down the freeway. It put him at ease. It made Roy nervous. He was always worried that a car would run off the road and slam into them and kill them instantly and then his wife would find out that he was paying his cousin for sensitive information on high-class drug cartels. It was a thought process based purely on paranoia. Just because he's hit by a car doesn't automatically mean his wife will find out about his indiscretions, but that's the way his brain worked. Besides, he and Brad thought they were doing some good. Take out the bad guys and repurpose the drugs. That was Brad's responsibility though. Roy was the contact and managed Harold and the neurosis that came along with Harold and Brad took care of the loot. It was amazing that after all this time the cartel hasn't caught up to them. Maybe once the drugs leave Mexico they're forgotten about. He was surprised a caravan of drug lords hasn't tracked them down yet, or at least tracked down Harold. It was even more amazing they hadn't been fired or repurposed, because in the five years they've been doing this job, they only brought in two viable suspects with a payload in their car. And those suspects weren't charged because they lawyered up.

"Hey – hey – asshole-" Brad said to him as he punched his shoulder. Roy opened his eyes. He must have fallen asleep. "There it is." Brad pointed out to a red Dodge Charge license plate 19G R07. "Ten o'clock." Roy looked past Brad and saw it heading towards them. It was going a mile or two over the speed limit in the middle lane. Playing it safe. Going the exact speed limit is suspicious so these guys had the right idea but Brad and Roy had seen it before.

"Call it in," Brad said. It was protocol and they needed a record of the traffic stop. What happened during and after the stop was a different story and was to-be-determined.

"Base, this is – patrol thirty, we got a red bird – one – nine – Garbo – Ricin – zero – seven. Driving with suspended tags," Roy said into the walkie.

"Garbo? Ricin?" Brad said as he put on the flashers and pulled slowly out on to the feeder road.

"I like to make stuff up, man. It's boring sitting out here," he retorted.

"I bet, buddy."

"You ever seen Grand Hotel? Garbo? John Barrymore?"

Brad shrugged and pushed down on the accelerator. Roy let it go. In under a minute they were within feet of the Charger. Brad pumped the siren button and the Charger began moving towards the side of the road.

"License and registration," Brad said as he leaned down to the driver's side window. Roy was positioned just outside of the passenger's side. Protocol. Protect your partner no matter how innocuous the suspect. Everyone was a suspect these days. The driver rolled his window down and looked up at Brad.

"Did I do something wrong?" he asked. He was young. Maybe a few days short of turning twenty. He was Mexican but the accent told Brad that he had spent some time in the states. There was a guy in the passenger seat. Young, also Mexican, same short cropped hair and narrow nose. His twin.

"License and registration please," Brad said again. "I don't want to-"

"OK – OK – one second." the driver said and reached over for the glove compartment.

"Every fucking time, Roy. Don't people know where their paperwork is?" Brad said but Roy was watching the car. He put his hand on top of his firearm and watched as the driver pulled out some documents and handed them to Brad.

"I thought you weren't gonna find them there for a minute," Brad said. The driver just nodded politely at him. "Are you two identical twins?"

The driver nodded.

"Is that fraternal or – what is that called?" Brad asked as he looked over the registration and license.

"I'm not sure, sir."

"Do you know, Roy?" Brad asked.

"I think fraternal is correct."

"That's what I thought," Brad said and looked down at the driver. "Ariel Vazquez?"

"That's my dad."

"Right." Brad looked up at Roy. Roy nodded at him. "Please step out of the car."

"What did I do, man?"

"We got a tip that you're carrying illegal narcotics in this vehicle. You got anything to say about that?"

Ariel looked at his brother who just shook his head. He looked back at Brad. "You got shit sources, amigo."

"Good. That's what I was thinking. Then we got nothing to worry about. Step out of the car."

"What?"

"Step out of the car, both of you and hand me the car keys."

It took them a minute but they both got out and Ariel handed the keys to Brad. Brad tossed them to Roy who went around and opened the trunk. Empty. He reached in and pulled out the cover to the spare tire and then pulled out the tire and took out a switch blade jabbed into the base of the trunk and pulled the carpet lining back.

"What the fuck you doing, man - ?" Ariel said.

"Trunks empty," Roy said.

"Give it to me." Brad reached out and took the knife from Roy. "Keep your eye on them." Roy watched them as Brad went around and opened the passenger side door. He stabbed the knife into the lining of the door and pulled back on the upholstery. A handful of white powder poured out. "Fucking jackpot, Roy." He stood up and smiled and then looked at Ariel. "You are so fucked, my friend."

"How you want to play it, Brad?" Roy said. He had his firearm drawn and was pointing it at the ground next to the brothers feet. Cars on the freeway were slowing down to watch.

"Let's take these guys on a little ride," Brad said.

Brad and the twins followed Roy in the Charger off of the interstate then down a side street that took them into the heart of the east side. The east side was the perfect blend of new Austin and old Texas. Trendy bars and restaurants were opening up ad nauseam and steadfast residents were protesting the ever expanding development of new homes and shopping centers that were, according to them, making their neighborhoods less authentic. Roy went down Caesar Chavez and took a left onto a residential side street and pulled into the driveway of a small duplex that was flanked by low-income housing. He got out and approached the front door of one of the units as Brad was pulling up in the cruiser. Roy banged his fist against the door and waited. No answer so he started banging on the door again. Just as he was about to stop the door opened. A large bald man opened the door. He had on a pair of lime green reading glasses.

"I thought you weren't here, man." Roy said.

"I'm always here," he said and then lowered his voice. "I got company."

Roy dangled the keys out in front of him. "This just came in."

"She just got here, Roy."

"So?"

"So, how about you let me finish with her and then I'll take care of your car, OK?"

"You aren't paid to negotiate with me. Besides, we got those guys too–" Roy flipped his thumb back at the twins. "You can't just leave them sitting out there. People will get suspicious."

"Alright, I here ya." He turned back into the house and shouted. "Verma, let's go get some queso."

"What?" a woman's voice echoed through the house.

"My treat!" He looked back at Roy. "You owe me, asshole."

"You can't take her."

"I don't work for you, so I can take her."

"Whatever. It's your ass. We'll pick you up in an hour."

"You never - not once - have you ever picked me up, so don't think I'm gonna believe you this time and don't mess up my place too much."

"It isn't your place," Roy said as the large man pushed passed him with Verma. They got into the Dodge and drove away. Roy signaled to Brad who got out of the cruiser and ushered Ariel and his brother into the house.

The house was small and in relatively good condition. There was an open sleeper sofa and television in the living room. An Xbox was connected to the television and there was a wireless remote sitting on the mattress of the sleeper sofa. There was a kitchen towards the back but it appeared to be relatively unused. Next to the television was a door which led to a bedroom. It was closed.

"What the fuck, guys?" Ariel said.

"Keep your mouth shut and sit down," Brad said as he pointed to the sleeper sofa. Ariel and his brother sat down on the mattress. His brother nudged him and then pointed down at the floor. It was covered, from wall to wall, in clear plastic. Ariel looked up and saw that the walls too were draped in plastic.

"Where were you two headed?" Roy asked

"We ain't telling you shit until we get a lawyer," Ariel's brother snapped.

"Sure, sure, I understand." Brad said as he walked into the kitchen.

Ariel stood up. "Did you hear what he said, he said-"

"He heard you," Roy said as he pushed him back down on to the mattress and then went through the door to the bedroom. He let the door shut behind himself.

"Where's that guy going?" Ariel's brother said.

Brad came back in with a knife from the kitchen. It was a six inch paring knife. "He'll be right back," he said. "Which one of you wants to go first?"

"Go first with what? Aren't you a cop or something?"

"Sure," Brad said with a shrug as Roy came back into the room wearing a poncho with the logo of the Houston Texans on the front. They were the front line of defense on the war on drugs and they were expected to act like it.

"You want to do the honors?" Brad asked as he proffered the knife.

"Eh –"

"Come on, it's my Christmas present to you. Ariel said he wanted to go first."

"No, I didn't. He's lying. I didn't say that – go first at what?"

Roy took the knife and went over to Ariel and punched the knife into the side of his neck. Blood spurted out against the wall as Ariel shrieked in pain. Roy retreated and punched the knife into his brother's neck. It was too gruesome to watch so Brad went into the kitchen and opened the fridge. Empty. Figures. There was a soft buzzing in his front pocket. He pulled out his phone. He didn't recognize the number but picked up anyway. "Hello?" he said.

"Brad?"

"Ya –?"

"Hey man, it's Cleft – Peter's friend – I need your help."

29

"You got a second?" Cleft said as he went over and shut the door to his office so Marie couldn't hear.

"Who is this?" Brad said on the other end of the phone.

"Cleft. Peter's friend – we met at the hospital and like a dozen other times."

"Oh right, right – Cleft, of course. Sorry, man. What's going on?"

"I need help finding, Peter."

"You and the world, my friend – "

"It's important."

"So is his conviction under a fair and guided legal system. He's probably deciding whether or not he should turn himself in."

"You saw him go through recovery – you helped him – do you really think he could do something like that? Just kill her in cold blood?"

"You'd be surprised the sort of things a man is capable of. Crime of passion makes people do crazy things."

"I guess so, I just – he never mentioned her. Not once. Did he say anything to you about her?"

"A few times, yes."

"So strange."

"People bury things, Cleft. You would be surprised what people are capable of hiding."

"I guess so, but – "

"What is it that you want?" Brad said in a rather terse manner. Cleft must have interrupted him.

"Sorry, I didn't realize that you might be working."

"Yup, busy day. What is it that I can help you with?"

"I think I found something."

"What does that mean – you found something?"

"That's the thing. I don't really know. Something about Endo-chrone but what specifically I'm still working on."

"What about Endochrone?"

Marie came over and tapped on Cleft's door. He held a finger up. She hated that.

"Can you help me find a car? Put something on the radio or something?"

"What do you mean help you find a car?"

"See, here's the thing. I saw Peter. I saw him this morning. He came to visit me and he gave me some files. I don't know why he gave them to me but it looks like Endochrone is up to some pretty shady stuff and I need to tell Pete – warn him, I guess, I don't know. If we can find the car we can find him. That's the thinking. It's my secretary's car."

"Files?"

"Ya, it's just now – now I think he might be on to something. Maybe he didn't kill that woman, maybe this is just one big miscommunication. I don't know – I need your help."

"What do the files look like?"

"I don't know, they're double sided, doesn't matter – what's important is that these files contain duplicate information – "

"Did you show them to anyone – share them – has anyone else seen them?"

"No." Cleft said. "Why?"

"You at work?"

"Yes, but – "

"I'll be there in ten minutes. Meet me downstairs. Bring the files with you and keep them to yourself and don't talk to anyone. You can't trust anyone these days."

"Oh, OK – but I really need to-" but Brad had already hung up. Marie started tapping her finger on the glass again. "What is it, Marie?!" Cleft snapped at her.

"Vanessa Snowdin is here to see you," she said through the glass.

"God, what is it with people. Tell her that I'm not here – that I left and that you aren't accountable for me – "

"You know you shouldn't use the lord's name in vein, right, Cleft?" Vanessa said as she floated her head around the door frame. "Is this a bad time?"

"I'm just heading out actually," he said as he picked up the files. He thought about what Brad said about not sharing the files with anyone and not saying anything about the files to anyone. It was a rather specific request, especially if Brad didn't know anything about the files, and people don't make that type of request if they're trying to protect something good. This was assuredly bad, so Cleft was going to copy the files and pass them along to Vanessa. Her arrival was unexpected but he was going to consider her being there serendipitous. Freedom of fucking information. "Marie – can you make a copy of these for Vanessa and then bring them right back to me?" Cleft asked.

"Sure," Marie said as she took the files and retreated out of the office.

"What is she copying for me?"

"I don't know – call it a project," Cleft said as he watched Marie head down the hallway.

"I like visiting enemy territory." She let out a small smile. "Always a little mystery."

"What is it, Vanessa? Did they finally decide to lay you off and you want to make amends with me?"

"You hung up on me earlier."

"Force of habit," he said as he smiled at her. He didn't particularly care for her but he admired her tenacity. In a business littered with college graduates thinking they were one step away from Rockefeller Center, not realizing the true nature and progression of the world, he liked the fact that Vanessa was comfortable being stuck in the middle. She also cared about a good story and getting the facts right, no matter what.

"I actually wanted to ask for your help," she said.

"Help with what?"

Vanessa took out a DVD case and set it on his desk. "It's a story I just finished editing and I thought you might be interested in it."

"Interested in what? I won't air your story."

"I don't want you to air it. I just want you to look at it and tell me what you think."

"What's it about?"

"Harvey Marcona."

"Huh." Cleft said as he shifted some papers around his desk.

"Huh what?"

"Why would you do a story on Harvey Marcona?"

"Cause someone paid me a lot of money to do a story on Harvey Marcona. You know how it is in this business. You hit a ceiling professionally and you know there's a fraction of a percent that the networks will take you, so you're stuck on your six figure salary – "

"Wait. You make six?"

"Ya, why? How much do you make?"

"Six too," he said and leaned back in his chair.

"Anyway, you're stuck trying to make ends meet until you retire and live off whatever pension they have left for you. So, when someone offers me details on a good story and a payday, I'm reluctant to turn it down."

"While I'm all for your rationalization – why a story on Harvey Marcona?"

"Dealer's choice."

"Let me guess, it makes him out to be the patron saint of genetic research."

"Quite the opposite actually. Tax fraud, infidelity, a pretty well-orchestrated character attack."

"Anything in there about pharmaceutical fraud?"

"No. Should there be?"

"And you can back all the claims with evidence?"

"It was handed to me on a silver platter, even came with references to follow-up with."

"Who paid you?"

"A friend."

"Some friend. Why me?"

"Why you what?"

"Why are you here in my office sharing this with me? Of all the people you could go to."

"I was hoping you would get to that. Because my friend – my source - was the same person who paid me to write a slam piece on Peter and broadcast his downfall on the evening news."

"I thought you did that out of journalistic determination."

"My source paid me two thousand dollars to bring Peter in for a fake interview and then ask him questions in attempt to discredit him. And I think you'd be the first to admit that there's a pretty big grey area with what Peter says and what actually happens."

"You aired that, are you going to air this?"

"Don't see any reason not to air it. People don't remember this shit. Anyway, I just thought it was interesting, the connection, me doing a story on Marcona and then Peter killing Marcona's secretary."

"To be determined." Cleft said and looked around the room. He needed some new art work. "Who's the friend?"

"Ah, funny you should ask but my sources are strictly confidential," she said and then smiled at him. There was no follow-up though. Cleft looked down at his watch while Vanessa stared at him. He knew she wanted something but he had places to be and wasn't in the mood for the run around with her. Where the hell was Marie?

"What do you want?" he finally said.

"I don't know, Cleft. I'm feeling rather greedy these days. I have momentum."

"What you have is thirty seconds."

"Fine – I want-" she looked up at the ceiling and thought about it. *Her old job back, cold hard cash*, there were too many choices but she knew, whatever it was, she wanted Cleft to suffer and remember what she did for him. Cleft looked over her shoulder. Marie was headed back towards the office – she looked flustered. What now?

"Well?" he said as he tapped on his watch and looked back at Vanessa.

"I want you to apologize to me."

"For what?"

"For never giving me the benefit of the doubt and for always second guessing me. Every chance you got. I'm amazing and you never acknowledged it. So – apologize."

"I'm sorry."

"What are you sorry for?"

"For never giving you the credit you deserved. There you go – I – am – sorry."

"That was sweet."

Marie came back in. "Jesus, that was a headache. Miller was in there with-" she started to say.

"Marie, I need the papers and the copies."

"Oh, the copier was busted."

"Dammit, Marie. Can't you do anything right?"

"I can get them later, it's not really a big deal." Vanessa interjected.

"No, no – that won't be possible," Cleft said and took the files from Marie and handed them to Vanessa. "Here you go."

"What am I supposed to do with these?"

"I don't know but I think it's important."

"That's your job though, to think things are important. You assign value to things for people. School is delayed, there's a collision on the east side, teachers aren't paid enough – you decide all of that for people."

"Vanessa, work with me here. Take the files, look at them. Peter and Marcona, there's a connection. I think you're right. Look at them – put them on TV. Do what you do best."

"Well, OK then," she said and put her arms up in the air. "You always make these visits so much fun. I need a story for the 5 o'clock."

"You haven't even told me who the friend is yet."

"I can't tell you, it's confidential."

"What if I told you I know who the friend is," Cleft said.

"What do you mean you know? How could you possibly know? You're so full of shit."

"Fine, have it your way," Cleft said. "Don't believe me then ask me."

"Ask you what?"

"Ask me something about your friend. Go ahead. Anything. I don't care."

"If you know who it is you can just tell me. You know that, right?"

"Not nearly as interesting."

"OK." Vanessa said and pushed the sleeves up on her blouse. "Where was he born?"

"I have no idea."

"You said to ask you something."

"Ask me something different."

"Fine – what's his safe word?"

"What do you mean his safe word - ?" Marie asked. "What's a safe word?"

"It's a word you use – when – when you're doing something and you need an out." Cleft said.

"What - like driving?" Marie asked.

"No, something – something dangerous."

"Ahh."

"You're wasting my time, Cleft." Vanessa said. "Tell me his safe word or I'm outta here."

"What are you doing with him that you even need a safe word?" Marie asked.

Cleft let out a small smile and looked at Vanessa. "Cannoli," he said softly.

"Jesus."

"Cannoli?" Marie asked. "What's that have to do with anything?"

"How did you know that?" Vanessa asked.

"That's a great question!" Marie said and turned towards Cleft but he ignored her and turned around and grabbed some papers from his desk and shoved them into his briefcase.

"Doesn't matter. It was an obvious choice. I have a meeting and I have to go to," Cleft said and walked passed Vanessa and Marie. "Thanks for playing, Vanessa!"

"You know, the IPO is two days away, don't you?" Vanessa said.

Cleft stopped just before he reached the precipice of the door and turned back around. "What are you talking about?"

"The IPO for Endochrone. It's scheduled to happen Tuesday morning. So whatever you're doing, scrambling around and having secret meetings – you better figure it out." Cleft didn't say anything. Instead he dropped his head and walked out of the office. It wasn't defeat, or any sort of concession, he was just focused and needed to start putting the pieces together fast. "Be careful out there," Vanessa yelled at him as the door shut behind him but he had moved on. He walked past the elevator and headed straight for the stairwell. He went down a few flights to the lobby and opened the door. Brad was standing at the reception desk talking to a girl who's time should be spent thinking about what colleges she wanted to go to. Cleft didn't know, he was just guessing. *Baylor, Smith, UT,* who knew. The world was hers and she was wasting precious time listening to whatever Brad was going on about. Brad looked up as Cleft approached him and gave him a big smile. "I was beginning to worry about you."

"Sorry – there was a thing."

"I hate when that happens. You got the files?" Cleft held up his briefcase and pointed to it. "Great – I parked out back." He gave the receptionist a wink and waved his hand towards the back of the lobby. Cleft followed him through the lobby and out a security door which led to a narrow alley that was just wide enough for a garbage truck to fit through. Brad pulled out his keys and opened the trunk. "Just toss them in there."

"Actually, I'd rather hold on to them, if you don't mind." Cleft said as he stared into the trunk.

"Not at all, buddy. You know what they say – take the files and leave the cannoli."

"I know – you say that a lot." Cleft said and turned around. Brad was pointing his gun at him. "Are you going to kill me?" Cleft asked. He didn't miss a beat.

"Is that what you want?" Brad seemed more surprised than Cleft. "I'll kill you later. How does that sound?"

"You have what you need now, right? Seems like the logical next step."

"I'm not a monster, Cleft. Come on, we're pals. You know me better than that." Brad said as he raised the gun and slammed it against Cleft's temple. Cleft stumbled back and Brad rolled him into the trunk and slammed it shut.

30

The words ripped through me like a wild fire – make the wife and child watch. It wasn't possible. There's no way that they could have gotten to Cleft this quickly. Cleft probably didn't realize he had the files yet. It didn't add up but it was too late. Fritz was already moving up behind me. Quick to respond to his bosses orders. What was the plan here? Video chat with the wife and kid and then blow my brains out or were they somewhere close by? Maybe it was just an idle threat and they were going to toss me back on to the street like used garbage and hope I forget all about this. Maybe give me twenty bucks so I can catch a cab home in time for dinner.

"Wait – wait-" I said as Fritz set his hands gently on my shoulders. "A little to the right there – and just squeeze – "

"Very funny." Fritz said like we were just two buddies joking around with each other.

"Can I ask you a question? You know, before your friend here takes me away for ever and ever?"

"Sure," Hector said.

"What about my plea deal?"

"What about it?"

"I want it. I thought about it and I decided – I want to work something out. You have the files now so we're clear."

"You had your chance and you missed it," Hector said. I could hear Fritz smiling behind him. He thought this was funny.

"What is it, Fritz?" I asked.

"You're such a wag," he said. "You think you have this all figured out."

"I'm no good to you dead," I said. "Think about it, Janice is dead,

Marcona is dead and now the Richards family across the street is dead. That adds up to some pretty serious business. Someone is going to put it together. You may think you know what you're doing but you don't. We have to protect the brand."

"We don't anticipate anyone finding your bodies. As a matter of fact, as of this very moment your house was put on the market and someone is headed over to make an offer. You know how the market is these days, right? So everyone is just going to think you moved. And that's if people care, which I presume they don't. You're a nobody now and you always were."

"That's nice of you."

"I'll tell you what though. Since you've been a relatively good sport about all of this, I'll give you a choice."

"What's that?"

"I can kill you here or better yet-" but that's all I heard. The next words out of his mouth were trumped by a soft buzz that ran through my brain. A deep fog formed around my eyes and Hector quickly became a blur. The drugs – whatever shit the doctor prescribed me – was kicking in strong. Or, better yet, maybe the Ə-zero corporation hadn't fully tested their state-of-the-art blood pumping machines and mine was slowly teetering out on me, fighting against me. I felt numb and yet indestructible at the same time. I wanted to jump out of the chair and lunge at Hector and rip the vocal chords straight out of his neck and shove them down Fritz's throat. I raised my arm and reached forward but the only momentum I had was from Fritz picking me up and dragging me out of the room. He wrapped his arms around my torso and let my feet drag on the ground. I looked back to curse at Hector "I'll get you-" I tried to say to him but what came out was mumbled gibberish. I was an overdone lethargic noodle.

This new room was dark and warm. I could feel traces of mildew floating through the air and clinging to my clothes. Fritz dragged me to one of the walls and set me down. "I'm sorry-" I started to say but stopped when Fritz straighten me up against the wall. I wasn't apologizing to Fritz, although I'm sure he took it as some last ditch effort to save myself. I was mostly apologizing to myself for letting it end this way – again. I couldn't save my family and I let everyone down. *Oh, woe is me*, I thought as I took a breath and let out the few words I had left "Where is Prescott?" But Fritz didn't respond. He pulled my legs out so I was positioned against the wall like a neatly fitted Tetris piece. It was a good question and given the circumstances I wasn't entirely out of line asking it. Prescott was the missing piece and apparently crucial to this team of delinquents that it was curious, at least to me, that he wasn't around. Had Hector already bailed him out or was he rotting away in some prison cell forgotten about until the end of time? Maybe he was back home, laying low and playing family man with his psycho-sexual wife and the kids. Beats me. Fritz took a few steps away from me and pulled out a small handgun. From his other pocket he pulled out a silencer and screwed it on to the top of the gun and raised the gun towards me. He pulled the trigger and fired two shots directly into my chest. It felt like two pebbles trying to break through my skin and my chest muscles throbbed as I shut my eyes in preparation for the end. The back of my eye lids were black and then white and then black again. The colors went back and forth like my brain was playing with a light switch and couldn't decide. One second here and another second there in perpetuity until the lights stayed on longer and the interchange slowed down. It was white now and I could hear a voice to my left. Singing.

"Happy cows, make happy customers, right here in Steak Heaven." It was Dan singing that ever familiar jingle. We were sitting next to each other at the counter looking out at the long corridor of sequential letters and escalators. He was halfway done with his burger master-piece. I looked down and mine was seemingly demolished. "Thought I lost you there for a minute," Dan said. "Where did you go?"

"I don't know," I said. "What happened?"

"One minute you were here and the next you were gone."

"How long was I gone for?"

"A few minutes, maybe. Two tops. I ate your burger, I hope you don't mind. I can get you another one if you want."

"No. That's OK." I said as I watched a golf cart move swiftly down the corridor. "Come with me," I said as I got up and waved my hands like a lunatic. The gentleman behind the wheel saw me and pulled over.

"Where you going?" Dan hollered after me.

"Gonna hitch a ride – let's go, unless you want to walk around this place forever."

"You're a man of action, I like it!" Dan said as he tossed his burger down on the counter and got up to follow me.

"Where you two going?" the driver asked. I proffered him the slip of paper that I had. "That's a long way," he said and then looked over at the steering wheel protruding from Dan's chest and snickered. Dan and I squeezed into the back as the driver pressed down on the accelerator. I was jolted back but settled when he evened out at a top speed of eight miles an hour. A cool breeze filled the corridor as we flew past various stores and restaurants. Sun blasted through the skylights and washed us in warmth as we slowly progressed on our unknowing journey. I looked up through the skylights and could see the massive redwoods looming over us. We went by teenagers in Technicolor swimwear playing in a stream that ran along the outer edge of the corridor seemingly unaware of their surroundings. We were surrounded by people, swiftly and indolently, heading to their pre-determined destination. This place was half airport terminal on a weekday morning and half family resort on premium grade Quaaludes.

"We're here," the driver said as he slammed on the breaks. I looked up – we had made it.

"What do I owe you?" I said as I reached for some cash. He reached his hand out and tapped on the dashboard where it said courtesy shuttle in large black typeface. "Thanks." A solid win for courtesy shuttles.

"No problem, but if you don't mind, please fill out one of these comment cards. Put your name on it too. Doesn't do me any good if your name isn't on it." He handed me a five by seven notecard with about ten questions on the back: performance, speed, generosity, music selection and so on. The front had an address on it – a P.O. Box followed by a dozen or so letters.

"Where are we?" I asked but the driver just pointed towards the escalator and waved as he drove away with Dan.

"See you later, man!" Dan shouted at me as he shrunk in the distance. I turned and looked up. The escalator was empty. I got on and rode the escalator up. It took about five minutes until I reached the top. I stepped off into a small office with a desk and door towards the back. The walls were covered with display cases filled with a variety of oddities: cash, a pair of sneakers, bars of gold, pipes, concert tickets, vinyl albums and so on. In the middle was a large case showing off a foot long machete with an inscription below it. I leaned in to read it but a buzzer went off and the door towards the back opened. A short rotund man came out and signaled his hand towards a chair facing the desk.

188

"Have a seat," he said. I took a few steps towards him and the chair. "Do you have your ticket?" he asked. I reached into my pants pocket and pulled the ticket out and handed it to him. "Thanks, have a seat." he said again but I didn't move.

"Where am I?" I asked.

"Have a seat and I'll explain everything to you," he said as he ruffled through the pages of a clipboard. His half smile slowly faded.

"Is there a problem?" I asked.

He looked at the ticket again and then up at me. "What's your name?"

"Peter Richards."

"You aren't supposed to be here yet."

"I don't even know where I am."

"How did you get here?"

"Well - funny you should ask – I was outside and then I came inside, they gave me that ticket and then – "

"Well, you need to go back. There simply isn't room."

"Room for what?"

"You, to be perfectly honest. There isn't room for you."

"Where am I?" I said. I wanted to shout it but couldn't find the strength. He flinched his hand towards the chair. I obliged and sat down. Do as you're told, Peter.

"Peter – life – living – whatever it is you call it – it's complicated. You're conceived and then you're born and you go about living and events happen and you have fun, sometimes it's not fun, but mostly it is and you assign value and importance to things and then you die and you come here. Got it?"

"OK. That's a very bland and depressing perspective."

"I'm pragmatic."

"What's important then? What really matters?"

"Are you asking me about the meaning of life?"

"I guess so, yes."

"That's up to you to decide. Whatever makes sense for you. Money, kids, sex, family, adventure, learning, sex – "

"– you said sex twice – "

"– because it doesn't matter, Peter. It means whatever you want it to mean. If you want to go around giving money to homeless people that's entirely your choice."

"That's a rather divine example though –"

"Same goes if you wanted to spend your life burning copies of the bible – we don't care. The human race has the ability to govern itself. We function in an entirely judgment free zone."

"That must be nice."

"Shall I continue?"

"Sure."

"Here we decide where you go next."

"So this is like purgatory?"

"No, purgatory is a word you made up to rationalize the distinction between heaven and hell."

"I think it's a little more complicated than that actually."

"It's not."

"So this is heaven?"

"No, also something entirely made up."

"Actually, heaven is in the bible – "

"Peter, did you come here to argue with me or would you like me to explain?"

"Sorry, yes, explain please."

"You're life, as you know it, is nothing but a small spec of sand on a beach the size of a million galaxy's pasted together. You existed somewhere else before you're born and you will continue to exist somewhere else after you die, in perpetuity. Your life on earth as a family man, a bachelor, a Jew, however you choose to live is just one frame of an epic motion picture. You came from somewhere and you're headed somewhere else."

"Where was I before I was born?"

"I can't tell you."

"Can't or won't?"

"Won't and that's because it's irrelevant. Also, it will take ages to dig up the paperwork."

"Well, for what it's worth, I certainly don't remember being somewhere else before I was born."

"Do you remember being born?"

"No."

"Do you remember learning to crawl?"

"No."

"Well, there you have it. There is only so much space in your brain for memory."

"But I was there when my daughter was born, I saw it happen."

"It's not a question on the legitimacy of child birth. No one is arguing that, but at some point that memory will be washed away by something else."

"But I was alive – I lived – I have a conscience and can feel things and I remember things."

"But memories fade and as you transition from one place to the next those memories and feelings weaken and become obsolete. You dream and have suggestions of the past and allusions to the future but that's it. You just move from one life and one experience to the next."

"Then what?"

"Then you keep going. It's like a donut, circular and unending. Similar to the universe. No clear starting point and no end, at least not yet."

"Everything ends."

"Not yet."

"Alright," I said and lowered my head. It felt exhausted and mentally inferior. "I'll play. So, where am I going?"

"Nowhere."

"Nowhere?"

"Unfortunately, yes, there just isn't room, as I said. It looks like you got the call too soon and you need to go back. This doesn't happen often and I apologize for any confusion. You can take it up with Supervision but I promise it's not worth your time."

"There isn't room? People die all the time."

"Precisely the reason why there isn't room."

"So now what?"

"So now you go back and continue your life until there is room for you and this just becomes some fuzzy drug induced dream that you'll think about for a few hours but inevitably forget."

"Well, I was shot. Twice. In the chest. I have a drug addiction. I'm sure my chances for living are negligible."

"There's one thing you're forgetting."

"What's that?"

"That Kevlar vest you're wearing."

"Excuse me?"

"Yes, you remember, right? You started wearing it after the events in

Boston. You were habitually determined that someone was going to kill you that you started wearing it on a regular basis. It was routine for a while and then when you moved to Austin it became semi-regular. You were wearing it when you had your heart attack. When you went to the hospital the orderly's took your clothing along with the vest and then you took it before you left. Hector and Fritz didn't know."

"I forgot."

"You didn't forget, you were just focused on other stuff and you were conditioned to it. You got comfortable."

"That's funny."

"What is?"

"A minute ago you were asking my name and now you're telling me about events in my own life."

"Sometimes it takes a minute. Lots of people come in here. Lots of information."

"So are you like regional or something?"

"I guess so."

"How long have you been doing this for?"

"Time isn't – it's just a – a way people document events."

"I guess I should have expected that answer."

"Now, if you just go through this door – someone on the other side will be able to assist you. There may be a little paperwork involved. Actually, who am I kidding, it's a ton of paperwork, but you'll forget about it and the feeling of frustration will wear off in no time." He went over and opened the door and signaled for me to go through.

"Can I ask you something?"

"Sure – just one question though."

"Who killed John F. Kennedy?"

"Who do you think killed him?"

"The CIA."

"It was the Russians. Good guess, a little obvious though."

"Really?"

"Yes, well, Oswald shot him but the Russians killed him. The KGB was pretty pissed about the Cuban Missile Crisis. They felt like they needed to send a message to the United States. A message that wouldn't go unnoticed. Someone in the KGB had met Oswald a few times, they had conversations about Oswald defecting to Russia. See, he was a Marine and had been thinking about it for some time. The Russians loved American defectors. They had a pretty significant budget allocated for recruitment too and sent him on an all-inclusive vacation to the Bahama's so he could think it over. He came back and said yes and they got him all set up. He worked as a spy for a few years, gathering and sending important information back to the homeland, and then he was given the order, directly from Khrushchev too. Anything else?"

"No, I think I'm good."

"Thanks for visiting, Peter. I'll see you next time," he said as my eyes slowly drifted shut.

<h1 style="text-align:center">31</h1>

I bought my vest from a well-known and respected manufacturer who specializes in making armored vests for a wide range of government and private organizations. They had three categories of vest: good, better and outstanding, as well as a wide array of price points within those categories which essentially correlated to how afraid you were for your own life. If you were a hobbyist and liked the idea of having a vest but truly didn't think you were in any sort of legitimate danger you would probably purchase something on the affordable end of the good category. For a few hundred dollars more you could get yourself something nice in the better category which usually appealed to local law enforcement on a shoestring budget. The better category also tempted most militia organizations who needed sufficient protection but didn't want to be screwed over by the outwardly greedy pricing of the outstanding category, which they thought was simply a 'fuck you' from American capitalism. The outstanding vests, the crème de le crème, were for Secret Service, FBI, U.S. Marshals, CIA and any government organization that went around engaging in periodic gunfire. After the events in Boston I had an elevated sense of self and was suffering from a rare bout of paranoia. I thought, for sure, whomever killed Clover was also out to get me and for good reason. Clover was allegedly sitting on a treasure chest of information and I was the perfect catalyst. I made a general inquiry online and a sales rep called me within a few minutes. After she got over the initial disappointment of me wanting to buy a single vest and not dozens for a large conglomerate she started going through the pricing. I told her to skip the pitch and that I needed something in the outstanding category. This rerouted her mild disinterest and she ran through some of the design options. Was I a defective agent for the KGB and I was worried the motherland was going to catch up to me? There was a special kind of Kevlar for that. For the most part, weapons and ammunition are similar but when you go from region to region they each have their own idiosyncrasies, so you should expect to pay a different price if you were worried about Russia than if you were concerned about a homegrown militia. I suspected it was some unprovable nonsense but decided to go with the thickest and priciest Kevlar available, something that would assuredly protect me from hell-fire in Gaza to a grassroots lunatic who locks down the local shopping mall. I had an exciting career so I needed to be prepared. Also, since I was an on-air personality, I convinced Cleft to let me expense half of it. I didn't see the difference between them giving me a fifty percent discount at Sport Clips, for a consistent and outwardly non-changing appearance, and them splitting the cost of a Kevlar vest. It was all the same as far as I was concerned.

I must have been out for a few minutes but it wasn't from the two bullets smashing into my chest, the vest protected me from that. Each bullet carried enough velocity that I stumbled back and banged my head on the concrete wall behind me. I could have been out for a few minutes or a few hours but it didn't matter. When I came to Fritz was gone and the room smelled like burnt ammunition. My legs were stretched out in front of me and my head was propped up against the wall. I looked down and saw two tears through my shirt and two bullets nesting peacefully in the folds of the Kevlar. The bullets made it about halfway through and the vest properly paid for itself. I reached down to pull the bullets out but they were still hot. Fritz was gone but he didn't go far.

"Tell me where it is," his voice said from the other room.

"I don't know, I'm sorry – I didn't know – I didn't do anything." It was Cleft. He was pleading, desperate and afraid, head totally under water, not sure what to do. He was probably thinking about his family that he had so meticulously kept together. "What did I do-?" he asked trying anything to stay alive. I heard some shuffling, followed by more pleading and then Cleft let out a scream that echoed against the walls. It took the reverberation a few seconds to hit me but it was bad. I reached down and pulled the Kevlar off and rolled to my side. My body was in bad shape and I was certain the bullets cracked a few ribs but I was alive and had all my functions. I put my hand on my chest

196

and pressed down. I could feel the nuts and bolts of my ə-zero heart churning away, a seamless connection between human and machine. I rolled on to my stomach and then stretched my legs out and arched my back so I was halfway between a beginner Yoga position and a baby waking up in the morning. It felt good.

"Tell me where it fucking is!" the voice said again, but this time it added the universal I'm-not-messing-around tone. I crawled towards the doorway and saw Fritz standing over Cleft with a pair of garden shears in one hand. Cleft's face was flush and his hands were drenched in blood. Fritz was using the garden shears to meticulously pull out each of Cleft's finger nails until he got whatever information he needed.

"Where are the folders?" Fritz asked him.

"I don't know what you're talking about," Cleft said. He was broken or close to it.

"I'll ask you one more time." Fritz said and clenched the shears down on Cleft's thumb. "Where are the folders?"

"Hey, Fritz—" I said as I pulled myself up on the precipice of the door. Fritz held his position over Cleft and turned his head towards me. "Ya, it's me asshole. You're a real crummy shot, you know that, right?" Now is a good a time as any to admit that I didn't really have a plan. Fritz let out a small smile and pulled out his gun with his other hand and pointed it at me. He pulled back on the hammer and made a small circle with his mouth as he focused his aim on my face. In what I calculated to be about half a second Cleft did what I never thought him capable of. He took his left foot and shoved it into Fritz's crotch with whatever force he had left. It wasn't a huge amount of velocity but it was enough to make Fritz flinch and look back at Cleft which gave me a two second window to rush at Fritz and take him to the floor. His head slammed back on the concrete and the gun slid to the other side of the room, out of reach from all of us. The serendipitous firearm transfer wasn't happening so with all my strength I straddled Fritz and grabbed the short strands of hair on his head and slammed his head into the concrete.

Crack.

"Peter…?" I looked up, Cleft had a look of shock on his face.

"You OK?" I asked. He just nodded. "Let's get out of here." I said as I ripped a sleeve off of Fritz's shirt and wrapped Cleft's hands. The blood seeped through instantly. It was going to take a few minutes for the fibers on the shirt to stop the passage of blood.

"How did you get here?" I asked.

"Brad – it was him. I needed help finding you, wanted to tell you about the files you gave me. I thought Brad would know where you were so I called him and told him I needed help tracking you down. I thought of all the people he would know how to find you. He met me at my office and then stuffed me into the back of his car. Now I'm here with no fingernails, thanks to you."

Shit. "Does he have the files?"

"Nope. I gave him a briefcase full of job applications. I gave the files to Vanessa."

"Vanessa?!"

"It was an in-the-moment decision. What the hell did you get me into, Pete?" he said as I reached over and pulled out a set of keys from Fritz's jacket pocket.

"I'll explain in the car," I said and lifted Cleft up. I pulled his arm around my shoulder and led him out of the room. We headed back towards the elevator bank and made our way to the stairs that led up to the attached parking garage outside. Cleft was lagging and Fritz's shirt was drenched in blood from the absence of fingernails. There was only one car in the garage, a dark silver sedan with a dented tail light. I took Cleft over and the opened the passenger side door and lowered him in.

"I need to go to the hospital," Cleft said.

"Sure." I said as I reached over and buckled the seat belt for him, shut the door and got into the driver's side and started the car.

"You can take me to the Seton-" he added.

"I gotcha, don't worry," I said as I looked down at the blood drenched shirt. Seton, or any hospital for that matter, was the last place I wanted to take Cleft. He was just going to have to see this through. Besides, they weren't going to tell him anything different than what I was going to tell him.

"Just keep pressure on it, Cleft."

"Fuck, man." he said and leaned his head back. "Just take me to the damn hospital."

"You know that's a stupid idea." I said as I reached over him and opened the glove box and pulled out the registration. The car was registered to Endochrone. "Figures." I said.

"What figures? Peter, you need to come to terms with what's – "

"I'm not taking you to the hospital so stop asking me!" I snapped at him. "I will let you bleed to death in this car before I take you anywhere near a hospital. I need to find Paula and Joyce." I said as I looked over at the small four by four screen on the dashboard of the car.

"What do you mean?"

"They took them." I said and went over the recent events with Hector and the video feed of my family. I reviewed how Brad set me up to take the fall for Janice's murder. I told him about how Brad introduced me to Marvin the realtor and how smoothly everything went with making me the fall guy up until a week ago when I didn't pass out from a medical grade roofie provided to me in the most clandestine fashion by Brad.

"Shit, Peter." he said as I ran my finger over the navigation screen. I pressed on RECENT LOCATIONS and selected the first address.

1501 East 7th Street.

East of downtown and just a few blocks from where we were.

"What's the plan, man?" Cleft said, trying to cover up the pain from his finger nails.

"Fritz came from somewhere – might as well start with the last place."

"That's just the last place he didn't know how to get to, not the last place he was. There's no guarantee they'll be there."

I shrugged. Cleft was right but I didn't care. I pulled the car out of the garage and took a right on to 7th street. East 7th was a few blocks down on the other side of the interstate and it would only take a few minutes to get there. We drove in silence sans a few grunts of pain from Cleft. I was thinking about where Paula and Joyce might be and why they got pulled into this whole charade. Better question was, *why did I get pulled into this charade? Was what Hector said really true? Was I just set up to be a fall guy for a murder of someone who got their hands on some valuable information? What was it all worth to them?* Before I could answer we reached the intersection of east 7th and Chicon Avenue. Even though the east side was flourishing it still had a way to go. Right at the corner was 1501 East 7th Street with a small parking lot and a single drive through ATM. It was a bank.

"Shit." Cleft said, followed by "There was no way you could know, you just made a guess."

"Maybe." I said as I looked up at the entrance to the bank. It was called the Korean Bank of Central Texas which serviced the growing Korean population of Austin as well as other clients. Above the name was a large red circle, the same circle that I saw in Hector's office.

32

"So now what – you don't think Paula and Joyce are in the bank?"

"I don't know–"

"I mean, he could very well keep them any–"

"I don't know, Cleft – let me think!" I snapped at him.

"A red circle is a pretty common image is all. It's just a circle – that's all it is. It probably doesn't mean anything." he said but I ignored him. His hands were looking better but I felt bad. "It's not what you think, Peter. It's not a sign, it's just a coincidence."

"What does that mean?"

"It means I don't want you to let your imagination run wild just because you saw two red circles in the same day."

"That's not fair and you're an asshole for saying that."

"Look, we'll find Paula and Joyce, but you have to get over yourself, Peter."

"I saw how you looked at me when I was in the hospital. You thought I killed her, didn't you?"

"You had no idea what I was thinking. The police had a pretty compelling case."

"That was the whole point: to be so rock solid that even I thought I killed her."

"I was pretty sure you killed her, it lined up and made sense when I thought it through, but Paula said it wasn't possible. She didn't think you had it in you." There it was again, a lower left hook to the groin taking whatever wind was left right out of me. My own wife, not believing in me simply because she didn't think I had it in me.

"You know something, Cleft?" I said.

"What – do I know what?"

"Avery sold me my prescription meds for two years."

"What?"

"Yup – that's right. Two years. He was buying them from some pharmacist in Lakeway and then reselling them. Good stuff too and I was his number one client."

"God – you're such a – you're such a dick, Peter." he said. "I'd beat the shit out of you right now if I had it in me."

"I'm just telling you, wanted to get that out there. It's probably the first honest thing I've said in a long time." But he looked out the window again. It was late. The radio in the car said it was just past one a.m. and it was cold outside and I didn't know where my family was. "Look, I'm sorry – I can take you over to Seton. It's fine."

"It's not fine. I'm going to help you. You got me in to this shit and I'm going to get us out." Cleft said.

"OK - fair enough."

"When you left those files in my briefcase, like an asshole, I gave them to Vanessa."

"Why would you do that?"

"Because I needed help and you weren't available."

"You know she'll air anything, right? She wants air time and she doesn't vet stuff. I wouldn't be surprised if she had a story about it to-night. News Director Investigates Mystery Medical Files, tonight at five."

"She knows a guy at Gracie Smith Klein. This guy Ronald Wexler, her contact, is the chairman of the safety committee there."

"So?"

"So Gracie Smith Klein is a middleman between drug companies and the FDA. They help navigate the approval process," he said. "And something didn't make sense in the files you gave me. All five of the people had been approved for Memoton but on the other side only four of them were prescribed something called Eflixer. Have you heard of that drug?"

"Cancer. The FDA approved it for use in cancer treatments. It's supposed to be highly effective. It's something Endochrone worked on with Green Pharmaceuticals." I said.

"Right and it's not out yet – not for another couple of months and when I asked this Wexler guy about it, he got real shady, didn't want to say anything."

"Their IPO is scheduled for Tuesday morning," I added. "That's how Janice found those files in the first place – she was collecting stuff for the auditors."

"How does Prescott fit in?"

"He's the money," I said. "I imagine that Endochrone gets its money from some pretty unsavory people."

"Like the dairy industry?" Cleft asked half joking

"I don't know. But let's find out." I said as I looked up the Korean Bank of Central Texas.

"How we gonna do that?"

"We're going to rob a bank."

33

David Prescott rested his head on Adrienne's lap and ran his hand over her thigh as she flipped through an issue of *US Weekly*. It was a few weeks old but she liked looking at the pictures of celebrities taking their kids on walks through Central Park. David ran his fingers down her calf and then took a piece of skin and pinched the back of her leg.

"Ow – what the fuck, David?" she snapped at him. But he just laughed.

It was a few minutes after one and they had finished lunch: a chef prepared salmon and dill flatbread with spinach and goat cheese salad. David and Adrienne didn't have any dietary restrictions or any specific food preferences. They simply gave the chef a credit card and sent him to the grocery store. There wasn't time or energy to specify what they wanted for every meal every day of the week for the rest of time. All he did was go to the local HEB, troll the aisles, sometimes for hours, and think about what rich people like to eat: salmon, dill, caviar, goat cheese, nuts.

Rich people really like nuts, especially on salads.

Flatbread too. That sounded about right. Rich people hate bread, unless it's flat.

The chef made Adrienne and the kid's egg whites with jalapeno sausage for breakfast. David detested the idea of breakfast and usually drank a pot of coffee and had half a bagel for sustenance until lunch which was usually some sort of delivery to the office that required minimal attention and effort. David didn't like to take time away from his day and busy schedule to eat but things were different now. David had been at home for close to twenty four hours and didn't have the freedom to leave. Adrienne had moved things around in her social calendar to be home with him and support him but she was waning. She wanted to get out, see the girls and enjoy a day of luxury down at the Four Seasons with champagne and a well-deserved spa treatment. Once again, he was holding her back. She didn't see the point in sitting around all day with him, watching reruns of some indecipherable crime drama on TV. David had ceased to live, as far as Adrienne was concerned. She would ask, from time to time, *how long are you under fake house arrest for? Why are you under fake house arrest? Does someone want you dead? Are we safe? Do you have a pulse?*

But he just gave non-answers and said they were indeed safe and things needed to cool down.

Simmer.

Sort out.

Just fucking relax and the world will be fine.

After the IPO is David's phrase of choice. The IPO was only a day away, so maybe then he could get out – enjoy the sun, go golfing or something – anything really. Just leave.

"Do they really have to sit out there?" she asked. She was talking about the run-down Honda Civic that sat at the end of their driveway with an interchangeable and consistently replaceable rent-a-cop.

"It's what they want."

"What do you want?"

"It's fine. Tomorrow is a big day, and things will be different after the IPO. We're going to make a lot of money, Adrienne, and we don't have to worry about Harvey anymore." he said and smiled at her but it hurt. She didn't know much about Harvey but the mention of his name made her think about Janice and what happened to her. Harvey seemed like a decent enough person, Janice had good judge of character, she thought. After all, her and Adrienne were the best of friends. As awful as murder is, maybe David had his reasons. Now he was a prisoner in his own home, at least until after the IPO. They didn't want him out there killing anyone else, she thought. Better to take precautions. Safety first.

She missed Janice and felt like she didn't need to go the way that she did. She also felt a little bad about calling the police and reporting the Tesla as stolen. She only spent a few hours with Peter Richards and, guilty or innocent, she liked his style. She had a vague suspicion that what he was telling her was true but if the cops caught him in her husband's car and it got back to David she was going to have a lot of explaining to do so she called it in and reported it stolen. He was a smart guy so he could figure it out on his own. A few hours later a police officer called her and said they found the car without a scratch on it. She was relieved, more relieved that Peter Richards wasn't found as well.

Someone from the police station brought the car back to the house and then waited in their kitchen for an hour while they sent another officer out to pick him up. Shortly after that, David was home. He hadn't spent more than eighteen hours in lock up until he was bailed out. He was guilty to the core, he'd be the first to tell you, but he had money and the county liked money. He also had a big company event in two days and needed to be available to speak with investors and advisors, especially now that Harvey Marcona was dead. He was the appeaser and David Prescott wasn't going to let a murder charge get in the way of that. Some big wigs from Wall Street wanted to fly him to New York for the IPO and have him and Harvey ring the opening bell at the New York Stock Exchange but he wasn't feeling it. He didn't think it would look good to the investors in the light of Harvey's murder.

"Can I ask you a question, David? Actually, I have three questions." Adrienne said and looked down at him.

"Uh, sure, I guess. What's up?" he said. She knew she was interrupting his show, he was irritated, but she didn't care.

"OK, first question: Did you pay an albino to bring a box here from Janice's house?"

"Yes." David said.

"Why?"

"Is this the second question?"

"It's more of a sub-question to the first question, if you will."

"Housekeeping - going public - need to know where everything is." He said and moved his hand away from her calf.

She wasn't enjoying it anyway.

David hadn't thought about the box. He gave the albino a few hundred bucks to bring it back to the house and then he put it away and went and took care of Harvey. Had to tie up all those loose ends. He didn't know about the visit from Peter Richards, Adrienne hadn't told him and she certainly didn't mention anything about giving him the Tesla or the banker's box.

"Who do you think killed Janice, David?" she asked and she was sincere. She thought for sure it was Peter Richards until she met Peter Richards. *Poor guy,* she thought. *In over his head,* she thought.

"That guy – Peter Richards." he said. "They were having an affair, he has a shady past - was a drug abuser, a philanderer. I mean, don't get me started."

"What do you mean, don't get me started? What else you know about him? Again a sub-question here."

"I know what's in the news. Like I said, he was all sorts of messed up. Only inevitable if you ask me. Some shady shit in Boston." he said. "Last question?"

"Do you know how much it costs to transfer an airline ticket to another person's name? Let's say you aren't going on a trip, due to unforeseen circumstances. Call the airline, hope you don't have a non-transferrable ticket. I'm asking because I think it's strange. Peter and Janice were supposed to go to Cabo the exact same days we were supposed to go to Cabo. Same airline too. It's strange, right? What a weird and troubling coincidence, David. What do you think about that?"

There was a soft buzz on his belt buckle. "I have to take this. It's Wall Street." he said as he removed himself from the couch and went into the adjoining office and shut the door. He had been in and out of that room at least a dozen times since he'd been home. Conference calls with the board of directors and auditors. Making sure everything was in place for the IPO and making the required adjustments in management and oversight now that Harvey Marcona was gone. David had been a part of Endochrone since the start and everything he did, every decision he made, was leading up to this moment and it was sweetened by the fact that Harvey wasn't around to spoil it for him. He didn't know why Adrienne was asking about the boxes or the albino – Janice must have mentioned something to her right after it happened. It's the only logical conclusion. The trip to Cabo was a careless mistake that Hector Ramirez shouldn't have made. He was too fucking enthusiastic.

If the police think they're going to Cabo it will make him look more guilty, is what he said and went ahead and changed the tickets. David didn't care. He knew that Adrienne wasn't going to want to travel after she heard the news of Janice's death. She was going to want to stick around and help out, plan things. How she knew about Peter and Janice's trip to Cabo was beyond him. Probably someone in the police department leaked it to the press and she saw it, believing everything she sees on television.

When he was off this call he needed to ask Adrienne what she knew. *What did Janice say to her? Was it just something she mentioned in passing or did Janice figure out what was in those files?* It was hard enough getting to this point – a point of full containment – he didn't need additional problems. If Adrienne knew what he knew she would be enraged. She wouldn't sit there and let him massage her legs. He knew what Adrienne was like when she was upset: uncontrollable and unilateral with no ear to reason whatsoever. She would call the police, FBI and the FDA. She might even pull one of the knives in the kitchen and cut his throat.

He wasn't going to ask. It was decided.

There was no point in asking Adrienne what she knew and there were a multitude of other things to focus on. Like dinner. Janice was supposed to make a reservation downtown for dinner tomorrow night to celebrate. David, Adrienne, Harvey and a few of their most generous investors. Janice tried to charm her way into dinner through Adrienne, but she would have been out of place. He admired her for trying but, honestly, what was she going to talk about, he thought to himself? Her husband? That ship had sailed and no one wanted to listen to that swan song anyway. David hoped that she remembered to make the reservation before Fritz got to her. Eight people at eight o'clock. The investors want barbeque and want to listen to some music. Janice would have to figure out the rest of the details. But she was gone now and David was in a lurch.

"David, can you hear us OK?" a voice said to him. David spun around in his chair and looked up at a wall of video monitors in his office: investors and advisory board members staring down at him.

"Loud and clear, team." he said.

"Great. Look, David, I know we need to review the management structure again and make sure everything is finalized but beforehand, I know there are few people on this call – Mister Khang – "

"Hi, David – " Mister Khang said from the lower left screen.

"Hello, Mister Khang – "

"– would like to hear about Memoton again. I thought maybe you could walk him through the highlights again. Only a few minutes if that's OK with you David. I know you're the money man, but still."

"Yes, of course. I would be happy to." He knew that Marcona had gone through the details a handful of times and Khang had the peripherals but fine – he could humor them.

"Just want to make sure my money is being used correctly, money man."

"Yes, of course, sir." David said as he leaned over and pressed a few keys on his keyboard which brought up a pre-packaged presentation on Memoton. Harvey was the mastermind behind this and made Janice slave for hours over its structure, but it was David who needed to speak to it. He didn't have a full grasp of the science, how could anyone, he just saw letters which moved around to create words and sentences of information. He would let his audience conclude what they wanted to from that.

He took a small breath and started, fully aware of his diverse audience, Mister Khang and, of course, their friend at Gracie Smith Klein, Ronald Wexler, who was omnipresent but mostly silent through these proceedings. "Memoton, also known as P39i during trial is a Cholinesterase inhibitor which prevents the breakdown of acetylcholine, a chemical messenger vital to learning and memory. Additionally, it supports communication among nerve cells by keeping acetylcholine levels high." He cleared his throat. "Acetylcholine is a neurotransmitter in the autonomic nervous system."

"Ya, ya, ya." a voice said.

David continued. "Memoton is the result of our extensive testing on Chromosome 16 which binds cells together that are crucial to learning and memory functions in the human brain. Essentially, it delays worsening of symptoms for six to 12 months, on average." David cleared his throat and looked out the window. His girls were outside walking the invisible tightrope on the edge of the swimming pool – typical. "If side effects do occur," he continued "they ordinarily include nausea, vomiting, loss of appetite and increased frequency of bowel movements and so on."

"What's the so on?" a voice said.

"Excuse me?" David said and looked up at the monitors.

"What's the so on?" the voice said again.

It was Larry Kingsman on the center monitor. He was one of the investors in Endochrone, first dollars in is what he likes to tell people. In fact, Kingsman and David had worked on numerous ventures together and David had made a very nice living for himself managing the assets of both Larry Kingsman and Mr. Khang. David started out managing the profits of Kingsman's adult publishing business – Depravity Press – where Kingsman was making over five million in profit each fiscal year. Kingsman was so impressed with David's diligence and attention to detail that he suggested he take on more work and gave him the portfolio of a Korean businessman who had cash – hundreds of millions of dollars in cash – and wanted to break into the American market. The dream.

David Prescott, Larry Kingsman and Mr. Khang – *the dream team.*

David had never met Mr. Khang, not in person at least, Kingsman said it wasn't necessary and, if you did meet him in person that probably meant you weren't doing your job correctly. David was fine with that. He preferred staying under the radar and getting his work done.

"I'll defer to Gracie Smith Klein on that one, if you don't mind." David said and looked at Ronald Wexler.

"Thanks, David." Ronald said as he leaned towards the microphone on his computer. "During the initial human trials of P39i a select group of subjects reported mild to severe headaches, difficulty walking as well as seizures. Under the advisement of Gracie Smith Klein, these subjects were removed from the testing process. It was later discovered that they had suffered from a rare form of brain cancer that was caused by Memoton."

"But it was negligible, right?" Kingsman interjected.

"Right, to a point, but cancer should never be considered negligible. This was a very lethal form of cancer." Ronald added. "Utilizing our relationship with various educational institutions, who cannot be named at this time, we sanctioned a study on P39i to find out what was causing the cancer. A team of scientists discovered that it tied back to a chemical agent that Endochrone was using in the drug making process.

"I would just like to point out that we sanctioned a third party for the actual production." David said.

"Fine – but it's still your drug and your creation." Ronald said. "Gracie Smith Klein advised Endochrone to remove the specified chemical agent from the drug making process and test it again. In a second round of testing, with the new and improved Memoton subjects reported no signs of terminal brain cancer."

"Interesting story, Mr. Wexler, but I'd like to hear about how this relates to Eflixer and where my money is going." Mr. Khang said.

"Right, of course." Ronald said. "One of the key findings was made by a local oncology student, Katy Price. She was reviewing tissue samples from the cancer patients and discovered that they all had the same malignant protein. Katy Price then spent her junior year developing a cheat code that eliminated the protein from patients. Harvey Marcona and Endochrone agreed to pay the rest of her tuition and patented her findings and then used those findings to develop Eflixer. Based on the initial tests Eflixer is going to be revolutionary, competing with Bevacizumab and Temozolomide."

"So you fixed Memoton and created Elflixer?" Mr. Khang asked.

"I'll defer here." Ronald said and his screen went dark.

"We did one better than fixing it, Mr. Khang." David said. "We enhanced it."

34

"You got a plan here?" Cleft asked. The sun had broken free of the horizon. The thermostat on the dashboard said it was thirty eight degrees. Outside, a car pulled into the parking lot and drove around to the back of the bank.

"No." I said and I meant it. "Just follow my lead, OK?" I got out of the car and shut the door. Cleft was a few steps behind me.

"Are you sure about this, Peter?" he asked.

"I guess so, sure as I'll ever be. You got another plan?"

"No – but can we talk about this?" his voice went up a few octaves when he got nervous. "Maybe Fritz does his banking here. Maybe he put the wrong address into the GPS – it could be anything."

"It's not anything. In fact, I'm pretty certain that it's something. He didn't put in the wrong address."

"How can you be so sure?"

"I don't know, but I have to go with something right? I have to make a choice, right? Can't just sit there." I said as I reached the door and went inside.

The bank was sparse and about thirty years out of date. The floor was covered with a faded pea green carpet. To one side was a small waiting area with a couch and two arm chairs. On the other side was a bank teller counter that stretched from one wall to the next. Behind the teller counter was a steel door.

"I'm just – your heart – I don't think you should be-" Cleft started to say.

"Save it." I said and walked over to the teller counter.

Back in 5 the sign said. It was me, a nervous version of Cleft and a sign. *Back in 5*. I reached my hand out and slammed it down on the bell.

Ding.

"One second and we'll be right with you." a voice said over an intercom. The voice was heavily accented and didn't sound like it was from any region in the United States. Based on where we were I would put my money on a Korean dialect. I looked up. There was a security camera behind the teller counter watching us.

"What are you going to do, man?" Cleft asked. It was nice not to be the nervous one for a change.

"Just relax." I said. "I'm just going to slit his throat and take the money." I said and smiled. "You're OK with that, right?" Cleft didn't appreciate the humor.

There was a loud bang from the other side of the steel door followed by "It's OK – be right with you." Then the steel door opened and a short elderly Asian man came out from the back. He couldn't have been an inch over five feet. "There's a sign out front – you have to read it – no solicitors." he said and waved a reckless finger in our direction.

"Oh, we're not here to sell anything." I said. "I just want to open up a checking account."

"A checking account?" he said. There was a hint of outrage in his voice, outrage at the practicality of my request.

"Yes, can you help us with that?"

"No, no – no checking accounts here, very sorry you came all this way."

"It's OK. We were just around the corner. What sort of account can I open?"

"No, accounts – no new customers."

"It's not new – existing." I said and reached into my back pocket and took out the registration for Fritz's car and set it on the counter. He looked down at it.

"Endo-" he started to say but stopped.

"Right, Endochrone. You familiar with it?"

"You police?"

"I'm not, but he is." I said and jabbed my thumb into Cleft's chest. "So you better be very careful what you say. What's your name?"

"No – no name, I don't have a name. You don't know me and you were never here."

"Sure, we were. I'm Peter and that's Cleft. What's your name?"

"John Smith," he said.

"Seriously?" I asked. He nodded. "Well, John Smith, we need your help. I need to know where my wife and daughter are. It's very important."

"I think you have me confused with someone else," he said.

"But you know Endochrone, right? You've heard of that?" He was silent. "What about a guy name Fritz? You know him?" He shook his head. "He knows who killed Kennedy." I added. "He tell you about that?"

"Ohh, yes, mister Fritz. Very grumpy guy," John Smith said. "Wouldn't tell me about Kennedy."

"Right – that's good. I need to find my wife and my daughter. It's very important you help me."

'I don't think I can help you with that. I'm very sorry. I don't know anything about that." he said as a woman's voice yelled from the other side of the steel door. It was unintelligible and the dialect was probably Korean. The man shouted something back at her.

"Why did you tell him I was the police?" Cleft asked.

"Just calm down, OK? You're gonna give me a heart attack."

"Can you please leave?" the man said as he turned back around towards us. "It's very busy today."

"What sort of operation you running back there?" I asked him.

"Don't worry about it." he said as he looked at Cleft. "Just business as usual, nothing you need to be concerned about." He flashed a smile and then pulled out a roll of hundred dollar bills. He pulled a few off and passed them to Cleft. "Just between us, right?"

Cleft hesitated but I reached over and took the cash. "Can we look back there?" I asked.

"They aren't there." he said. "Your wife and daughter aren't down there."

"OK – that's fine, we just want to take a look. Is that OK with you?" I said as I looked up at a security camera. I nudged Cleft and he handed him back the hundreds and then pulled out some more cash and handed it over.

"Follow me." he said as he turned and worked his way to the steel door. He pulled out a key chain and unlocked the door and went through. "Watch your step." he said as he went down a metal staircase.

"After you." Cleft said and gestured towards the stairs. I took the lead and went down. The staircase turned twice before we reached the bottom.

"What the hell?" Were the first words out of Cleft's mouth and he couldn't have been more right. We had descended on an industrial sized laboratory. There were at least twenty long lab tables and a team of four people at each table. They were wearing white labs coats with white surgical masks. In the center of the room was a conveyor belt that was carrying hundreds of small blue pills. At the very end were two technicians loading the pills into medicine bottles. The ceiling was covered with security cameras.

"Happy now?" John Smith asked.

"What's going on down here?"

"They just pay me – that's all. They give me a thousand dollars a week to show up here seven days a week. I make sure the technicians do their job. Two hundred bottles an hour. Ten hours a day. That's all I know. If someone shows up late I fire them. If they leave early, I fire them."

"What are you making?"

"You know – children's vitamins. Flintstones- the best kind." He gave me a sly look.

"Who?" Cleft asked. "Who pays you?"

"I think you've seen enough. I have your money so you can go now." John Smith said. Cleft was about to say something but then a phone rang. "Excuse me," John Smith said and walked over to a phone that was hanging on the wall.

"How did you know, Peter?" Cleft asked.

"Know what? That there was a top secret lab down here? I didn't. It was blind luck."

"What do you think they are making?"

"I don't know, but whatever it is they really don't want anyone to know about it." Cleft said as John Smith came back.

"Everything OK, John Smith?" I asked.

"They want to see you."

35

"So we're manufacturing a revolutionary Alzheimer's drug that gives people cancer?" Kingsman asked. He knew the answer but he liked running through it to appease Mr. Khang.

"It doesn't give people cancer." Prescott corrected. "It's a drug that treats Alzheimer's and cancer is a possible side effect. It's actually a pretty good Alzheimer's drug."

"I would also like to add, for the record, that all sorts of people get cancer for all sorts of reasons." Kingsman said.

"And there's no possible way that someone, at some point in time, will find out that you knew about this before going to market?" Ronald Wexler asked.

"No. Every possible loose end has been eliminated. We are one hundred percent contained."

"That's very nice to hear, Mr. Prescott." Mr. Khang said. "I'm very happy with what you've been able to do with my money. Very impressive work."

"Thank you. I know there have been a few roadblocks but – "

"Makes the end all the sweeter, David."

"I'll have to agree on that one." Kingsman said. "David, let's get on to more important things, like – where are we having dinner tomorrow night? We have lots of cash and I want to make sure we use it wisely."

A beep came from Kingsman's line. "If you'll excuse me, gentleman, I need to take this." His line went dark.

"There's a place downtown – great barbeque and live music." David said. "How does that sound?"

"That would be great, Mr. Prescott. My plane arrives in the afternoon."

David's cell phone buzzed in his pocket. He pulled it out and glanced down at it. It was a text.

NOT CONTAINED!!! ASSHOLES!!

"Everything OK, Mr. Prescott?" Ronald Wexler asked.

"Yes, everything is great. Mr. Khang, we'll send someone to pick you up."

"Very well." Mr. Khang said and disconnected his line.

"You OK, David?" Ronald asked again.

"Yes, no problem. Thanks for all your help with this Ronald. Couldn't have done it without you. We'll wire the money to you tomorrow."

"I'm aware." he said as his screen went blank. David looked at the text message again. It was from Kingsman:

NOT CONTAINED!!! ASSHOLES!!
What happened? David texted back.
You employ retards.
What do you need?
Get the fuck over here. Fix this.
Be there in ten.
Make it five. We're going to kill the wife.
What? Whose wife?
Peter Richard's wife and kid.
WTF?!?!
Brad got 'em this a.m. They're here.
ARE YOU INSANE?!
Total containment, dipshit. Do you not know how anything works?
FUCK OMY
What's OMY? You dumb too?
ON MY WAY!
Oh right.

David shoved the phone back in his pocket and went back out into the living room. Adrienne was still on the couch. "Everything OK?" she asked.

"Ya, sure, it's fine. Just in the final stages of everything – you know how it goes."

"I guess so," she said as she stretched.

"I'm going to go run an errand you need anything?"

"You can do that – just go out and run an errand? The cops like that?"

"I was gonna go out the back and use my bike. You got an issue with that?"

"I don't give a shit, David."

"Alright, fine – just asking. Hey, I meant to ask you – when did Janice tell you about the Albino?"

"What do you mean – *when did she tell me?*"

"About me paying the Albino to get the box from her house."

"She didn't tell me."

"Oh, well then how did you find out?"

"What does it matter how I found out? I found out."

"What else did she say about the box – about what was in it?"

"You're acting real paranoid right now, you see that about yourself, don't you?"

"It's just, you know – the IPO and everything."

"Was there something bad in the box?"

"What? No. Why would you think that?"

"Because of your behavior."

"I was just curious."

His phone buzzed again and he looked down at it.

You're not here!!!

Kingsman really had a way of getting through to people.

"Is there a problem?" Adrienne asked.

"No, things will be better, I promise, after the IPO."

"You should get that tattooed on your face – *after the IPO*. I'm so tired of hearing that."

"They will. Things will be better."

"OK."

"What's the problem?"

"You killed a man, David. That's the problem. Don't you see that? You killed someone in cold blood. That's pretty messed up. Someone you knew and trusted and loved and you're just walking around here like it's no big deal."

"You didn't know him." David said. "You didn't know Harvey."

"You don't know anything about me and you have no idea what I know."

"I just wanted to know what Janice told you, that's all. Calm down."

"You calm down, you piece of shit. If Janice said anything important I would have told you but now you're acting like a crazy man and I know something's up."

"Fine, if she didn't tell you - how did you find out?"

"You know who told me? You know how I found out? I'll tell you. Peter Richards told me. That's right, he came over here and told me about the Albino and the box at Janice's house. Then I tied him up downstairs and had sex with him. It was good too, none of that frat house garbage you try and do to me. He was classy and I came – a lot. Then you know what I did after I came? I gave him the banker's box and the Tesla and he left."

"Whatever, Adrienne, you're delusional. It's the only consistent trait you have."

"Am I?" she said and pulled out her phone and handed it to David. "Look at that." It was the picture she took of Peter in all of his naked glory.

"Seriously?" he asked.

"Look closer if you're still unsure." she said as she moved the phone closer to him.

"You gave him the car?"

"Yes, I certainly did. Told him to go real fast too."

"You're unbelievable. You have no idea what you've done. You live your life like there are no consequences." he said and walked out.

"We need milk!" she shouted at him.

David went out to the garage and grabbed his bike and took it through the sliding doors that led to the backyard. He went up the steep incline and tossed the bike over the fence and then hoisted himself over. He took the bike through his neighbor's yard and rode down Falcon Ledge to Lost Creek which took him up to the Estates of Barton Hills. Kingsman's house was on the left and protected by an eight foot brick wall and a guard house. David rode passed the guard house and left his bike behind one of the cars that was parked in the cul-de-sac in front of the main house. The main house was a massive red brick structure that covered half a dozen acres and had a view overlooking the Barton Creek Country Club. There was a smaller guest house to the north and a club house to the south which led to the swimming pool and tennis courts. David had been here before and thought it was over the top and absurd, opulence at its finest and fitting for a man like Larry Kingsman.

"I thought about buying a place like this once." a voice said behind him. David turned around. Hector was leaning against a pickup truck smoking a cigarette.

"It's like forty degrees outside, Hector."

"I like the cold. Keeps me sharp." Hector said. The phone in David's pocket buzzed again. He was sure it was Kingsman berating him for his tardiness.

"What's going on inside?" David said and gestured towards the house.

"We have a containment issue."

"I heard about the files."

"Sounds like your wife and my client had a – thing – a rendezvous of sorts and she passed along some very important information."

"He's not really your client."

"Not anymore, especially since he doesn't seem like he's interested in working out a deal. I'm quite good. Too bad he doesn't know that." Hector said. "Why did you pay someone to take the box out of her house, David? Fritz and Brad were going to take care of that when they killed her. It was the plan."

"I panicked."

"No shit you panicked. You shot Harvey Marcona in the lab, David!"

"He was going to figure it out. He kept asking me questions and I think Janice mentioned something to him about it."

"It's done now so count your blessings."

"We should have destroyed those files ages ago.""

"You know what they say about hindsight."

"That it's always right?" David said and then turned towards the house. "Is his family in there?"

"We had to take the necessary measures. I certainly hope, for your sake, Adrienne doesn't know anything."

"She has no idea."

"I hope that's right, David." Hector said as a grey compact car drove past the gate house towards them.

36

As soon as the words "They want to see you," left his mouth John Smith hung up the telephone and pointed towards the door that led back to the bank. "Go back through the bank and get into the car," he said. "The car will take you to where you need to go."

"That's it, huh?" I said. "Is that where my family is?"

"I don't know, please go now. You've caused enough problems for me and my operation already." John Smith said and hurried back down the stairs.

Cleft and I turned around and walked back through the bank and outside where, believe it or not, there was no car waiting for us. We were just standing in an empty parking lot watching a group of vagrants stare at us from across the street.

"This is a fucking joke." Cleft said as he pulled out a phone.

"New phone?"

"I had to borrow Marie's since, well, you took mine after you tied us up."

"You think you and Marie are headed somewhere?"

"Funny time to ask."

"Seize the day."

"Marie and I are working on things, Phyllis and I are working on things. Lots to sort out. I'm exhausted, I won't lie." he said as he punched the numbers on the phone.

"What are you doing?"

"I'm calling the police."

"Don't − "

"Don't what, Peter? I'm not going to turn you in so don't worry about that. They have Paula and Joyce, I'm doing the right thing here for your family."

"They're going to kill them, Cleft."

"Maybe, but they are definitely going to kill us, so I'm going to take my chances here. You have a better plan?" he asked as a light grey Honda Civic pulled around from the back of the bank. John Smith was in the driver's seat and honked the horn. It was blistering cold outside but he had the windows rolled down nonetheless.

"Get in!" he said.

I looked at Cleft. "Trust me on this one, alright?"

I could hear a voice on the other end of Cleft's telephone "One second." he said into the phone. "Peter, they're just going to kill us. There's absolutely no reason for them not to at this point."

"Hector said if I agree to a plea deal for the murder of Janice –"

"Peter, think about it, that's never going to happen. You go in there and tell them you'll play along – what do you think they'll do? Let the police help."

"Get in the car or I'm going to get out and break your legs and put you in the car!" John Smith yelled but Cleft hadn't decided yet. "I'm not joking around." John Smith added.

"Come on, man – help me out here." I said and put my hand on my chest. "Do it for my heart."

"Alright, but I need you to be right on this."

"I'm always right." I said and opened the back door to Civic and got in. I slid over and Cleft got in next to me.

"Put these on." John Smith said and tossed two black sacks over the seat. "Put them over your head." Cleft and I put the sacks over our heads as the car sped out of the parking lot on to east 7th Street. John Smith had the radio on the local campus station but other than that no one spoke. I stared out the window. There wasn't much to say and even if there was, I didn't know where to start. Maybe a few years in jail for a crime I didn't commit was a better option than my current situation. At least then, Paula and Joyce would be safe. Paula would be hysterical, maybe even enraged, at how I tore the family apart but at least she would be alive and safe. Her and the girls would inevitably move, get away from the nightmare across the street that her husband created but that too, in time, would pass. Joyce wasn't old enough to absorb what happened and to-be-determined wasn't even here yet, so Paula could freely litter Joyce's mind with whatever story she wanted. But that was only possible if she was still alive.

We took a hard left at Chicon and headed south as my heart started to beat against the inside of my chest. It was quick and felt almost as if I just finished a marathon or a double cheeseburger and a deep dish pizza.

"What is it?" Cleft asked.

"My heart." I said and pressed my hand against the center of my chest where my heart was. I felt faint and disoriented and my chest was covered in sweat. I pulled out the Ciclosporin, the immunosuppressive that I'm supposed to take religiously no matter what. Come the fury of hell and the overlords have emerged for the Reckoning but dammit fool take that Ciclosporin, your life depends on it.

"Tell me about Boston." Cleft said. "Don't think about your heart and tell me about Boston."

"What do you want to know?"

"Start from the beginning."

"It's three different stories, actually." I said and thought about Roy Cardinal. "The first is Roy Cardinal. He was a wide receiver for Boston College. Good kid. Freshman and way out of his element. He grew up in Dorchester so he had roots in Boston. His dad was a maintenance worker at South Station and his mom worked the register at a local Stop & Shop. He had a few siblings, two brothers maybe. Being part of the football team and the Greek system he was exposed to some rather unsavory people. A few weeks before the Christmas break he started selling marijuana to his teammates. He did such a good job with his customer base that he also started selling crack cocaine as well as a wide variety of methamphetamines. Sometime in the early spring a student by the name of Julia Weitzer overdoses at a frat party. Her parents pressed for an investigation and the campus review board opened up a formal case which didn't gain much traction until a student by the name of Garret Waingro came forward and said he knew who Julia Weitzer got the drugs from: rising BC sports star Roy Cardinal. Waingro said Cardinal was knowingly selling shit product that was laced with tile cleaner and that he offered it to Julia Weitzer at a discount because she wouldn't sleep with him. Cardinal didn't deny that he was selling, he needed money for his family so they could make ends meet. He also acknowledged that he gave Julia Weitzer a discount but that's only because he was into her and wanted to impress her; he thought the product was pure. It was from Mexico after all. A few weeks later, according to authorities, Roy Cardinal shot Garret Waingro. I never met Roy Cardinal but he seemed like a good kid, got into some serious shit for what he thought were the right reasons."

"What did he think the right reasons were?" Cleft asked.

"He needed to support his family."

"And the second story?"

"Charles Clover." I said as we hit a pothole. We only made one right turn so I think we were headed west towards downtown. "He started working at the District Attorney's office right after he graduated from college which was about ten years before I met him. We met at a friend's wedding, got to talking and he said that if I needed anything I could reach out to him. We had lunch and he agreed to be my source and pass me information from time to time on cases and stories I was investigating. It was mostly to verify or discredit information. A week before Roy Cardinal was shot Charles got pulled over for a broken tail-light on Route 1. The officer on scene suspected he was driving under the influence and asked him to take a breathalyzer. He agreed and tested at two times the legal limit. He was arrested, released on bail and then promptly put on leave from the DA's office. Before he was arrested for drunk driving he was put on a homicide case that involved a Boston College student who was shot while walking to his job in Harvard Square. Charles had someone in his office re-check the alibi's of the suspects, and most importantly the prime suspect: Roy Cardinal. He then called me up, said his office found something and needed to meet. That night I went to our usual place and he gave me a copy of a plane ticket which proved Roy Cardinal was in Florida when Waingro was shot. We only met for a few minutes and then I went home and started working on a draft of my story. Two hours later the police knocked on my door and wanted to know when the last time I saw Charles Clover was and then brought me downtown. I was in custody for only a few hours and then released because there wasn't any physical evidence to connect me to his murder. When I got home, my apartment was in shambles and the copy of the plane ticket was gone."

"Who else saw the plane ticket?"

"Just me and Clover."

"Who did the due diligence for him – who found the plane ticket? That person would know, right?"

"Yes, but when I asked the DA's office they didn't want to assist me, didn't want to help someone who was suspected of killing one of their own. Their job was to prosecute people, after all."

"What airline was he on – where did he fly to?"

"American to Orlando." I said. "He was only there for a few days, but when I tried the airlines I couldn't get anything, I needed court orders and attorneys, they weren't just going to give some reporter that information. It was a dead end."

"Right."

"You two assholes done talking back there?" John Smith called back to us.

"What's the last story, Peter?" Cleft asked.

"Louis Kleiner."

"Oh right, mob boss extraordinaire." Cleft added.

"He's the last piece." I said. "He works at the ticket counter for American Airlines at Logan Airport. He's been there for three years. Before that – nothing. No other jobs, no friends, nothing. A man in his mid-sixties with a totally clean slate. He pays two thousand dollars in cash a month for a walk up apartment in Quincy and has only one bank account where he receives his bi-weekly paychecks from Logan Airport and pays for his and his wife's life insurance policies. He works the ticket counter part time and spends his time away from work secluded in his house. I have record of him making two trips to a Cambridge based plastic surgeon but that's it. Work, home, plastic surgeon, repeat. My theory is that Louis Kleiner and Ricardo Gianetti are the same person. Ricardo Gianetti and his wife disappeared when he was on trial twenty years ago for smuggling drugs through Logan. He was in lock up and then vanished. The trial was put on hold while authorities looked for him but they couldn't find him. The state pronounced him and his wife dead five years later and the FBI and DEA declared it a victory against organized crime. In the years since he went missing the landscape of border security and national security changed and it became increasingly more difficult to smuggle narcotics into the United States. But using his position at Logan Airport, and a tight web of confidants, Ricardo Gianetti aka Louis Kleiner figured out a way to transport nearly a billion dollars' worth of narcotics into the United

States each year. You see, it wasn't about stashing a modicum of drugs on one or two flights a day with the risk of someone being caught. That was petty crime, a misdemeanor, and the risk outweighed the investment. It was about getting a large supply into the United States quickly and relatively unnoticed. Gianetti used his position as a generous donor for a state senator to get close to the CEO of Boston's largest shipping company - LASS Incorporated. LASS had a fleet of unused 737's that were sitting in a warehouse next to Logan Airport. LASS was trying to break into air freight but wasn't able to compete with the likes of FedEx and UPS so their planes sat there unused and neglected. Gianetti offered the CEO of LASS a hundred thousand dollars a week to rent the planes so he could move product from Mexico City to Boston, Miami, Austin and San Diego. The security protocols for air freight were different and less strict than passenger planes. Also, in the wake of 9/11 Homeland Security was concerned about bombs on shipping vessels and passenger planes that the last thing it was looking for was a 737 packed with ten thousand pounds of Mexican White Gold. Meanwhile, Ricardo Gianetti got a few face lifts, changed his name and got a job working at the ticket counter for American Airlines at Logan. In addition to dealing with unruly ticket holders it gave him access to the flight data for every flight going to and from every airport in North America. It was a rather smart decision on his part actually. It gave him something to do during the day and at the same time he could monitor his loot without bringing attention to himself. He didn't need that job, but what else was he going to do – sit at home?" Cleft was silent. "So, to answer your question, at least your implicit question: No, I didn't set him up. I didn't wrongfully incriminate him and I certainly didn't kill Charles Clover. There was something bigger going on and everyone had a myopic perspective they couldn't see the larger, more inclusive story. Sure, I wasn't perfect, I made mistakes, I have a colossal amount of faults but destroying two innocent men for the sake of my career isn't one of them."

"I can't believe Avery sold you drugs." Cleft muttered. He'd get over it.

"We want to think the world works a certain way – that life operates in a way that we can easily understand – but it doesn't. Good guys and bad guys, right and wrong. That's what we want so we can easily judge and know where we stand. But life doesn't work that way. There are layers and dark alleys and back handed deals."

"Who shot Charles Clover?" Cleft finally asked.

"Roy Cardinal shot him."

"But he was in Florida."

"Was he? Clover had a copy of a plane ticket from American airlines, the same airline that Louis Kleiner worked for. I think Roy Cardinal got caught dealing drugs for Gianetti, panicked and then the feds started asking questions and he went berserk and shot Waingro because he felt Waingro was responsible for his imminent downfall. Maybe Cardinal didn't know anything about who he was selling for – maybe he knew a lot, doesn't matter, but when he shot Waingro Louis Kleiner knew Cardinal was uncontainable and didn't want him to talk so he brought him in and protected him. Kleiner fabricated a plane ticket with Roy Cardinal's name on it. There were witnesses in Harvard Square who say they saw Roy Cardinal shoot Waingro but there was a plane ticket that put him in Orlando and how can you argue against something like that? The cops dropped their charges and it all went away."

"How do you know all of this?"

"Because I went to Orlando to visit Roy Cardinal's grandmother."

"Oh great – and what did she have to say for herself?"

"Nothing. She doesn't exist."

"We're here, assholes." John Smith said as the car came to screeching halt. I should have suspected as much. We had just taken a hard right turn and made a slow incline before stopping. John Smith got out and came around and opened the doors for us and took off our ski masks. I got out of the car and could feel the cold air press against my face. It was cold and sunny. We were parked in the cul-de-sac in front of a massive house and the only thing I could see was David Prescott charging towards me. He stopped a foot in front of me and screamed "You asshole!" in my general direction and then pulverized my face with a left hook.

I went down. I think I saw Hector behind him but I couldn't tell for sure.

37

"I bet you're wondering how I got a dentist's chair in here." a voice said to me. My eyes were closed, shut tight enough I could see the blood pumping through my eye lids. "I asked you a question." The voice said to me again. "I bet you're wondering how I got a dentist's chair in here."

I opened my eyes.

I was sitting on a couch in the middle of a large living room. It was one of those nice couches I always saw at West Elm that Paula thought was too impractical for our lifestyle. We didn't want to bring attention to ourselves after all. Cleft was next to me and our hands and feet were tied together. There was a set of tall sliding doors to the left of me which led out to the back which had a swimming pool, guest house and a small guest house which was probably for all the pool equipment. In front of me, on the other side of the living room, was a large kitchen with plenty of square footage and tall windows that looked out on to the backyard. Adrienne and her husband were standing at the enormous island in the center of the kitchen. Hector was with them and vigorously shaking an absurdly large martini shaker reserved specifically for pending IPO's and the imminent demise. David and Adrienne each had a martini glass at the ready. David was watching Adrienne but she was too busy staring outside past the pool, past the pool house and the guest house – watching nothing with a discerning look on her face, wondering how everything went so wrong.

"Did you hear me?" the voice said again. A few feet in front of me was a shiny silver dentist's chair and next to it was Larry Kingsman in his wheelchair. "You see, there's no retail market for these, especially one of this size and capability." Kingsman said. "But I have a friend who runs the manufacturing company out of San Antonio and he got this for me on special. They usually run about five grand a piece and you have to buy at least three. I got a discount on one." he said and gestured over towards the chair. Brad was sitting in it with his head tilted back towards the ceiling His mouth was held open with two plastic bridges – the kind they use in the dentist's office.

"I think I'm going to be sick." Cleft said.

"Where's my family, you maniac?" I asked Kingsman but he gave me a half-hearted grin and rolled his wheelchair over to the other side of Brad.

"Brad here – I believe you two have met –" Kingsman continued "– he's been complaining lately of some upper-mouth pain." Kingsman pushed the joystick on his wheelchair and spun around to the other side of the dentist's chair next to a tray filled with an assortment of dental tools. "Normally I would suggest he go and see a dentist – a professional, but since we have all the tools here I thought I might as well help him." He reached over to the tray and picked up a battery operated dental pick. "When I was in the Korean War, where I left my legs, I was in a prisoner of war camp for at least a year. I was an American combatant and the Koreans saw me as a threat. I was captured at night from our base and they took me and my crew to an undisclosed location. They tortured us for information on our battle plan. One method of torture was to bring in a local dentist who would extract teeth. Every time we didn't proffer the information they wanted, information they thought we had, they would take a tooth out. But they didn't have the luxury of contemporary dental tools. Sometimes they would just take a blade and cut around the tooth and let it fall out or, better yet, tie a rope around the tooth and yank it out. Whatever they were in the mood for." He took a breath and set the dental pick down on the tray. "Adrienne, if you could be a doll and come lower this for me that would be great." Kingsman said and rotated his wheelchair around a full 180 degrees so he was facing her. Hector and David looked at her and David whispered something and took a sip of his cocktail. Adrienne set her martini glass down and then lifted up her other hand. She was handcuffed to the oven door on the other side of the counter.

"Oh right." Hector said and took out a key and unhooked her. She took a sip of her martini and slowly made her way towards Kingsman. She passed the precipice of the kitchen and glanced outside again this time her eyes stopped on the pool house. It was only a fraction of a second but I knew what she was telling me, or at least I think I did.

"I know where they are." I said to Cleft under my breath.

"What?" he said

"Shut the fuck up over there! I'm trying to work." Kingsman said as Adrienne stopped by his side. "If you could be a dear and lower this for me. That would be lovely." Adrienne looked back at David and he nodded at her – it was all OK, you're doing the right thing here playing along, keeping your mouth shut. Adrienne obliged and pressed her foot down on the foot petal and Brad descended so he was level with Kingsman's waist. "Perfect – thank you." he said as she made her way back to the kitchen. Kingsman reached over to the tray of dental utensils and picked up at pair of pliers. "Don't move," he said as he shoved the pliers into Brad's mouth. Brad squirmed and bit down on the mouth guards. Kingsman wasn't in there for longer than ten seconds before he retracted the pliers with one of Brad's teeth. A gush of blood shot out and Brad let out a small muffled scream.

"Keep it to yourself, will you?" Kingman said. "Don't embarrass yourself." But Brad squirmed in the chair, weakness and vulnerability oozing out of him. With a hint of kale.

"Shit." Cleft said and leaned forward and threw up on the floor.

"Keep it together, man." I said as Kingsman shoved the pliers into Brad's mouth again and pulled out another tooth. Blood dripped from Brad's mouth and hit the floor. I kept my eyes on Kingsman, trying to give him a whiff of the confidence brewing inside of me.

"Your friend is next and then you." Kingsman said and waved his hand in the air signaling for someone who was off stage.

"That's fine. I already had my wisdom teeth taken out and Cleft's a big boy he can take care of himself." I said and then shouted into kitchen. "Hey Hector – I'm ready for that plea deal now!"

"Forget it, Peter. You're a dead man." he shouted back to me. I could hardly hear him over Brad's shrieking. Kingsman lowered his hand as John Smith came in from the foyer and approached him. Kingsman said something to him in what I'm pretty sure was Korean and then John Smith leaned towards him and Kingsman whispered something into his ear. It only took a few seconds and then John Smith nodded his approval and pulled out a small handgun and fired a single shot into Brad's temple. The bullet went straight through and exited the other side with a stream of guts and slammed into the door frame.

"Well done!" Hector shouted from the kitchen and raised his glass.

John Smith slid the gun back into his pocket and sliced off the hand ties around Brad's wrists and ankles and let them fall to the floor.

"Put him out back." Kingsman said as John Smith pulled Brad off the chair and dragged him to the back door. He dropped the legs and fiddled with the lock on the door. "Push the lock up, you idiot." Kingsman said. John Smith obliged and opened the door, took Brad by the legs and pulled him outside. The door slammed behind him. "Who's next?" Kingsman asked as he looked at me and Cleft.

"Me." I said.

"Very well." he said and waved Adrienne back into the living room.

"Peter, what are you doing?" Cleft asked me.

"What time is it?" I asked him.

"I don't know – like five something – why?"

"You'll see" I said as Adrienne arrived at the couch. She leaned down and slowly started to undo my hand ties.

"Don't take all day, Adrienne." David said from the kitchen.

"Are you sure about this?" she asked me.

"What choice do I have?" I said and smiled at her. Peter Richards charm. "You having fun in the kitchen? Some celebration you have going on over there."

"They like doing this. They think it's fun watching Kingsman do this." she said as she leaned down to untie my ankles. "You nearly ruined their entire enterprise but now they feel like they've won. Cocktails and murder, it's the perfect combination."

"If you say so." I said and stood up and walked towards the dentist's chair.

"A willing participant – I like that." Kingsman said and patted the seat on the chair.

"Go easy on me." I said as I leaned back in the chair and stared up at the ceiling.

"Open wide, you piece of trash." Kingsman said as he leaned over me with the pair of pliers. "You scared?" he asked. "You look like you're about to piss yourself."

"Can I make just one request." I asked him. There was no harm in asking and, at worst, he could say no.

"What is it?" he said.

"Can you turn on the television?"

"What? This isn't a fucking resort." he said with an infinitesimal amount of outrage in his voice.

"Come on, think about all I did for you."

"You've done nothing except make things more difficult." he said. There was the outrage I was waiting for.

"Come on, Larry – just let him do it." Prescott said.

"Don't call me that." Kingsman said to him. "You've done enough harm as well and Mr. Khang is going to deal with you directly when he gets here tomorrow. It's hard enough containing myself so I don't go over there and rip your lung out and serve it to you dutiful wife."

"Eat shit, Larry." Prescott said to him. It was good to see the criminal foundation was holding strong.

Kingsman looked back at me. "What channel?"

"Channel five." I said. "I think you'll like it."

"Hector could you make something of yourself and come in here and turn the television on. This man has requested channel five."

"Sure." Hector said and set his drink down. He came into the living room and grabbed the remote off the coffee table and turned the television on, flipped through the channels and stopped at channel 5 where Travis Holt was holding strong behind the anchor desk.

"Is this what you want?" Kingsman said as he pushed the pliers into my mouth.

"This is perfect." I said and then there was a loud cracking noise in my mouth as the pliers bit down on one of my molars. I felt a wave of pressure along my gum line as the small calcified box in my mouth was being squeezed by the twin tongs of death. The pressure was followed by a very acute stinging sensation and then absolute relentless pain that went from my tooth, through the veins in my gum all the way down through the blood canals arriving finally at my heart and then knocking on the door. *Fuck you, Larry Kingsman,* I thought. Then relief – or total numbness as he pulled the pliers out and let my tooth fall to the floor.

"You like this garbage on television?" he asked me.

"Yes – turn it up please. It's hard to hear over the grinding in my mouth." I mumbled. The words were clear in my head and I can only hope he heard them. He waved his hand violently at Hector and the television slowly got louder. Message received.

"You're being such a good sport. I cried the first time this happened to me." Kingsman said. I could feel it, we were bonding. He was going to be so disappointed in me. "The second time too, I think, but let's be honest, I can't remember. Man, Korea really did a number on me." he said and started laughing. I tried to laugh with him but he shoved the plier's back in and started digging around again.

"Thanks, Travis." a voice said on the television. It was Vanessa and she sounded lovely. "I'd like to start off tonight by issuing a retraction as well as an apology. I am retracting the story I did recently on Peter Richards where I unfairly implied that he was responsible for the death of a district attorney in Massachusetts, Charles Clover. I was given information from a source that later proved to be unreliable. It is my understanding that Peter Richards had no direct involvement with the death of Charles Clover and that it was simply a result of some rather poor timing of some very unfortunate events. It is also my conclusion that Peter Richards is a decent and honest man."

Kingsman looked down at me. "Is that what you wanted to hear?" he asked. I nodded. It was rather nice actually. "You a narcissist or something?"

"Something like that."

"Now to my story." Vanessa said and swiveled in her chair so she was facing a different camera. "Genetics and Greed are two words that don't normally go together." she said. "We live in a time where there have been significant advances in genetic research and science. We also live in an age where financial greed is at its worst, so it's no surprise that these two things have finally merged together. Austin company Endochrone purchased the patent rights to chromosome 16 a few years ago and has since made extensive breakthroughs with their research. One such finding they sold to Green Pharmaceuticals for a cutting edge Alzheimer's drug - Memoton – which increases short-term memory function in patients. Just ask Carol French, Peter Davis, Roger Reddinger and Becky Williams." As she said the names their pictures appeared on screen. "They, along with many others, were all part of Endochrone's trial for Memoton and now they are all dead. Don't believe me? Just ask David Prescott who was recently arrested for killing the head of Endochrone, Harvey Marcona." A picture of David appeared on screen.

"What the hell is this?" Kingsman said.

"Just keep listening." Cleft said.

"In addition to curbing some of the conditions of short-term memory loss, one of the key side effects of Memoton is brain cancer. But if you read the side of the bottle or went and asked Endochrone they would deny this. They would just tell you to see a doctor who would then prescribe you with Eflixer, another Endochrone product that treats brain cancer. How did Endochrone do this you may ask? They had the help from an oncology student by the name of Katy Price." A picture of a young and enthusiastic student appeared above Vanessa's head on screen. "Katy Price reviewed the data from Memoton's test subjects and found a malignant protein. She developed an antidote for the protein and Endochrone put that into Eflixer which it markets as a state of the art cancer killer. Katy Price was unavailable for comment."

The phone in Kingsman's kitchen started to ring.

"Nobody answer that." Hector said. "Just stay where you are and remain calm – she doesn't have anything to back this up."

"If you join me at ten o'clock this evening I'll be sitting down with a source close to the Endochrone family and someone who was integral in getting Memoton to market."

"She's lying through her teeth." Hector said.

"And tomorrow I'll have a story on how Larry Kinsman is laundering money for the Korean mafia." Vanessa added. "Up next, we have financial news and how one Austin company hopes to make it big tomorrow with their IPO."

"God dammit." Kingsman roared and looked back at Hector. "Fix this pile of rubbish."

"Of course, sir." The phone rang again. "Nobody answer that until I get this under control." Hector said but Adrienne reached out and picked it up.

"Kingsman residence." she said. "Why yes, please hold." She pressed the phone up against her chest. "It's for you Larry – It's a Mr. Khang. He sounds rather upset. Says he wants to see you first thing when he gets here tomorrow."

Kingsman looked down at me.

The pliers were still in my mouth and there was another loud crack. "You're lucky you aren't going to be around to see what I'm doing to do to your family." And then he squeezed the pliers together and yanked out another tooth. When I had my wisdom teeth taken out I was given both a general anesthetic and laughing gas which sent me into total and complete euphoria but I didn't have that luxury here. It was just me, Kingsman and his tools. The pain was so acute, and so unforgettable, that my body went into shock. My eyes drifted to the back of my head and images of Paula and Joyce filled my brain. I wish I was with them now instead of here. I wish this would all go away and then, again, I was out.

38

When you lay down at night to go to sleep you close your eyes twice. The first time is a soft close where you allow your eyelids to drop and then you can scan the back of them. If you pay close enough attention you can see loose fibers and skin and hints of light from the outside. The second close brings complete darkness and disconnect from the outside world. This is where you can fall asleep or, as I was experiencing, transition from my understood reality to a pre-determined purgatory where, in addition to not feeling completely welcome, the entirety of my future was up for debate. I was getting accustomed to this transition and felt confident that I had at least a partial understanding of what a time warp felt like. It wasn't so much that my body was whisked away and pulverized into a trillion pieces only to be pulled through the sky and reassembled in some ethereal utopia. Rather, I didn't move at all, I stayed put in the dental chair as the Carousel of Progress went into effect and transitioned out of one setting, in this case Larry Kingsman's house, for another in record time. The transition was confirmed by a soft beep and a faint sound that I suspected was an applause although I couldn't tell for sure. The second more fortified layer of my eyes opened allowing a strong beam of light to penetrate the weaker more linen like qualities of the first layer. I felt a breeze, picked up the soft hint of pine and heard the distant sound of people talking.

"I said thanks for visiting, Peter, and I'll see you next time." a voice said to me. I succumbed and opened my eyes. The rotund man was still sitting across from me or, better yet, I was still sitting across from him.

"I – I did – but I think I'm back now." I said. "How long was I gone for?"

"For the love of God." he said and reached his hand out and pressed on a button that was implanted in his desk. I suppose some practicalities are unavoidable. "I need an ninety-seven-three form in here quickly, please." he said.

"A ninety-seven —" a voice started to say back to him. Unsure.

" — three. It's an override form. We need to make room for one more. He simply won't stay away."

"No – no – no." I said. "That isn't necessary. I can go back. If you don't have room for me than it's fine. No room, no problem." I ran my tongue around the inside of my mouth; circled it around my gums and shoved it into the back of my mouth. It seemed as if all my teeth were intact and I didn't get a lingering taste of blood.

"Don't worry about it. It's the system that's broken. You didn't do anything wrong." the rotund man said. "There's a typhoon headed towards the coast of Australia, thousands are planned to perish. I'm sure we can save one poor person and make room for you. It's been known to happen."

"I need to see my wife and my daughter."

"Look, I know this is strange and a bit unusual but there will always be some sort of withdrawal. It happens to everyone and, like everything else, those feelings will fade into obscurity."

"You don't understand – they're in trouble and I'm the only one who can help them."

"You have a rather high opinion of yourself, don't you?"

"Press the button again and tell them that you were incorrect and that you don't need an override form." I said

"It's Supervision, they won't understand."

"Make them understand." I said as I stood up and took a step over to the display case with the machete. The inscription below it said: THANK YOU, KURTZ.

"What do you think you're doing?" he said as I lifted up my elbow and smashed the glass and grabbed the machete and pressed it up against my neck. "That was a gift!" he shouted at me.

"Press the button and tell them you were incorrect or I'm going to slit my throat." Holding one's self hostage usually isn't the best position to take when you're trying to gain the upper hand in a negotiation but this was an uncommon situation so I needed to do something that was in line with this weirdness.

"No – no – don't do that." he said and put his hands out as if he were reaching for a long lost childhood pet that I was about to drop into an open flame. This is the sort of reaction I was going for. Always thinking.

"Press the button and tell them you don't need the form." I said and closed my eyes hoping and praying I would go back. "Do it."

"You don't understand what will happen." he said. "If you kill yourself here there's nothing we can do to help you."

I pressed the machete against into my neck and tilted it down. "Try me." I said. "It can't be any worse than what I've been through."

"You will be out of our control and you will find yourself in a place of total darkness and total uncertainty where you will wait for eternity."

"Wait for what?"

"Someone to save you – to acknowledge you. But it will never happen and you'll be there for the rest of time and then when time finally does end you'll have been forgotten about but you'll still be waiting."

"Send me back."

"Do you know who gave me that machete?" he asked. "It was given to me by Colonel Kurtz who was murdered with it during the Vietnam War. He was hacked to death by an American Captain. Assassinated. He had some very bad luck. Wasn't a good man but it didn't matter. We don't discriminate."

It sounded familiar: Kurtz and Vietnam. My brain shuffled through the various bits of random information and memories it was able to hold on to. I had to reach for it, and it took a second, but I got it. "But that's – you're talking about a movie – a fiction." I said. "Captain Kurtz isn't a real person. He's character in a movie, the invention of someone else, played by an actor who is a real person." I hadn't seen the film since college but it's a classic.

"I'm not sure I follow."

"What do you mean you aren't sure if you follow? Have you ever heard of *Apocalypse Now*?"

"What's that?"

"You have to be kidding me. It's a movie! It's not even that – it's a classic piece of American cinema." I said and lowered the machete about half an inch from my Adams apple.

"I've heard people speak of movies but I've never seen one."

"This is insanity." I said.

"You're the one who's acting insane. Not me." he said. Assured. Buoyant. Irritating.

"So if this Captain Kurtz died, *died in a movie* and came here – " I said. My brain twisted around itself.

"Everyone comes here."

"Right. If that's what happened, a fictional character showed up here, then when Marlon Brando dies he comes here also?"

"Everyone comes here."

"So Marlon Brando comes here twice is what you're saying. And you do a profile, or whatever you call it, on Kurtz, who I should remind you is fictional, and you send him somewhere, to the aforementioned post-life, and he continues to exist in perpetuity?"

"That's the general idea."

"Interesting."

"If you say so."

"So what about Roger Rabbit?"

"Who?"

"He's a character in a movie."

"How did he die?"

"Well, he didn't."

"Then it's a moot point. If he didn't die the he wouldn't come here. What's the movie called?"

"*Who Framed Roger Rabbit?*"

"If he didn't die in the movie then he didn't come here and he ceases to exist outside of the movie."

"OK, what about a character who dies in a movie and then comes back to life in another movie? A sequel or a spinoff perhaps."

"I guess it means that we refused them and they weren't ready. Not dissimilar to yourself."

"But when you sent them away why did they go back to the movie and not real life?"

"We don't make a habit of putting people back into a world they are unfamiliar with."

"Why not? Certainly seems like it would be more enjoyable. People get over you when you die – it takes time but it happens eventually, might as well have some fun with it."

"It's complicated and I don't like to go into detail."

"What happens when you die?"

"I'm already dead."

"Are you a hallucination?"

"If that's what you want to tell yourself. If it makes stuff easier for you."

"What a surprise."

"Peter, it's been nice getting to know you. You are an unusual and unique person and our time together has been nothing less than interesting but you can go. I'll send you back and you can save your family and take care of the things that you need to take care of and do whatever your life requires of you. But only under one condition."

"What's that?"

"I don't ever want to see you here. Not for a very long time, understand?"

"Deal. I'm taking the machete though." I said as everything when back to black.

39

The blackness flashed to white and back again a few times until I heard the rage bellow from Kingsman's stomach. "Find out who's she sitting down with tonight." he screamed. My eyes popped open and I looked up at him. "You still alive?" he asked. "You're a spirited piece of litter aren't you?" The pliers were out of my mouth and dangling from his thumb with a small smear of blood on them. I circulated my tongue and felt two confirmed openings in my mouth. One was on the left towards the back and the other was right in front on the bottom. He got me good and lesson learned. I felt the handle of the machete against my left palm. I flipped it around and pressed the blade against the wrist tie on my right side and cut it off. I reached over and grabbed the handle with my other hand and moved the blade quickly towards Kingsman and drove the blade down hard into his leg. The machete broke through the fabric of his pants then protruded effortlessly through his skin but stopped when it hit the bone. He didn't flinch. "Don't you know I'm paralyzed from the waist down, you idiot?" he said as a gush of blood squirted out of his leg and across my face. He grasped the handle and tried to wrestle the blade away from me. "Hector – Help!" Kingsman shouted. "The moron is getting creative!"

Hector set his martini glass down and rushed out of the kitchen towards me. Adrienne and Prescott stood by, inert and unsure. Just before Hector reached me, Cleft emerged from his seat in the audience and rushed towards him. His hands and feet were still confined but he plowed into Hector with a full body blow and took him to the floor.

"Good hit, my friend." I said as I yanked the machete out of Kingsman's corpse of a leg and slammed the butt end against his chin. His head flipped back and he rolled away from me. I used the machete to slice off the leg ties and then cut Cleft free of his ties.

"Don't let him go anywhere." I said as I handed Cleft the machete and went over to the glass doors that led out back.

"Hey – Peter." Adrienne said. I stopped and looked back at her. She tossed me a key.

"For the pool house." she said.

"Thanks." I opened the glass door and ran outside. Brad's body was floating in the pool face down. John Smith was on the edge trying to pick the remnants of Brad's brain out of the water with a pool net.

"What are you doing roaming around out here?" John Smith asked. "Help a buddy out with a dead body?"

I made my way to the pool house and shoved the key in and opened the door. It was dark and musty but the sunlight came in and revealed the face of Joyce and then Paula. Joyce was asleep across Paula's lap and Paula had her head tilted back so she was staring up at a small opening in the roof. There was a small cup of water next to them and an empty plate. Paula saw me. "Peter." she said with a hint of surprise. She shook Joyce gently to wake her up. I went over to them and gave them a hug.

"Daddy." Joyce said as she looked up at me. "How was your vacation?"

"It was nice."

"What happened?" Paula asked me. "We've been in here – it's been at least a day. A week maybe. What did you do, Peter?" But it wasn't accusatory and didn't have the faintest hint of anger. She wanted information so she could put the pieces together in her head.

"It's a long story. I'll explain when we get home." I said and hugged Joyce again. "I'm sorry."

"Not as sorry as you're going to be." a voice said from behind me. I turned around. Prescott was standing in the door frame pointing a handgun at me. "Stand up and step away from your family." he said and shook the gun so I knew he had it.

"Is that the gun you shot Harvey with?" I asked as I stood up and took a step forward sealing the divide between him and my wife and daughter.

"It is, as a matter of fact." Prescott said.

"Did he know you were laundering money for the Korean mob?"

"He didn't know anything."

"What about the cancer? He figured that out."

"He was working on it. He had allusions that things weren't right but he was sort of a bore, a dull knife if you will. He wasn't sharp. Not like you."

"Thank you. It's a rather odd compliment, especially coming from a man pointing a gun at me but I'll take it nonetheless. Too bad so many people had to die."

"But I'm going to make so much money."

"I guess that's what it's all about, huh?"

"It's the American Dream, Peter." Prescott. said to me. "Everything we do is for money, cash or equity. The possibility and potential for more. Whether you admit it to yourself of not. Just make sure you do it correctly."

"That's a very cynical way to look at life." Paula said from behind me. "Clearly you've never been loved. Not the correct way at least."

"Shut-up." David snapped. "I wasn't talking to you. You're not even American."

"Don't talk to my wife like that." I said and then "Is Mr. Khang going to let you keep all the money you laundered for him? Is he going to let you keep all the money you and Kingsman laundered for the Korean mob when he meets with you tomorrow?"

"Yes." he said as he looked down at Joyce. His confidence was wavering. "Most of it."

"What do you get? Ten percent? Five percent?" But he didn't answer. I can't imagine a meeting between David Prescott and Mr. Khang turning out favorable for Prescott. I didn't have the slightest idea who Mr. Khang was, what his position in the Korea mafia was, but the meeting wasn't going to be something Prescott was going to walk away from feeling happy about. That is, if he walked away at all. "Cause he doesn't seem like a guy who tends to understand things and this is quite a big mess you've created for yourself."

"There isn't a mess that can't be cleaned up. I'm sure you can understand that."

"For your sake I hope that's true."

"And I'll have so much money tomorrow it won't matter. I can pay people to forget and to make things clean."

"Money from the IPO?"

"Right. It will all be better after the IPO." he said and cocked the gun and massaged his pointer finger around the trigger. He took a small breath. Right when he was about to exhale a large iron mallet swung around the door frame and slammed into the back of his head. I heard his skull crack as he dropped the gun and fell to his knees.

"I always hated how he said that." Adrienne said as she dropped the mallet and came around the corner. "You OK, Peter?" she asked.

"Yes. Are you?"

She nodded.

"Who are you?" Paula asked as she stood and picked Joyce up. "You know my husband?" Amazing how things can go from scary and uncertain to plain awkward.

"Oh, I'm sorry. Paula, this is Adrienne Prescott. She's David Prescott's wife." I said and pointed to the body on the floor.

"I'll probably change my last name." Adrienne said as she proffered her hand to Paula. "It's nice to meet you. Your husband is a good man."

"Nice to meet you." Paula shook her hand, I stepped outside. John Smith was reaching into the pool trying to pull Brad's body towards the edge. Cleft was inside tying Hector up and Kingsman still seemed like he was out of it. I stepped back into the pool house and leaned down to Joyce.

"Sweetheart. This lady is going to take you and mommy around to the front yard where you'll wait for me, OK?" Joyce nodded. "I'm going to go inside and take care of something but I promise that I'll be out soon."

"OK."

"I love you."

"I love you too, Daddy." she said and gave me a hug. In an instant, Prescott, Kingsman and all that was bad had disappeared.

I looked over at Paula and Adrienne. "Take them around the back, there's some rubbish in the pool."

"Sure thing." Adrienne said and put her hand on Paula's shoulder. I stepped out and walked past John Smith back into the house. Cleft was tying Kingsman's hands to the wheelchair.

"Seems a little redundant, doesn't it?" I asked.

"Just taking the extra step." he said. "We don't need him rolling away on us."

I looked over at Hector who was down on his knees with his hands behind his back.

"You didn't have much fight in you, did ya?" I said and leaned into his jacket pocket and pulled out his cell phone.

"Peter —" Hector started to say. "- as your attorney I'd like to advise you on the options available to you, given the current state of affairs."

"Oh, shut the fuck up." I said as I punched numbers into the phone. It rang a few times and then there was a click.

"Hello?" a voice said.

"Detective Skelly?" I said.

"Yes?"

"This is Peter Richards. I'd like to turn myself in."

40

I gave Skelly the address of where I was, he hung up and then probably put the call out that he was apprehending a grade-A suspect and got the nearest cruiser to tag along for backup. I didn't tell him anything else. I didn't say who the address belonged to and I didn't explain the situation at hand. I was burying the lead. He showed up twenty minutes after we hung up and rang the doorbell. I opened the door and invited him in and told him to have a seat next to Kingsman who was still passed out in his wheelchair. Skelly agreed, took a seat in the living room and I walked him through the events, as I understood them, while the two officers shook Kingsman to his senses and read him his rights. They also arrested Ramirez and pulled Brad's body out of the swimming pool. John Smith was long gone. Cleft sat next to me the whole time and confirmed my story.

"That's a pretty big story you got there, Peter." Skelly said to me fifteen minutes later. Paula and Joyce were on their way to the hospital to get checked out. Treat the dehydration, address the tragedy.

"That's what I was thinking too." I said.

"And you were just this pawn?"

"Seems that way." I said. *Way to minimize my involvement here, Skelly.*

"That's nuts." he said. "Do you have copies of these files – the files that Janice had?"

"Yes, some are here and then Vanessa Snowdin has some over at KVAN. We had to divide the assets. I'm sure you can understand."

"And this is everyone, right? Kingsman, Hector Ramirez and the guy they pulled out of the pool?" he asked letting it all sink in. "Shit. I thought I was just coming here for your sorry ass."

"I wanted to surprise you. I'm sure you can understand."

"Well, there is one other person." Cleft said.

"Who?"

"His name is Khang. Mr. Khang."

"Who's that?" Skelly asked.

"I think he's the money."

"Definitely the money." I added.

"Where is Mr. Khang now?" Skelly said as he scribbled a note in his notepad.

"Somewhere in the sky between here and Korea. He gets here tomorrow for the IPO. He wants to listen to live music and eat barbeque, is my understanding."

"OK noted." Skelly said and wrote some junk down on his notepad. "I think this is great and helpful but I still need you to come down to the station while we check on this. We'll ask you some questions, formally and on the record, and give you the all clear."

"That's fine." I said. "But only under one condition."

"I don't think you get to offer conditions here but go ahead."

"Cleft and I want to take Mr. Khang to ACL tomorrow night."

"Excuse me?"

"We do?"

"Yes, we do. Willie Nelson is doing a show. We got tickets months ago and I want to take Mr. Khang. Maybe we'll take him to Lambert's beforehand."

"That's – that's not going to happen." Skelly said suppressing the snicker.

"Kingsman too. I have four tickets. Paula and I were going to go with Cleft and his wife but I think this is a much better idea."

"No. I'm going to arrest him at the airport. In fact, the FBI is going to get involved here and they'll probably lead the investigation. I'll most certainly get shut out."

"No, don't do that – don't let that happen. I like my idea much better. If he shows up at the airport and you're there and the FBI is there he's just going to get back on that plane and fly home and you'll have nothing."

"We'll probably hide behind something and sneak up on him. That's how it usually works. We don't simply stand outside waiting for him waving our hands and badges in the air."

"I've never met this Mr. Khang but I think Peter has the right idea."

Cleft added. "Lure him in and butter him up. Get him on tape talking about the money and the crime. It would play great during the six o'clock hour. If you arrest him at the airport you'll have nothing."

"Guys this is great and I appreciate your offer but I'm going to politely decline." Skelly said. I voiced my objection but eventually submitted my concession. Skelly didn't want to listen to reason so who was I to tell him he was doing his job wrong. It's the order of the law.

"It's fine. You're right." I finally said. I probably should be at the hospital now with Paula and Joyce anyway. We were just going to have to let Mr. Khang go and let the authorities handle this. As much as I wanted to know what sort of outfit Mr. Khang was running I had to listen to Skelly and take care of my family. Paula and I only had a few minutes to speak before her and Joyce were escorted away. She apologized for subjugating me and not listening to me when I tried to explain things to her. She said once the dust settles, and the smoke clears, we need to discuss things and figure out what we want to do. I guess I thought things would work themselves out but Paula told me it's not as simple as that. Marriage takes work. Family takes work and commitment. Investment is the word she used. She's my hero so I was going to figure out a way to make the pieces fall into place.

41

I spent a few hours at the hospital with Paula and Joyce and then drove them home and helped them get settled. Paula let me put Joyce to bed and then showed me the door. There wasn't a big reunion, no heart-to-heart, where she bore her sole about how she misjudged me and wanted to make things better. She needed to process and think things over. Settling dust, clearing smoke. She said she'd call to set up visits with Joyce and I could come to her doctor's appointment next week. After I left the house, I went and booked a room at a small boutique hotel off South Congress where the selling point is invisible service: no front desk, no bellman, none of the arbitrary unpleasantness of every-day life. Just a confirmation code that you punch into a keypad to get into the hotel and then your room. I was anticipating a big payday from this charade so I made sure I got a head start on the reckless spending now. I took a shower and laid down to get some rest. I was planning on heading over to Perla's later to grab a drink and some oysters but ended up sleeping well into the next day. I woke up around noon and went outside and poured myself a glass of wine from the self-service bar and sat outside and embraced the cold weather. I was thinking about what to do next when the phone in my room rang. I went inside and picked it up. "Hello?" I said.

"Peter, it's Skelly. What are you doing?"

"Enjoying a nice glass of wine and wishing that it would snow. How did you find me and what do you want?"

"Paula told me and I need you to come outside. I can't seem to find the front desk."

"That's sort of the point." I said. "What do you want?"

"I need you to go to Pflugerville and meet Mr. Khang when he lands. It's for the FBI actually."

"I thought you said no to that sort of behavior."

"The feds don't want to send Kingsman by himself. He said he'd cooperate but they don't trust him. You have to go with him."

"Send Prescott."

"Send Prescott and Kingsman? We might as well give them a private jet out of the country. Mr. Khang has never met Prescott so you're going to pretend to be him when Mr. Khang lands."

"When is that again?"

"In about thirty minutes."

"Can Cleft come?"

"No."

"What's in it for me?"

"Nothing. It's a civic duty."

"OK. I'll be down in two. This was my idea though so don't go taking credit for it." I hung up with Skelly and then called Cleft and told him to meet me at the Executive Airport in Pflugerville in twenty minutes. I didn't care what Skelly said. Cleft was going to do this with me. I took some heart medicine and the last sip of wine and went down to meet Skelly. We took South Congress to Caesar Chavez and cut over to the interstate and headed north. We hit some traffic getting out of downtown but were at the airport in a good fifteen minutes.

"What the hell is he doing here?" Skelly said as we pulled up to the entrance. Cleft was standing by his car waving at us.

"We're a package, Skelly. Dual-threat." I said. "If you won't let him come-"

"Ya, ya —I get it, Richards. You're so clever." he said as we pulled through the gate. Cleft followed us in his car and we parked outside the main building and went in. Kingsman was looking out the window with a gaggle of federal agents behind him. He didn't look over at us. He was probably thinking about everything he had built and how best to keep it together. Complying with the feds was a good step but probably wouldn't keep everything together, especially when they find out how much of his empire was built with dirty money. They were going to take it away piece by piece, slowly and painfully. He may help them with Mr. Khang but he was screwed.

"Who's the asshole going to be?" Kingsman said.

"Hi Larry." Cleft said.

"I know you're playing Prescott." he said as he rotated his wheelchair towards us. "But what about you, Cleft?"

"I paid for the Willie Nelson tickets so I'm in." he said as a red and black Learjet hit the tarmac. It was pretty big which wasn't surprising. Mr. Khang was probably worth millions, if not more, and needed a big plane with enough fuel capacity to get from Korea to Austin. I should ask him if he watched any good movies on the way over.

"Larry has a wire on." Skelly said. "You need to get Mr. Khang to talk about his business and where he keeps his money. He probably keeps it all over the place, multiple accounts offshore, so get him to be specific. Bank names and account numbers if you can. This is our only shot." Got it.

"I told him this was preposterous." Kingsman interjected. "But they won't listen to reason. It's the fucking Korean mob, guys, not Enron."

"Remember he's mad at Prescott. Wants to kill him probably."

"Right."

"Good luck out there, boys." Skelly said as I rolled Kingsman's wheelchair outside. Cleft was a few steps behind us. We left the main building and stopped a few feet from the base of the plane.

"You'll never be the man Prescott was." Kingsman said to me as the door to the plane opened.

"Thanks for the vote of confidence, Larry." I said

"Don't call me that, you sack of shit." he said as a short Korean man with long black hair appeared at the entry way of the plane. He was wearing a Keep Austin Weird t-shirt and sunglasses and looked like he was in his mid-twenties. He saw us and headed down the stairs of the plane. "Mr. Khang – it's nice to see you, sir." Kingsman said as he extended his hand.

"Good to see you, Mr. Kingsman." he said.

"I'd like to introduce you to my colleague, David Prescott." Kingsman said and waved in my general direction.

"Nice to meet you, Mr. Prescott." Mister Khang said. "You're not as handsome in person as I thought you were going to be."

"You're not very good looking yourself, Mr. Khang." I said.

I felt Kingsman groan when I said this but Mister Khang smiled and put his hand on my shoulder. "I'm really upset with you two. There will be consequences. But first things first. Let's party." he said. "I want to meet a nice Texas girl and have her cover my body with melted cheese."

"It's called queso, Mr. Khang." I said.

"Please, call me Bob."

"Of course, Bob." I said and looked over at Cleft. "Could you please show Bob and Larry to the car, Junior?"

"*Junior?*" Cleft said as he squished his face together.

"Yes. Is there a problem, Junior?" I asked.

"Not at all." Cleft said and signaled to a black stretched limo that pulled up next to the plane. "Follow me." he said as Mr. Khang followed him over.

"I hope you're enjoying yourself, you dirty turd." Kingsman said to me as I pushed him over to the car.

"Very much so. Yes. Thank you."

"I hope you know that you are no better than a bag of dead dicks," he said to me as I opened the back door for him. He was going to have to hoist himself in. I had my limits.

"Have you ever seen a bag of dead dicks?" I asked. "If so, I'd like to do a story on it. Criminal millionaire found carrying a bag of deceased penises in Austin."

"I hate you." he said as he unbuckled himself from his wheelchair.

"I was really hoping we could become friends."

"I've had shit that had more personality than you."

"He never told you his first name, huh? Did he?"

"Come on girls." Mr. Khang shouted back at the plane. Two girls came out and got into the limo with Mr. Khang and Cleft. They couldn't have been a day over twenty, if that. Once Kingsman was in his seat I helped him push his legs in. I folded up his lightweight aluminum wheelchair and shoved it in the truck of the limo.

"Where's lunch, Mr. Prescott?" Mr. Khang asked me once we were all squeezed in the limo.

I tapped on the glass divider and the driver lowered it a few inches. "Can you take us to the east side, please? Sixth and Chicon." I said. There was a hot new restaurant that opened up recently from a world-renowned celebrity chef. It was originally just small plates and then they changed it to just a tasting menu. In the past few weeks they transitioned away from the tasting menu and now only feature the essence and aroma of food. For a meager seventy dollars you can get the scent of grilled beef tongue wafting below your nose. They still have a full bar though. Ingest some Beef tongue fragrance while sipping on a bourbon cocktail. Bob Khang could cover himself in queso later. We had business to take care of.

"Mr. Prescott." Mr. Khang said. "It's too bad your wife couldn't join us." as we sat down at the restaurant. He was at the head of the table flanked by the two girls. "We've been working together for so many years, it's only natural that I should get to meet your family. Then kill you."

"Yes, it's too bad she couldn't make it." I said. "We'll have to make some time to stop by the house and see her. But I'm happy that we have time to talk. I have some business ventures that I want to discuss with you."

"You do?" Cleft said.

"Yes, I do, actually, *Junior*." I said. "Is that a problem?"

"Who are you again?" Mr. Khang asked Cleft.

"He's my personal aide." I retorted. "Junior Muskrat, at your service."

"You're really something, Peter." Cleft said. "You know that, right?"

"Who's Peter?" Khang asked.

"Gentleman." Kingsman interjected. "Can we stay on point please?"

"What's your idea, David?" Mr. Khang asked. The waiter came by and set a teapot in the center of the table. It steamed.

"Seasonal fruit, ice, milk. A starter. Compliments of the chef." the waiter said.

"Urn Charms." I said to Mr. Khang.

"Jesus." Cleft said.

"Urn charms? Tell me more." he said.

"Well, it's sort of a multi-layered idea. You have the charms. They aren't dissimilar to wine charms. You put them on urns so people know which urn their deceased is in. Simple enough. They come in multiple colors, can probably do some licensing deals too. Marvel, Harry Potter. I see endless possibilities."

"Interesting." Mr. Khang said. "But so what? What's the market?"

"Here's the interesting part. You aren't actually burning any bodies. You're just filling the urns with recycled newspaper and selling body parts on the black market. The grieving get a personalized urn with a limited edition charm. A collector's item to show off to their friends."

"You have a channel for this? Do you have relationships with distributors?"

"Absolutely. I wouldn't even think to tell you unless I had it setup. Ready to pull the trigger, just need to secure the funding."

"How much do you need to get started?"

"Well, let's have that discussion." I said as the scent of seasonal fruit drifted under my nose.

"What do you think about this?" he asked and looked over at Kingsman. Kingsman shrugged. "It's a thing." he said.

"But I should warn you," I added. "I'm meeting with a few investors."

"Why would you do that? I'm your man. Whatever you need, Bob Khang is here for you."

"You heard him." Cleft said.

"I guess my concern is that there will be a lot of eyes on this. A lot of due diligence. It's a very particular business."

"The urn business?" Kingsman asked.

"The business of death."

"We just funneled millions of dollars through the American scientific community. I paid a consultant five hundred thousand dollars to lie to the FDA and provide them with false information," Mr. Khang said. "I'm sure we can handle this."

"But aren't you mad?" Kingsman asked.

"Ehh, it happens." he said and waved his hands.

I hope Skelly got that. A crime on American soil. My job here is done.

"I'm curious as to how your business is structured." I said. "I have it set up over here in the States but I'm interested in how the backend works. In Korea."

"Oh, is that so?" Mr. Khang said as he leaned closer to me. All eyes were on me. "What makes you think I'm going to tell you that?"

"Because if you want to make some real money, cold hard black market cash, you're going to need to break into the international market. I only have connections in the United States. I know the banks and back alleys. But you, my friend, have the other piece. You and me, we can have the whole world."

"I like the way you think." Mr. Khang said. "You never told me how creative he was." he said to Kingsman. "I should kill you on principal."

"Surprise?" Kingsman said.

The waiter came back. "Just give us a bit of everything." Mr. Khang said as he pulled a small plastic bag out of his pocket. White powder. "Do you want some?" he asked as he offered the bag to me.

"I'm good." I said.

"I'll have some actually." Cleft said.

"Ya, me too." Kingsman chimed in.

"Help yourselves gentlemen. It's the good stuff. It's called North Korean Explosion." he said as he passed the bag over to them. He looked back at me. "I know you've been working for me for a few years, Mr. Prescott, and I like your style. I think you have an interesting idea, it has potential. I don't make a habit of discussing my business practices with anyone so you'll just have to accept that about me. I make enough money already so maybe I'll just pass on your idea."

"But more money. Do you know much money you can make from body parts on the black market?" I said and looked over Mr. Khang's shoulder. Skelly was standing by the hostess stand near the bar with a collection of federal agents. He watched me as he sipped a bourbon cocktail. He was taking his time.

The waiter came back and put another teapot on the table. "Zucchini chicken pot pie inside a crab shell." he said. "Enjoy."

"It's got to be at least a billion dollars." I said.

"Peter – that's enough." Kingsman said. "I think we got what we need."

"What?" *What the fuck was he doing?* I had Mr. Khang, I was luring him in.

"Who the fuck is Peter?" Mr. Khang said. He pushed his chair back and stood up. "What the hell is going on here?" He reached down and pulled a hand gun out of his back pocket and pointed it at me. "Who are you?" he said as he pulled the hammer back. But before I could respond two officers approached Mr. Khang and restrained his arms.

"Mr. Khang." It was Skelly. "You're under arrest for money laundering and drug possession."

"Took you long enough to get over here." I said. "He almost shot me."

"You should try that bourbon cocktail. It's delicious." Skelly said.

"What about Willie Nelson?" Mr. Khang asked as the officers escorted him out of the restaurant. "We were going to see Willie Nelson!" He was pretty pissed. He didn't get to see Willie Nelson and he didn't meet a nice Texas girl to pour melted cheese over his body. He seemed like an OK enough guy, I'm sure he would have found someone who was willing to do that. He just wanted to come to Austin, check on his minions and have a good time. As far as I was concerned there wasn't anything wrong with that.

Skelly took the wire off Kingsman, thanked us for our service and dismissed us. The three of us stuck around for a few minutes and finished what was left of the zucchini pot pie. Kingsman told us a story about Korea and asked Cleft if he was hiring. I don't think it occurred to him, or maybe it did and he didn't care, but he was probably going to go to jail for a very long time. He struck me as the type of person who wouldn't be bothered by that sort of development. He left and then Cleft and I took the limo downtown, had a drink at the W and saw Willie Nelson play at the ACL theater behind the hotel. It was perfect and a great way to end the night. Afterwards, I said good-bye to Cleft and walked back to my hotel, took my heart medicine and fell asleep. I had no plans for tomorrow so maybe I would make it over to Perla's for some oysters.

THE END.

ACKNOWLEDGEMENTS

Sara Barney, Jack Barney and Bobbie Kroman.
April Litz, Brian Carden, Caroline Hotchkiss,
Dave Roberts, Claudia Chahin and Todd Pate.

ABOUT THE AUTHOR

Dana Barney is a Bostonian turned New Yorker turned Los Angeleno turned Austinite with a strong proclivity for the absurd and conspiratorial. He has a BA in writing from Bennington College in Vermont. He enjoys exploring the underlying, and sometimes inevitable, dark side of every-day life. He lives in Austin with his wife, and two daughters.